Let Me Die Yesterday

By the same author
Christ in Khaki
The Honey Gatherers

Non Fiction
Murder in Dorset

Let Me Die Yesterday

Theresa Murphy

ROBERT HALE · LONDON

ISBN-10: 0-7090-8173-1
ISBN-13: 978-0-7090-8173-9

Robert Hale Limited
Clerkenwell House
Clerkenwell Green
London EC1R 0HT

2 4 6 8 10 9 7 5 3 1

Typeset in 10/13pt Palatino
Printed in Great Britain by St Edmundsbury Press
Bury St Edmunds, Suffolk
Bound by Woolnough Bookbinding Limited

one

McCabe was lonely in the new darkness. There was only the crunching of gravel under his feet for company. The sound broke the vast rural silence that made a city man uneasy. Twilight was eerily darkening the surroundings into silhouettes as he approached Abbeyfield Manor. The manor was a neglected building owned by the past, and he could sense that the long dead resented his intrusion. Each window had its scar tissue of peeling paint. Carved stone columns rose upward for fifteen feet, overshadowing a huge oak door. The lintel over the door was an arch held in place by an engraved keystone. McCabe's Latin was too rusty for him to decipher the carved inscription.

He stood undecided at the door. Out of place and out of time, he regretted not having obeyed the feeling he'd had on reaching the outskirts of Abbeyfield. Standing on a hill, with the sun gone and long shafts of sullen light pouring through distant towns and rolling countryside, he'd had an urge to flee the unknown and return to the crowded streets of London and the habits and prejudices that fed his life. A new and potentially lucrative assignment should not bring a chill down his spine. As the darkness had thickened he made an uneasy truce with himself, agreeing to stay because he needed the money.

The heavy metal doorknocker was stiff from disuse. It separated his three knocks into the ritualistic sound of a secret society. A bird disturbed by the noise startled McCabe by scolding him shrilly from the woods to his left. From nearby came the panicking scamper of some small night creature. True to the horror-movie setting, the door creaked loudly in protest as it was slowly opened.

Prepared to face some wrinkled, reeking crone, McCabe was pleasantly surprised by the sight of the woman who stood silently in the gap of the partly open door. In her forties, there was something deeply sensual about her unkempt appearance. Her unnaturally blonde hair was long and uncombed. She wore a pale-blue crop top and a pair of faded, frayed jeans. The casual, subdued clothing should have made her uninteresting, but it had totally the opposite effect. Her offbeat beauty was as much internal as it was physical.

Her detached manner appealed to McCabe. Her blue eyes went past him to where he had parked his modest Vauxhall Cavalier. A tendency towards obesity was suggestive of self-indulgence. That was a trait that McCabe had learned came as a bonus in a woman. When she shortened her gaze to focus on him he was certain that she was seeing him for the first time.

'OK, I give up,' she said wearily, in the kind of low and husky voice he had anticipated. 'You look more like a boxer than a salesman – so what are you?'

'What would you like me to be?' he challenged her.

'Anything, as long it's at least a hundred miles from here,' she countered.

'You've got a good case against that charm school.'

'A comedian.' The blonde sighed in exasperation. 'Listen, mister, we get all kinds here; beggars begging on the doorstep, buggers doing buggery in the bushes, peepers peeping in the windows. Which of those categories do you come under?'

Taking a step back, McCabe made an exaggerated show of studying the old building. Face serious, he asked, 'Which is your bedroom window?'

That put a twinkle of amusement in her eyes, but only momentarily. Suddenly she became even more withdrawn. Eyes blank and her expression bland, she gave the impression that she was strolling through some inner landscape. Normally as self-sufficient as the surrounding hills, McCabe felt hurt at being shut out by her.

Returning to reality, she studied him intently. It was as if she expected to read in his eyes the answer to a question she had yet to ask. She pursed her lips dubiously. 'Could you be the man my father is expecting?'

'If your father is Colonel Simon Farquahar.'

'Oh dear, a major cock-up,' she said. 'I'm not much good at apologizing.'

'No problem,' McCabe assured her. He liked her direct way of speaking. Nice talk had somehow become a status symbol. Often people who used the nicest sounding language had the meanest hearts.

'That's very kind,' she said. 'Your name is?'

'McCabe. Gerry McCabe,' he replied, enjoying her first smile. It put on show white and even teeth that were large in keeping with her oversized mouth.

'I'm Beth Merrill,' she introduced herself, disappointing McCabe by not proffering her hand. Her handshake would be a greater thrill than an intimate caress from a lesser woman. She went on. 'Beth Farquahar that was, as they say around these parts.'

Detecting an echo of regret in her tone, it suggested to McCabe that she was a divorcee. Catching sight of a gold band on the third finger of her left hand, he revised his diagnosis to that of an unhappy marriage.

Leaning casually with her back against the doorjamb she gestured for him to enter the house. Passing close, McCabe inhaled her fragrance. It was not a manufactured perfume, but an exquisitely raw and natural female scent.

The interior of the manor was in a far better condition than the exterior had led McCabe to expect. The hall was a huge chamber, dark with oak-lined walls and old paintings. An ornately framed portrait of King George VI held prominence. Wearing naval uniform, the bewildered King looked out from a distant yesterday into a today that he didn't understand. Facing McCabe were imposing Doric columns flanking a broad staircase.

A little away from him now, she was standing awkwardly, her superb self-confidence seemingly having abandoned her. Head bowed, she was frowning and teasing at her lower lip with her teeth, staring off into nowhere. McCabe broke the awkward silence between them by asking a question.

'Is the missing woman your sister, Mrs Merrill?'

'*Is* she, *was* she? Which tense should I use, Mr McCabe?' she answered, with a question of her own. 'It's been more than thirty years.'

'I don't know enough about the case to answer that. Were the two of you close, Mrs Merrill?'

An energetic nod had her hair tumbling about her face. Raising both hands to push it back, she put unshaven armpits on display. McCabe found a strange eroticism in a sight so unusual in an age of artificial women. A strange and powerful eroticism. She was nibbling on her cosmetic-free bottom lip again.

'There were just the two of us,' she told him sadly. 'Time is not a healer, Mr McCabe. All the passing of years does is to dig more deeply and painfully into the unhealed wound.'

Fixing him with a steady look, uncertainty made a little furrow on her forehead. Her blue eyes were no longer cool. She was no longer poised and talkative. Without warning, she started off down a corridor. Catching up with her, McCabe said, 'It must be upsetting for you.'

'It's not easy, and my father doesn't help,' she said conversationally rather than in complaint. 'He has turned this place into a mausoleum for the 1960s, Mr McCabe. It wouldn't surprise me to see Sandy Shaw walk by any minute with no shoes on. A resurrected John Lennon would feel instantly at home here.'

They continued in silence, with Beth Merrill's depression deepening along the way. Coming suddenly to a halt, she turned to speak. She stood close. McCabe was very conscious of her warm breath stroking his cheek.

'I should warn you, Mr McCabe, that my father's mind tends to wander. Please make allowances for him. Grief prevents a person from growing old gracefully. Also, we have suffered much over the years from hoax callers. I accept that this is different, that you are *bona fide* as it were, because my father's solicitors arranged with a firm of London solicitors for you to investigate. But I live in constant dread of my father being cheated. However, in the short time that I have known you I feel that I don't have to ask you not to take advantage of him.'

Warmed by this compliment, McCabe assured her, 'If I take this case, Mrs Merrill, then Colonel Farquahar will pay only for what he gets.'

'Thank you,' she said softly, then swiftly switched the subject. 'Tell me, Mr McCabe, what do you think of Abbeyfield Manor?'

Substituting diplomacy for total indifference, he replied, 'It's very impressive.'

They walked on, McCabe assuming that she wasn't going to comment on his opinion of her home. But he was partly wrong.

'The place is a trap,' she sighed. Her lips moved, and for a moment they remained parted as she stopped by a door. 'You're a man of the world, Mr McCabe, tell me how you see life.'

Surprised by both the question and the surfacing of his own bitterness, he asked quietly, 'Do you want the truth?'

'Of course. And in your own vernacular.'

McCabe gave her the truth, but modified his language. 'It's a right bastard.'

The nod of her head was not for him. She was confirming to herself that he had agreed with her. She seemed to be waiting. Everything seemed to be waiting, somewhere. Holding the door handle, she put out her free hand to him in an involuntary move. She swiftly withdrew the hand before the fingers could make contact with his arm. Blushing faintly, she was for a moment or two attractively vulnerable. They exchanged glances. It was no more than a brief look, but in their eyes, their expression, or whatever breath of a motion one makes if only to exist, live, breathe, they had communicated well with one another. McCabe wondered whether he was richer or poorer for the tacit exchange.

'From the start I recognized you as a kindred spirit, Mr McCabe,' she said quietly.

Instantly, they returned to being strangers as she opened the door and an overpowering heat prevented McCabe from immediately following her into the room. Then he stepped into a study lined with overflowing bookshelves. A log fire burned brightly in an old-fashioned grate. It touched on a forgotten memory for McCabe that came rushing at him, winking and exploding, too swift for definition. Recovering, he saw a white-haired old man sitting at a bureau in one corner of the room. Getting unsteadily to his feet, the old guy toppled sideways. McCabe made no move, knowing that often the aged and the infirm proudly preferred a cracked skull to a helping hand.

Recovering before he hit the floor, the old man came up sideways like a boxer anxious to beat the count. He extended a skeletal arm in McCabe's direction.

'My dear fellow, how good of you to come all this way.'

McCabe took the cold, dry-skinned hand. Red-rimmed, watery eyes that had seen much but remembered little, surveyed him. A shock of lively hair saved the old face from being a skull. A heavy white moustache, tinged brown either by food or tobacco, lifted obliquely in a smile.

McCabe said, 'It's a pleasure to meet you, Colonel Farquahar.'

'Sit you down. Sit you down.'

Returning shakily to his corner, the old man was slammed back down into his seat by a fit of violent coughing. Beth bent to take a book from an armchair before gesturing for McCabe to be seated. Then she seated herself on a straight-backed chair.

'November is a bad month for old people,' Farquahar commented to himself, as he stretched both hands to the fire. Then he turned his head to McCabe. 'You come highly recommended, young sir. Your solicitor chappy in London assured my solicitor chappy that you are the best.'

McCabe stayed quiet for a moment. Clement Phillips, a solicitor with a grubby office in Kennington, was a total chancer who often put work his way. In London, a recommendation from Phillips would be regarded as a black mark. Not wanting the old man to expect too much of him, McCabe said, 'I don't think I could live up to that, Colonel.'

'Nonsense,' the old man scoffed. 'I'm a good judge of men, and I like the cut of you. You'd have made a fine soldier, a first-class officer of the old school. A Yard man, I take it?'

'I served in the Met for a while,' McCabe replied cautiously. Having spent twelve years trying to forget his police career, he didn't want to be reminded of it. With his marriage to Carol rooted in something that was eternal, he had stupidly begun a hollow affair. Bewitched by Ali Quenton, a dark-complexioned, gorgeous detective sergeant, he had behaved like the lovesick teenager he had never permitted himself to be during his adolescence. That mental lapse had cost him dearly. When an ambitious Ali had planted drugs on a suspect, McCabe had, out of some distorted sense of chivalry, taken the rap. He had spent three years in prison and lost his wife and daughter. Ali Quenton was now a detective inspector.

Aware of his unease, the perceptive Beth Merrill came to McCabe's rescue. 'Forgive my father, Mr McCabe. He has a Humphrey Bogart fixation. Philip Marlowe and all that.'

'Beth believes that I am senile.' Simon Farquahar looked fondly at his daughter. 'Are you a married man, McCabe?'

'Dad ...' Beth Merrill gasped reprovingly.

Not expecting so direct a question, McCabe thought carefully. He had no intention of revealing anything of his private life. Neither Carol nor he had been able to fathom why he had gone so wrong. He gave a one-word reply that wasn't the truth, but neither was it a lie.

'No.'

'Stout fellow,' Farquahar congratulated him vehemently.

Unable to understand the old man's attitude, McCabe looked to Beth Merrill. But she had retreated into her inner world. On a shelf behind where she was sitting was a framed photograph of a woman with a 1950s' hairstyle. Though there was a resemblance to Beth, the woman's features had symmetry that the blonde's face lacked. McCabe decided that this had to be Mrs Farquahar, wife to Simon and mother to Beth. Where was she now?

Simon Farquahar arranged one of his moustachioed half-smiles. 'Well, are we going to do business, McCabe?'

'This must be kept in perspective, Colonel,' McCabe responded. 'As three decades have passed I would advise that you adjust to the likelihood that your missing daughter is dead.'

'Your frankness is appreciated, McCabe. We've had all the pious words and pretentious platitudes we can take. What we need now is action. The current of life carries us swiftly onwards, and I have no time to spare. Do you see your way clear to take the job?'

'Though both Mrs Merrill and you, Colonel, are charming people,' McCabe answered carefully, 'all I know at present is that your elder daughter went missing in the 1960s.'

'1969 to be exact. That was a bad year, McCabe.' Farquahar

was shaking his head in the incredulous reminiscence of someone viewing old family photographs. 'History holds a record of special years that were turning points for good or bad, and 1969 was one of the latter. This country of ours has been in decline ever since: grossly inferior politicians, *and* the royal family steeped in immorality.'

Maybe the old guy was right, but McCabe hadn't driven down to London for a philosophical treatise. He steered the conversation back on course. 'That was the year when your daughter left home, sir?'

Farquahar corrected him. 'No, she didn't leave home. Katrina disappeared, completely, McCabe. The years since have been wasted years.'

'All our years are wasted years,' his daughter added flatly, in the background.

'What were the circumstances of that disappearance, Colonel Farquahar?'

'Beth can tell you that better than I can, McCabe. I wasn't here at the time. I was working for the government. I was one of the team aboard HMS *Fearless* off Gibraltar when that damned fellow Wilson lost out to Ian Smith.'

Beth Merrill dropped her air of detachment to block her father's excursion into the past. 'I was only fourteen, Mr McCabe, three years younger than Katrina. But I remember enough to answer your questions.'

'Had there been any family arguments, Mrs Merrill?'

'Nothing other than the occasional squabbles that occur even in the best regulated families. My mother was here then, and the three of us got on really well together.'

McCabe noticed that she had given no hint as to where her mother was now. With it likely that Mrs Farquahar was dead he asked no questions. He would delicately probe the matter later.

'Can you think of anything that might have caused your sister to leave?' he asked.

'Katrina got in with the wrong crowd, McCabe,' Simon Farquahar interjected angrily.

Beth Merrill explained, 'My sister was a hippie, Mr McCabe.'

'Nothing but unwashed, undisciplined scum, McCabe,' the

old man said in disgust. 'No doubt you remember that shocking affair that took place in Oxfordshire?'

McCabe and the daughter exchanged mystified frowns. She asked, 'What are you talking about, Daddy?'

'Come, Beth,' the father protested. 'They are still prattling of it today as if it was some laudable event. Where was it now? Wood-something or other. Woodstock. That's it, Woodstock.'

'That was in America, Daddy, New York State.'

Beth had spoken in a gentle way that revealed a deep love for her ageing father.

Simon Farquahar defended himself. 'Well, there is a Woodstock in Oxfordshire. The flower people! My God, that was a misnomer, an insult to nature. Remember their vile slogan, McCabe, *Make Love not War*? No more than a damned excuse for sexual licence.'

Suspecting there was a clue in Farquahar's complaint, McCabe asked tentatively, 'Was your sister promiscuous, Mrs Merrill?'

A shake of her head set her long blonde hair swinging. 'I wouldn't say so. Katrina had a steady boyfriend.'

'Was he a hippie?'

'No; in a way he was a local boy. He came here from Bristol to work for Ryan Pavely, who owns the largest farm in the district. Though Andy, Andrew Fairview is his name, did join Katrina when she mixed with the flower people.'

This was a better break than McCabe could have hoped for. He followed up with another question for Beth. 'Is this Andrew Fairview still living locally?'

'No.' A frown laddered Beth Merrill's brow. Deep in contemplation, she puckered her lips. Her cheeks sank slightly, accentuating her already prominent cheekbones. She was most attractive that way. 'You should have been told this right at the start, Mr McCabe. Andy went missing at the same time as Katrina, and neither of them has been seen nor heard of since.'

This answer brought McCabe relief. It was rare for a girl to be found alive when missing for so long as Katrina Farquahar, but the possibility of an elopement made things look brighter. Hearing the old man muttering, he turned to him.

'Someone had betrayed us, of course, McCabe,' Farquahar was saying angrily. 'But all that was quickly covered up.'

'I don't understand, sir,' McCabe said, before catching Beth's covert warning signals.

'The damned sanctions against Rhodesia, of course,' Farquahar snapped testily. A drop of sweat rolled down into his eye and he blinked, but that was all.

The old man took a large format book from his bureau and opened it. Seeing newspaper clippings pasted to the pages, McCabe looked questioningly at Beth. Shaking her head, she mimed, 'Rhodesia, UDI.'

McCabe was sympathetic to the old man in his time slips, but ancient details of Ian Smith's Unilateral Declaration of Independence would be no help in finding Katrina Farquahar. Getting up from her chair to pick up a log and bend over to place it on the fire, Beth surreptitiously moved close to McCabe to whisper, 'Direct your questions to me, Mr McCabe, but discreetly so that my father doesn't feel left out.'

Moved by her kindness to the old man, McCabe gave a close to imperceptible nod of agreement. When Beth was seated once more, he asked, 'Did your sister take her possessions with her when she left, Mrs Merrill? All her clothes?'

'Only the kaftan she stood up in,' she said wryly. 'Oh, and her handbag, with three shillings and ninepence in it.'

'As it was so long ago you are very precise as to the amount, Mrs Merrill.'

'That's because Katrina was flat broke, Mr McCabe, and that was all the spare money I had to lend her when she asked me earlier that day.' She paused reflectively. 'What would that be in new money … around twenty pence. No one would get very far on twenty pence today.'

How far could Katrina Farquahar have got on three shillings and ninepence in 1969, McCabe wondered? It wasn't a great sum with which to begin a new life. Why was it necessary for her to borrow so paltry an amount from her sister if she was leaving with her boyfriend?

'Did her boyfriend have any money?' he asked.

'That Fairview chap have money!' Simon Farquahar snorted

derisively, coming back to the present with a rush. 'Katrina, destined to become lady of this manor, McCabe, went off with a penniless farm labourer.'

'Whatever money either of them had they squandered on ridiculous clothes,' Beth said.

This struck McCabe as odd. If the missing girl had been fashion conscious, albeit fashion on the fringe, it wasn't likely that she would leave home without taking her beloved clothing with her.

Beth Merrill increased this mystery by saying, 'Her wardrobe is crammed full. Would you like to see Katrina's room, Mr McCabe?'

McCabe nodded assent, and they left the room without Farquahar noticing. Sitting with his bony elbows resting on the flap of his bureau, he slept with one eye partly open.

Upstairs on the landing, Beth paused outside of a door to warn McCabe. 'My father believes that life, like good music, is full of recurring themes. He has this weird idea that if he preserves Katrina's bedroom exactly as it was, she will return one day and everything will be as before. Sad, isn't it? There's no going back. Nothing can ever return to what it was.' Turning the handle of the door, she added numbly, 'I just go along with my father's wishes.'

'Your support must be a great comfort to the colonel, Mrs Merrill.'

She shrugged, her favourite gesture. 'I don't have a choice. Have you ever wondered why it is we can be unfaithful to a partner but not a parent?'

Aware that she hadn't asked a question and didn't anticipate an answer, McCabe followed her into the room. There was a hint of perfume made musty by the passage of time so that it had the mildly polluted smell of cut flowers in a graveyard. Not wanting Beth to notice, he fought hard to control an icy shiver that ran through him.

If Katrina Farquahar was still alive she would be in her 50s, but this was a young girl's room. Garishly coloured posters of the pop stars of yesteryear adorned the walls. Wearing something like a cross between a bowler hat and a Stetson, the paper ghost of Jimi

Hendrix concentrated on plucking a guitar, while on the opposite wall a black-eyed Dusty Springfield held a phallic-shaped microphone close to her wide-open mouth. Personal items were left around as if they had been used recently. The bedroom was an unsettling anachronism of immense proportions.

'There are some kinds of memories that make you want to crawl back into the void,' Beth whispered sadly. She switched on an outdated record player, carefully guiding the arm on to a spinning disc. She told McCabe, 'I'll set the scene for you.'

She moved away to open the double doors of a wardrobe as Cilla Black's strident voice sang *There's Always Something There to Remind Me*. Adopting the role of an unenthusiastic boutique assistant, Beth took clothes from the wardrobe. She laid miniskirts of various colours on the bed, identifying them for McCabe. 'Mary Quant.'

Next taking out a black skinny-ribbed polo neck jumper and an ice-blue pair of hipsters, she held the items up to study them. At that moment she was neither woman nor child, but with much in her of both, as she remarked with a touch of envy, 'Katrina was very slim and could wear this kind of thing. I was born out of time, Mr McCabe, with big boobs and a lot of bum when no designer was interested in that kind of figure.'

McCabe had a ready, sex-slanted argument against the gorgeous Beth's self-denigration, but this was neither the time nor the place, so he gave her a feeble smile. With a strong-voiced girl belting out a song of long ago, something seemed to be gathering in this room. Whether it was attached to Katrina Farquahar or was some kind of phantom from his own past, he didn't like it.

'The Apple Boutique,' Beth said, as she laid pairs of flared jeans on the bed, followed by several kaftans in psychedelic colours.

Having to clear his throat before he could speak, McCabe managed a weak, 'She certainly had a lot of clothes.'

A slip of the tongue made him refer to Katrina in the past tense, but Beth hadn't picked up on it. Standing, running a hand over a kaftan, she spoke absently. 'It was the Beatles.'

'What was the Beatles?'

'They owned the Apple Boutique in London,' she qualified her comment, as she gathered up the clothes, asking by raising one eyebrow if McCabe had seen enough. When he nodded she began to replace the garments in the wardrobe, talking as she did so. 'Katrina and Andy went on several shopping trips to London. I know that our memories play tricks, but life rolled along happily then, clean and fresh and eternal. It is all so different now.'

Though in whole-hearted agreement, McCabe didn't want to indulge in nostalgia in the eerie atmosphere of that room. He offered no more than a neutral shrug, glad that he hadn't touched any of the clothes because they were alive with the invisible vibrations of their owner. The chance of Katrina Farquahar still being alive was fading fast for him.

Taking a photograph from a drawer, Beth passed it to him with a wry smile. 'This is the sort of thing that makes my father rant on about the decadent sixties.'

McCabe took the monochrome photograph. It was an outdoor shot of a sexy girl wearing only a scanty pair of briefs under a see-through dress. A memory clicked automatically into McCabe's head, and he identified the picture. 'That's Jane Birkin arriving for the premiere of the film *Slogan*.'

'Very good,' she congratulated him, with a moist-lipped smile that stirred him. 'I didn't have you down as a film buff, Mr McCabe.'

'I'm not really, but that era has stayed with me.'

'As it has everyone who lived through it,' she said wistfully, rummaging around in the drawer to take out a second photograph. 'I feel I lost myself to my new friends and novel lifestyle at that time and I've been unable to find myself since.' She handed the photograph to McCabe, speaking reverently. 'This is Katrina.'

Cilla Black reached the end of her song. In the new quiet, McCabe looked into a pair of eyes that were deep despite being two-dimensional. The schoolgirl in the photograph didn't resemble Beth. A dark band kept a fair-headed, early-Lulu style in place.

'Keep it if it will be of use to you,' Beth offered.

Delaying his reply, McCabe looked again at the young and innocent face in the photograph. Whether the real woman was dead or alive, this young Katrina Farquahar had gone forever. To soften his refusal as he handed the photo back, he said, 'What with changing hairstyles and that sort of thing, Katrina's picture won't help.'

Beth Merrill put both photographs back in the drawer and closed it. She had a way of slowly raising her eyes to look at the person she was speaking to. There was a level of intimacy in the mannerism that had a profound effect on McCabe.

He enquired, 'What action did the police take, Mrs Merrill?'

'Very little.' She became uncharacteristically evasive. 'In short, they did nothing.'

'That's unusual,' a puzzled McCabe said. 'There was enough suspicious about Katrina Farquahar's disappearance to warrant a serious police investigation.'

'Perhaps not, considering how things were then,' Beth said quietly, almost sheepishly. 'You see, Mr McCabe, we didn't report my sister's disappearance right away.'

'You waited for your father to return home?' McCabe guessed.

'Oh no. Father came back less than a week after Katrina had gone,' Beth answered. Suddenly looking very weary, she bent her body intending to sit on the bed. But, as if suffering an electric shock, she jumped up before any part of her had touched it. She continued speaking, rapidly as if trying to divert his attention from her peculiar aversion to her sister's bed. 'Quite some time went by before we informed the police. That was mainly due to it not being the first time Katrina had left home. The longest she had ever been away was three months, so I suppose we took that period as a criterion.'

'So three months passed before you told the police?' McCabe checked.

'Probably several weeks more. Each day we hoped that she would come back.'

'These other times when your sister went away, did she go with her boyfriend?'

Shaking her blonde head, Beth replied, 'No, Andy stayed at work on the farm. On those occasions Katrina went with a close friend she'd made among the hippies.'

'A man?'

'No, a girl named Suzi Duoard. I know little about her. Like the rest of the flower people she turned up here one day out of nowhere.'

'What kind of girl was she, Mrs Merrill?'

'Really striking in appearance,' Beth answered, her eyes going vacant. 'I suppose that I became a devoted fan. Every young man in the area, and some that were not so young, fancied her like mad.'

'Was she, er ... easy, do you think?'

'It was difficult to tell in that era of free love,' Beth mused. 'But I wouldn't say that she was. Suzi was extroverted, but a strong-minded type.' She crooked an arm to glance at her wristwatch. 'We had better go back down to my father.'

They were moving towards the door when she suddenly turned her head away. McCabe realized that she was going to cry. He felt ashamed. This was entirely his fault. He had delayed her too long in this room. She put a hand on his arm to stop his stumbling apology.

'It's all right,' she said, raising a dainty handkerchief to her nose. 'It's not now, not today, Mr McCabe. It's just ... I don't know, it's just – everything.'

He took the handkerchief from her and gently wiped the tears from under her eyes. Her mouth quivered into a faint smile, and they were both perturbed to discover that in her distress they had completed whatever had passed between them earlier outside the colonel's study.

They both became lost in a vacuum of quieting emotions. She was different. The harsh lines in her face had gone, and there was no wise look about her eyes. They went out on to the landing.

Shutting the door, Beth went down the stairs ahead of him, turning her head to speak over her shoulder. 'Please be certain about taking this case, Mr McCabe. Have you ever lived in a rural district?'

'Never,' McCabe admitted.

Stopping partway down the stairs, she said, 'That is the point I am trying to make. Neighbours are constantly changing in a city, but in Abbeyfield they have stayed in place for generations. Folk hereabouts are not only struggling to keep their own transgressions secret, but also striving to conceal the sins of their fathers and grandfathers.'

'You are suggesting that I will run into trouble, stir things up, by asking questions.'

'Not *suggesting*, Mr McCabe, I am *saying* that you will.'

Though appreciating her thoughtful warning, McCabe didn't view the hostility of local people as seriously as she did. He said, 'Surely I will only worry those with something to hide?'

'Everyone has something to hide,' she replied dully. 'Believe me, Mr McCabe, it would be very easy to start a war in Abbeyfield.'

'That won't worry me, Mrs Merrill, providing that I win.'

'At the end of most wars it is impossible to distinguish between the victor and the vanquished,' Beth Merrill cautioned, as she turned and went on down the stairs.

He watched her go on ahead of him. There was an aura of desolation around her.

two

B ack in the study, which was as swelteringly hot as a green-house, Simon Farquahar was awake and wanting to know if McCabe was going to take the case. 'Well, McCabe, have you completed your preliminary stocktaking?'

'Almost, Colonel. I have just one more question,' McCabe said guardedly.

'Then ask away, my dear fellow,' the old man said, unable to conceal his impatience as with strained politeness he added, 'your caution is understandable.'

'It's Mrs Farquahar.'

Father and daughter exchanged glances. It seemed to McCabe that each was silently begging the other to answer. Beth said, 'My mother left not long after my sister went. Katrina going upset her badly.'

'Pah!' the old man protested. 'Don't make excuses for that woman, Beth. The truth is, McCabe, that Maria, my wife, went with a man. A damned fellow young enough to be her son.'

Learning this complicated everything as far as McCabe was concerned. He had found that most cases led to a secondary intrigue, or even a series of related incidents. But to have two closely connected events in the same family at the outset was bad news.

'Was it a local man?' he enquired.

'He was from Kilverham, the nearest town to here,' Beth explained. 'He is a solicitor.'

'*Was* a solicitor,' her father corrected her, with a touch of glee in his tone. 'They went off to London together.'

'It wasn't a fairy-tale romance, Mr McCabe,' Beth said. She was distant again now. Their rapport had vanished completely. 'There was no living happily ever after. Sylvester Hartley left my mother within a few months. She is living in London, alone.'

'Do you keep in touch with her, Mrs Merrill?'

'We exchange Christmas cards every year, I don't think,' Simon Farquahar responded.

Beth saved McCabe from asking an obvious question. 'I know what you are thinking, Mr McCabe, but the answer is no – Katrina has made no contact with my mother.'

Standing, Simon Farquahar took several uncertain steps in McCabe's direction. With his jaw thrust out and his eyes glittering black buttons under bushy white eyebrows, his pose would have been pugnacious had age not defeated him. 'I believe that answers your final question, young sir.'

'There's just one more thing I don't understand,' McCabe said awkwardly. 'Why have you brought me here now? Why didn't you hire a private investigator all those years ago?'

Beth stood silently as her father slumped back heavily into his chair. He spent some time thinking and breathing hard. A clock chimed hollowly somewhere in the house. With the echo still in the air, the old man made the striking of the clock his priority.

'My goodness, Beth,' he spoke incredulously. 'Seven o'clock already. You'd best get Roland's dinner ready. Off you go now and take care of your husband. McCabe and I will muddle along together until you rejoin us.'

Watching her reluctant departure, McCabe was surprised to learn that Beth's husband lived at the manor. He had assumed that they were either estranged or living apart because her husband worked in some other part of the country.

'Roland is head of the senior school in Kilverham,' Farquahar explained. 'He's an excellent fellow, an excellent fellow. Comes from a very distinguished family. His father was a confidant of the Duke of Windsor, would you believe.'

'Really,' McCabe said with feigned interest. The old man had delayed answering until Beth was out of the room. McCabe repeated the question, 'Why have you left it so late to begin looking for your daughter, Colonel?'

Holding up a thin hand, palm toward McCabe as a signal not to say any more, the old man opened his bureau. 'Times change, McCabe. Once we had eighteen employees on this estate, but now I'm reduced to one part-time gardener who is damned near the same age as myself.'

An earthy smell linked the old man's statement and his search in the bureau as he brought out a clear but mud-stained polythene bag. In the heat of that room, McCabe suddenly felt cold, a hard cold, like steel exposed in a blizzard.

'Take a look inside there, my dear fellow,' Simon Farquahar ordered.

Carefully peeling the polythene bag open, McCabe took out the rotting remains of a plastic handbag. It was sticky to the touch and gave off the dank stench of clay. McCabe asked, 'Katrina's?'

Colonel Farquahar nodded. The nodding went on involuntarily until he cupped his chin in his hand. More minutes passed before he was able to speak. 'Beth knows nothing of this. Open up the handbag, McCabe.'

Prising apart the stiff hinges, McCabe removed a powder compact that had been dulled by dampness, and a flaking, discoloured tube of lipstick. There was an envelope with a handwritten letter inside that moisture had made illegible. Finding an old-type driving licence with a stiff red cover and most of its pages stained brown, McCabe could make out *Katrina* and the part-name *Farq* ... Taking out a tiny purse he tipped its contents into his palm. There was a florin, an old shilling, a sixpence, two pre-decimal pennies and two halfpennies. Three shillings and ninepence in total, just as Beth had told him.

'Bert Jakeman, my gardener, found it last week,' Farquahar said. 'He dug it up in the rockery down by the tennis courts. I will show you the exact place at some time, McCabe, but we must not let Beth know what we are up to.'

'Of course not,' McCabe agreed. 'But this doesn't look hopeful, Colonel Farquahar.'

'I realize that.' The colonel's constantly watering eyes overflowed. He used the heel of a hand to wipe tears quickly away from his cheeks.

'Who else knows about this?'

'Only Bert and myself.'

'You can rely on him to keep it to himself?'

'Good heavens, yes, McCabe,' Farquahar stoutly defended his gardener. 'Bert is as loyal as the day is long. He fought under my command right through the campaign in Malaya.'

'With respect, Colonel, I must say that you should have told the police about this.'

Farquahar said in mitigation, 'I am an old man who is completely lost in this modern era. You could never comprehend how traumatic it is to watch the news on television and not recognize the world you are seeing. Good God, McCabe, they even have nancy boys in Parliament. That is the reason why I want you to handle everything. I must know what happened to my first-born, even if it is the worst kind of news.'

The awesome prospect of telling the old man that his daughter was dead prevented McCabe from coming to an immediate decision about taking the case. He badly needed this assignment. Though his payments to Carol were up to date, and Cindy's school fees were paid up until the end of term, there were some hefty expenses overdue. McCabe saw images of his wife and child, pictures that sharpened as they came out of a fog in his mind. The black-haired Carol laughing and lovely in the good times, sobbing and distraught when the bad times came. Too young to understand, Cindy had been a bewildered and unhappy observer of the result of her father's stupidity. How long ago was that? A week? A year? A lifetime? These stark memories helped to persuade him that there was nothing either ethically or morally wrong in taking Simon Farquahar's money only to tell him that his long-lost daughter was dead.

'I will investigate the disappearance of your daughter, sir,' McCabe said. 'But the chances of a happy outcome are extremely slim. All I have to offer is my very best effort.'

'I ask for no more than that, my dear fellow. There are no words to express my gratitude,' Farquahar exclaimed, taking McCabe's right hand in both of his cold and scaly hands.

At that moment the door opened and Beth came into the room. Taking in the handshake, she remarked, 'I assume that Mr McCabe will be staying with us.'

Standing in the doorway behind her was an unremarkable man aged around sixty. Bespectacled and narrow-chested, he was dressed in a tweed jacket and grey flannel trousers. His remaining hair was worn like a grey halo around his otherwise bald head.

As detached as ever, Beth introduced the man. 'This is my husband, Roland Merrill, Mr McCabe.'

'Pleased to meet you, Mr McCabe,' Merrill said as he shook McCabe's hand. 'Welcome to Abbeyfield.'

Merrill was somewhere between fifteen and twenty years Beth's senior. His smile was meaningless, a practised yet unconscious gesture for anyone watching. The pleasantries were all a sham.

Simon Farquahar slid a thin arm round his daughter's shoulder, delighting in telling her, 'McCabe has agreed to help us, Elizabeth. I'll leave you to prepare a room.'

'No,' McCabe cut in quickly. 'I appreciate your kind offer, Colonel. But I will work better from a separate base.'

'You know best.' The old man nodded his head sagely. 'I can see that it would be wise for you to be away from the manor and its influences.'

'And its distractions,' Beth said enigmatically. She went on, 'We'll have dinner and then Roland and I will take you into the village, Mr McCabe. Sharee Bucholz will fix you up with a room at the Fox and Hounds.'

'I'm sorry, Beth, but you'll have to count me out,' Roland Merrill apologized. 'I have a veritable mountain of papers to mark this evening.'

Eyes tightening, Merrill watched Beth intently. The eternal conflict between age and youth was always at its most destructive between an older man and his younger and attractive wife, with jealousy adding another dimension.

Showing no reaction, Beth said, 'That's no problem. Daddy, you go to your room and take a rest before dinner. Roland, why don't you take Mr McCabe into the drawing-room.'

'Whisky?' Merrill asked, when he and McCabe were settled.

'Fine, thank you,' McCabe nodded, taking a look around. The room was another anachronism. A portrait of Harold Macmillan, as saggy-jowled as a basset hound, held the drawing-room back from the present just as George VI did the hall. The room conjured up an image for McCabe of pre-television Sunday evenings, with a Farquahar family of old standing round the piano singing *Who is Sylvia*?

Passing a glass to McCabe, Merrill asked, 'Well, what do you make of this business?'

'That's difficult to say at this stage,' McCabe shrugged. 'Did you know Katrina?'

'I was her maths teacher, McCabe, just as I was Beth's. There was no impropriety, of course. Beth had finished schooling for more than two years when we started going out together.'

McCabe was studying a gold-framed portrait in oils of Beth. She sat at an angle, hands demurely in her lap. A gifted artist had accentuated her intelligence and somehow captured in full the inner Beth of which McCabe had caught fleeting glimpses. Her wide, sensual mouth was the focal point of the painting. Since leaving Katrina's room the electric spell of expectation between them had been broken. Intent on mending his marriage, McCabe was determined to keep it that way.

He said, 'I don't have much hope of finding the girl alive.'

'That is the only logical conclusion,' Merrill agreed. 'I'm at a loss as to why the colonel is stirring it all up again.'

'I can assure you that he has his reasons.'

Merrill ran a forefinger up and down the edge of his jaw. His voice had a cutting edge to it. 'Good reasons no doubt, McCabe.'

'Yes.'

'That suggests that you know something I don't.' Merrill was mildly challenging.

McCabe deliberately paused the conversation by slowly sipping his drink. 'Perhaps that is so, Merrill, but I owe a duty of confidentiality to Colonel Farquahar.'

'I take it that my wife is aware of whatever it is that has been kept from me,' Merrill complained.

'Mrs Merrill doesn't know, I can assure you,' McCabe said. 'If she doesn't suspect that there is anything to know, it will be for the best.'

'No, McCabe,' Merrill disagreed, pouring himself a second drink while ignoring McCabe's now empty glass. 'What would be for the best is for you to dine with us this evening, then drive straight back to London.'

'I am sure that the colonel wouldn't agree with you, Merrill.'

'My father-in-law has been taken for a ride by many fraudsters on this Katrina thing, yet he still doesn't learn.'

'I don't take people for rides, Merrill, I'm here to help if I can,' McCabe said quietly and evenly. 'Your wife has accepted that.'

'Beth!' Merrill spoke the name with a mirthless chuckle. 'Beth would accept anything provided that it pleased her father.'

'Believe what you wish,' McCabe shrugged. 'You must surely care about your sister-in-law.'

Turning a chair round, Merrill sat on it. Holding his glass in both hands he stared into it, folding his legs comfortably before replying to McCabe in a quiet and reasonable tone. 'I am as caring as the next person, McCabe, but Katrina destroyed an aristocratic family that can be traced right back to the Norman Conquest. The Farquahars and the Merrills were the two most highly respected families in these parts. The immoral antics of Katrina have deprived the Farquahars of that respect. Regrettably, my own family is tainted by association. My parents once dined regularly here at the manor. Then that damned girl disgraced the name of Farquahar when she mixed with those lawless itinerants. Though I live here, neither my mother nor my father now find it possible to bring themselves to visit the manor.'

'Surely you don't blame this on a young girl?'

'That girl is responsible for everything that has gone wrong here at the manor,' Merrill replied, anger raising his voice.

'Do you realize you might be bad-mouthing a child who has been murdered?'

'I am mindful of that possibility, McCabe. But those people Katrina mixed with demanded licence and got it. Licence leads to anarchy.'

'But—' a badly shocked McCabe began, but stopped as Beth had come into the drawing-room to announce that dinner was served.

Unaccustomed to the blackness of the night and unlit roads of the countryside, McCabe drove slowly. Beside him a silent Beth was dramatically illuminated by the soft glow from the instrument panel, a dashboard Madonna whose mystique was given added depth by her not having spoken since they had driven out of the car-park of the Fox and Hounds. Wearing a clinging, silky blue dress of a Chinese style, she had done nothing with her hair. The result was a half-sophisticated, half-untamed look that had affected every male in the public house, McCabe included. Beth had arranged lodgings for him with a landlady who had a German name, a local accent, and an outsized pair of free-range breasts.

Sharee Bucholz had been wearing a tight yellow woollen dress that did her well-fleshed body full justice. The open front of the dress hovered somewhere between immodesty and indecency. At the start of the cleavage of her magnificent breasts, a huge heart-shaped rhinestone pendant hung on a gold chain that had dazzled McCabe with highlights of colour when she had brought Beth's and his drinks to their table. Though on the threshold of middle age, in the pale-yellow light Sharee's face had a mature, unselfconscious kind of beauty. She looked deep into McCabe's eyes as if trying to communicate something. McCabe could guess what it was.

Beth had explained that the landlady was an Abbeyfield girl who had married a German. Her husband had been killed in an autobahn car crash on his way home to attend a family funeral. She warned, 'Years of widowhood have turned Sharee into a huntress, so watch yourself, Mr McCabe.'

The Fox and Hounds hadn't fitted in with McCabe's idea of a country pub. It was a rather pretty place with lightwood walls, parquet flooring, and red velvet draperies. There was no strobe lighting or chromium, the bar being an antique mahogany masterpiece. The tables and chairs were not modern plastic rubbish, but ornately carved, highly polished wood.

'This place must be Dullsville to you, Mr McCabe,' Beth had said apologetically. 'But unfortunately, this is where the people that you need to talk to do their drinking.'

'At least it's peaceful,' McCabe had replied.

Beth had introduced him to the folk of Abbeyfield, beginning with Ryan and Rita Pavely. Of average height and handsome in a weak kind of way, Ryan Pavely had the snobbish arrogance of those born into wealth. Yet McCabe had noticed that the man was totally devoted to his wife.

Beth now broke the long silence in a voice that was a little croaky from disuse. 'There's a lay-by just up ahead.'

Pulling in, McCabe switched off the engine. The headlights died a slow death to leave a darkness that wrapped itself tightly around them. The only sound was the occasional sharp crack as the engine cooled and contracted. There were stars but no moon in the sky. It was a perfect night for either the poacher or the lover. Being neither of those things, McCabe wondered why she had asked him to stop the car.

'Well, Mr McCabe, what is your professional opinion of the good people of Abbeyfield?' she said at last.

McCabe's grimace went unnoticed in the darkness. 'Most of them looked me over as if I was some kind of animal they were considering purchasing at a market.'

'I suppose they do appear odd to outsiders,' Beth said with a chuckle. 'It probably has more to do with in-breeding than it does good-breeding. How did Ryan and Rita strike you?'

McCabe paused. Though having every intention of giving an honest answer, he didn't want to cause offence. The Pavelys were lifelong friends of Beth's. On learning of McCabe's profession and his purpose in Abbeyfield, Ryan Pavely had alternated between ridiculing and patronizing him.

'I didn't like Ryan Pavely,' McCabe bluntly told her.

'I must confess that I found him embarrassing this evening,' Beth readily agreed. 'The Pavelys are a wealthy family, and Ryan has tremendous influence around here. Your presence made him edgy.'

'Why would I make him edgy?'

'Because of what you are. You are here to snoop, and an honest businessman is a contradiction in terms,' Beth explained. 'Goodness knows what you'll unearth when you start rooting around in the village. Rita was Katrina's best friend right from when they had started school on the same day. She is nice, isn't she?'

Unable to agree immediately, McCabe ran a few remembered impressions of Rita Pavely through his mind. The lean-faced woman had a certain something in her eyes and a way of holding her thin but sensuous lips slightly apart, that combined to hint at a semi-dormant nymphomania. She reminded him of the women who provided his main source of income from divorce investigations in London. There was a horrible ugliness in the infidelities of other people.

'She is preferable to her husband, Mrs Merrill.'

With a short laugh, she asked, 'Isn't it about time that you started calling me Beth?'

'I will,' he said, 'beginning tomorrow.'

'Why not now?'

'Because this is the wrong situation,' he replied evasively.

'Us being out here all alone in the night?' she mused. 'Don't tell me that you are a prude.'

'No, I'm just someone who has enough problems without adding to them.'

'Haven't we all?' she gloomily agreed.

Despite the limited light inside the car, she leaned sideways to use the rear-view mirror. Very close to McCabe, she used fingers to comb her hair. With most women such a move could be interpreted as either unthinking innocence or a deliberate come-on. But Beth Merrill wasn't like most women. Something of her always remained hidden. McCabe sat rigidly still until she returned to her seat.

'You didn't ask any questions in the pub,' she commented lightly. 'I thought that is what detectives do, Mr McCabe.'

'Not all the time,' he replied, checking his watch. 'It's late. We had better make a move.'

'No, not yet,' she said firmly, surprising him by opening her door and getting out.

McCabe also got out of the car. Beth was standing on a knoll, her body erect and arms outstretched like an ancient goddess performing some primitive ritual. The sweet scent of earth rose from the ground. Moving slowly, McCabe stopped several feet from her. He felt that to speak would be like interrupting someone kneeling at prayer in a church.

Having sensed his noiseless approach, she spoke without turning her head. 'I like the nights, Mr McCabe. There is something angelic in the darkness that I am unable to contact in daylight. When it is tranquil like this I can forget what *is* and glimpse what might have been. How would you term that, as pure escapism?'

'I would say that it is something to relax into, not analyse,' McCabe replied.

'For all your rugged looks, Mr McCabe, you are sensitive.'

'Perhaps it's my one virtue,' he suggested.

'I am sure that it's not.' Head tilted back a little, she moved in an arc to scan the star-sequinned, velvety sky. She spoke speculatively. 'Is Katrina here on earth, looking up at this same sky? Will she be watching tomorrow's sunrise? Sometimes I fear that I won't be able to keep the show on the road.'

Beth's three decades of worry over her sister, and the constant care of an ageing father, had McCabe understand. But she was a strong-minded woman who had admirably coped with the many difficulties in her life.

'You are a strong person,' he assured her.

She shook her head slowly in denial. 'I'm not strong. All I do is follow a route and routine that's well plotted. I meet the challenges, but never win the prizes.'

There was no self-pity in the way that she said this. McCabe accepted that she found it therapeutic to tell someone of the strain that she was under. It was easier to speak of such things to a stranger. Would finding Katrina help? Was it possible to stick together the pieces of an old and shattered life?

She spoke softly in contemplation, 'Maybe Katrina is not here with us at all. Where do you consider Heaven to be, Mr McCabe?'

'I'm the wrong person to answer that question.'

'I think not,' she disagreed sorrowfully. 'But it was wrong of me to ask you.'

McCabe put a consoling hand on her shoulder. Some kind of energy to pulsed between them. His hand seemed clamped to her by magnetism, and it took a great effort on her part to jerk away from him.

She half-whispered, 'Take me home now please, Mr McCabe.'

They drove off in the direction of Abbeyfield Manor without speaking. The high perimeter wall of the estate reflected the beams of the headlights. McCabe could see Beth's face clearly. Her sad look when out in the night had receded.

'Are you OK now, Beth?'

'Beth?' she smiled. 'I trust that you don't break your New Year resolutions so quickly, Mr McCabe.'

'Gerry,' he corrected her.

'Fine, Gerry. But you didn't answer my question.'

'I only ever made one.'

'Have you broken it?'

'Not yet, but is there another lay-by up ahead?' he enquired jokingly.

A musical tinkling of laughter burst from her. 'It sounds as if you made a resolution to be faithful.'

This was a subtle invitation for him to reveal more about himself. Good-looking women were seldom smart, but she was. He shut up shop, giving nothing away.

Beth underwent one of her quick-fire personality changes. Abandoning subtlety she asked. 'Are you married, Gerry?'

'Sort of,' he replied.

She spoke glumly as he drove through the manor gateway. 'Sort of! Is there any other kind of marriage?'

'Who knows? There aren't any guidelines, Beth,' McCabe replied. The car tyres scrunched noisily on the gravel drive. 'It's something like a parody on the Trinity, with every couple haunted by the eternal third party instead of the Holy Ghost.'

'I'll have to think that one over. You're too deep for me, Gerry.'

Stopping the car, he quipped, 'Home sweet home.'

'You're kidding. Do you know how I'd like life to be?' she asked, then answered her own question. 'Like in those old films when everything goes wrong for the principal characters one night. Then the next reel and it's morning and everything is much brighter and happier. I've been waiting a long time for the next reel.'

'You probably have to see the whole film, Beth,' McCabe advised.

'And hope for a happy ending?'

'They are very rare.'

With a laugh that was short on mirth, she commented, 'We're

a couple of manic depressives, aren't we?' Making no move towards getting out of the car, she enquired, 'Tell me, Gerry, are you one of those perfectionists who doesn't welcome advice?'

'I'd like to think not. Why do you ask?'

'Maybe this is silly, but it could be useful,' Beth was saying hesitantly. 'When do you intend going to Kilverham?'

'First thing in the morning. I want to call at the police station.'

'It might be worth your while to look up a chap called John-John.' Beth turned her face to him. 'In the sixties he was John Menson, a sensible, good-looking guy. He took a bad trip on LSD, and his mind never came back properly. He's a kind of religious freak now, which has earned him the name of John the Baptist locally.'

'You think that he might be able to help?'

'Maybe,' Beth said. 'He's the last of the hippie Mohicans, so to speak.'

A cold thought disturbed McCabe. 'Was he strange in the head before Katrina went missing, Beth?'

'Yes,' Beth nodded, and McCabe could detect fear in her eyes. 'That's been on my mind.'

'Where can I find him?'

'You mustn't go alone,' she said anxiously.

'Is he violent?'

'Who knows with someone as odd as John-John.'

'I'll watch myself,' McCabe promised. 'Where will I find him?'

Pointing through the windscreen as if it were daylight and she could see the landscape she was describing, Beth instructed, 'Go out of the village on the Kilverham road for about three miles, and you'll see a rough track on your left with a Perkins's Scrapyard sign. John-John has a battered old caravan.'

A light came on in a downstairs window of the manor. Beth sighed. 'Time to go. That's Roland's signal that he knows I'm out here.'

Getting out of the car, she held the door open to lean back in and say, 'I enjoyed this evening, Gerry, which makes it impossible for me to go back to how I was.'

'How were you?' he asked with concern.

'Conditioned to accept a life of quiet despair,' she replied numbly, then suddenly changed to a flippant mood. 'Watch your-self with the Widow Bucholz, Gerry.'

Beth slammed the door and walked away. He watched her go, then started the car and headed for Abbeyfield and the Fox and Hounds.

A light glowed in the kitchen of the public house as McCabe drove into the car-park. He walked slowly and reluctantly towards the building. He hadn't anticipated being distracted by two attractive women in a rural area. Striving not to make it obvious, Sharee was waiting for him with a bottle and two glasses on the table. The pale-green satin, thigh-length robe she wore revealed legs that were heavier than current fashion consid-ered desirable, but shapely. She smiled as she filled the two glasses. 'I couldn't call myself a landlady if I let you retire without a night-cap.'

Unable to come up with a viable excuse, McCabe sat and she pulled out a seat across the table from him. She raised her glass. 'Here's wishing you success in Abbeyfield.'

'I'm told that I'll need a lot of luck,' McCabe remarked.

'This is a very insular community,' Sharee nodded gravely. 'I doubted that they would accept Joachim, my husband.'

'Did they?'

'Yes,' she replied reminiscently. 'Probably because we were at the centre of the village here at the Fox and Hounds. We hadn't long taken over the place when the hippies arrived. They gave us a magnificent start in the pub business. The place was packed every night. One of them, a beautiful girl with long black hair, was a lovely singer who sang Julie Felix songs, probably because she looked like her. I just can't bring her name to mind....'

'Suzi Duoard,' McCabe volunteered.

Aghast, she croaked a question, 'How on earth could you know that?'

'The name came up earlier this evening,' McCabe admitted modestly. 'The 1960s seem to have made quite an impression on this area, Mrs Bucholtz. What attracted the hippies?'

She shrugged. 'I suppose they welcomed somewhere they could stay unmolested. Most farmers chased them off their land before they could get settled, calling the police to help if necessary. They were made welcome on the Pavelys' place, Perham Farm. That was before Ryan took over. Old Silas and Mary were running the farm. They always indulged Ryan, their only child, and still do. He was young then and something of a tearaway who liked having the flower people.'

'You're a valuable source of information,' McCabe told her gratefully.

'I've probably said too much,' Sharee said worriedly. 'This may be the twenty-first century, but a lynching might still be possible in Abbeyfield. I found the place to be suffocating when I was young and adventurous, so I left to join the army. That's how I met Joachim.'

'How long ago was it that you lost your husband?' McCabe enquired.

'Five years ago last Christmas. Christmas hasn't been much fun since, Mr McCabe.'

Not comfortable with the formal use of his name, McCabe didn't encourage familiarity by inviting her to call him Gerry. 'It must have been an awful time for you.'

'Losing Joachim took all of the joy,' she said pensively, looking around the kitchen as if she could see the whole pub. 'I get by putting everything into running the pub. Keeping busy is helpful.'

'I can understand that,' McCabe sympathized. 'I hope that I will be taken into the Abbeyfield fold as quickly as your husband was.'

'You won't be because you're asking questions,' Sharee told him with a decisive shake of her head. 'Joachim wasn't prying into people's lives. 'Like the sleeping dog, Abbeyfield's past should be let lie.'

Pursing his lips dubiously, McCabe asked, 'Even if a girl has been murdered?'

'Yes, even if a girl has been murdered,' the landlady said emphatically. Draining her glass she stood. With a tired smile she said, 'I have a brewer's delivery coming early, so I'm turning in.'

'Goodnight,' McCabe said.

'Goodnight, Mr McCabe.'

three

In the few short hours he had been here, Abbeyfield had come up with so much intrigue that he knew that he would have to be cautious from the start. The landlady's barely disguised plea that he should leave Abbeyfield in peace had set him thinking. It seemed Sharee wanted to defend the whole community. That was something that he couldn't comprehend.

If, as was likely, Katrina Farquahar's body lay where her purse had been unearthed, how many villagers already knew that? It was inconceivable that an entire community would wish to protect the killer.

Remembering Beth saying, 'Ryan has tremendous influence around here', set McCabe thinking. Sharee Bucholtz had tied in Ryan Pavely with the hippie commune at the time Katrina had disappeared. If the young farmer had been involved with Katrina's disappearance, his family apparently had the power to force the locals to be silent.

He put out the kitchen light and made his way wearily up the stairs. A large wedge of light on the landing warned him that the landlady had left her bedroom door partly open. Beth's joking warning about Sharee Bucholtz now became serious.

Going quietly into his room, McCabe quickly prepared for bed. When he was in bed the events of the day did a constant rerun through his mind to keep sleep at bay. Believing that he'd heard a movement on the landing, he listened intently. Hearing nothing, he told himself that he'd been mistaken.

Even so, a few moments later he got out of bed and locked the bedroom door.

*

Chair tilted back, Detective Inspector Solomon Quinn studied McCabe through professionally cautious eyes. Leanly handsome in the suffering kind of way women go for, the detective's vanity showed in the combed forward style of his auburn hair that concealed a receding hairline. Quinn had a capable look that said he could handle himself when the going got rough. The ruins of Katrina's handbag lay on the desktop between them.

'I won't bullshit you, McCabe,' Quinn said, indicating the handbag. 'What you have isn't enough for me to persuade the chief to excavate Abbeyfield Manor.'

'Just a rockery, not the whole estate,' McCabe pointed out.

The morning had so far gone well for McCabe after he had survived the awkward atmosphere at breakfast with Sharee Bucholtz. She had reacted badly to what she saw as rejection by McCabe last night. As she had stood to clear the dishes from the table, he reached out to grasp her wrist.

'It's not you, Sharee,' he had explained.

'I think I knew that, but thanks for reassuring me, Mr McCabe.'

'Gerry.'

This made her smile sweetly, and he had told her, 'Even so, it was a powerful test of my willpower.'

She had smiled once more, and neither of them had mentioned the subject again.

Now Quinn, who had nicotine stains on his fingers but no cigarettes, used the tip of his tongue to switch the match he was chewing to the opposite corner of his mouth. Picking up McCabe's business card from his desk he read it once more before enquiring, 'What's the Gerry short for, Gerald?'

'Gerrard.'

'Have you spoken to Bert Jakeman, the colonel's gardener, Gerry?'

Shaking his head, McCabe replied, 'I didn't think it necessary. The colonel said that he was one hundred per cent reliable. Surely he isn't known to you, Inspector?'

'Not in the usual sense,' Quinn answered. 'Uniform responded to a complaint from a member of the public last week. They found old Bert in Colwell Lane. He was wearing an army tunic and bush hat. He had a shotgun with him to flush a Malayan bandit out of a garden hedge.'

Disappointed, McCabe sighed inwardly. 'Are you saying the old guy is *non compos mentis*?'

'All I'm saying, Gerry,' Quinn responded, with a shy, boyish smile that didn't fit properly on his hard face, 'is that there are definitely no Malayan bandits in Kilverham.'

McCabe decided not to give up. How had the old gardener come by the purse if he hadn't dug it up? From the state of it, it was evident that the purse had been buried for thirty years. He changed tack. 'Do you know the officer who dealt with the Farquahar girl's disappearance, Inspector?'

'I *knew* him,' Quinn's reply was carefully worded. 'That was Charlie Peake, who died a couple of years back.'

'I'll risk one more question. What do you know of a guy called John the Baptist?' McCabe asked.

Getting up from behind the desk, Quinn went to stand and look out of the window with the bored expression of a man who had seen the same scene too many times. Several minutes passed before he spoke. 'I wish you'd spared yourself that question, Gerry.'

'Is it that bad?'

'Worse,' Quinn replied. 'If John the Baptist ever does have a good day now, then you'll be lucky to catch him on it.'

'It sounds as if you keep tabs on him, Inspector.'

'It shames me to admit it, but every time a flasher is reported on the common, or someone is seen hanging around a kids' play-ground, John-John is pulled in.'

'Simply because he is different?'

The inspector nodded. 'Exactly. It's unfair and unjust, but that's the way the system operates.'

'Well, thank you for your help, Inspector,' McCabe said, as he stood to leave. 'I'm going to call on John-John on my way back to Abbeyfield. Should I brush up on my martial arts first?'

'I've never known him to be physically violent,' the detective smiled. He extended his right hand to McCabe. 'This suggestion may not appeal, Gerry, but it's not often I see a new face. Pete Rendall, my superintendent, is a traction-engine enthusiast, while Will Short, my sergeant, brews his own beer. They do not make riveting company. Could we get together for a drink this evening?'

McCabe said, 'I'd like that.' Keeping a straight face, he added, 'I will be able to show you my stamp collection.'

'You do that, and I'll show you what police brutality is all about,' Quinn warned jokingly. 'Where will I find you, Gerry?'

'I'm staying at the Fox and Hounds in Abbeyfield.'

'I'll be there around eight o'clock, and you can drop the rank and call me Sol,' Quinn said. 'I'll take a look at the Farquahar file in the meantime.'

'If there's a file on Maria Farquahar, the girl's mother, I'd be interested.'

'There isn't, as she left home of her own accord,' Quinn explained. 'But if you come across the bloke she went away with I'd like to hear about it.'

'You will,' McCabe promised. 'Sylvester Hartley isn't it?'

'That's it. He's wanted for fraud. Not now but then, the 1960s.'

'I'm sure to come across him in my travels, Sol.'

Going out through the door, McCabe stopped when the detective called his name.

'A word of caution,' Quinn said. 'John-John might not cause you trouble, but you'll have to pass Abb Perkins to get to him. He's big and he can turn nasty, real nasty.'

Thanking him for the warning, McCabe went out to his car.

Though a town whereas Abbeyfield was a village, Kilverham had a rural allure of its own. Its character was preserved by an old cattle-market with eighteenth-century porticoes, and saddlers' shops and corn merchants that had resisted the passage of time. Woolworth's, although tiny and quaint, was an anachronism balanced out by a black and white Tudor building that bore the scars of once having been converted into a cinema, and was now a bingo hall. A large part of the town's attraction came from its urbane obedience that gave it an air of tranquillity rare in an increasingly violent age.

Running Beth's directions through his mind, he spotted the

scrap-yard sign and turned into the dirt track. He weaved through a maze of wrecked cars piled high, braking, as a giant of a man stepped out in front of him. Wearing a once-white vest and a pair of torn trousers, the man folded bulging-muscled, tattooed arms across his chest and stood in front of McCabe's car.

He checked McCabe's number plate before coming round to the driver's side. Long yellow hair fell forwards as he bent to ask, 'You looking for Vauxhall spare parts, mister?'

McCabe said, 'No, I've come to see the guy who lives in a caravan here.'

'He ain't in,' the man who fitted Solomon Quinn's description of Abb Perkins said, using a massive, thick-fingered hand to brush back his hair. 'McCabe, isn't it? I've heard you were around asking questions.'

'News travels fast around here,' McCabe commented.

'*Bad* news does.'

'When is this guy likely to be back?'

'Questions, questions,' Perkins complained. 'I sell car spares, not answers. Best you just turn your car round in that space over there, then drive on back out.'

'That sounds like a threat,' McCabe observed laconically.

'That *is* a threat.'

Though huge, Perkins, like most tall men, was an awkward mover. In addition, the scrap-merchant was so heavily muscled that he would be slow. McCabe told him in a conversational tone, 'Some other time.'

'Any time, McCabe,' Perkins offered belligerently.

Back out on the road heading for Abbeyfield, McCabe realized that he had just encountered yet another local anomaly. Abb Perkins didn't want him to talk to John-John Menson, but why? Perkins could have been no more than a boy at the time Katrina Farquahar had gone missing.

Entering Abbeyfield, he was driving past the post office when Beth Merrill came out. Spotting him, she waved, signalling for him to pull in behind a gleaming Land-Rover Discovery. With the collar of her sheepskin coat turned up, she came to the nearside of McCabe's car. Opening the passenger's door, she leaned in, her blonde hair as unruly as ever. She was one of those rare people whose image couldn't be taken with you when parting from them. McCabe felt a thrill as if seeing her for the first time.

'Gerry,' she greeted him brightly. 'I see you're out and about, earning your keep.'

'If I was paid by results, then I haven't earned a penny.'

'The natives have taken to the bush,' she guessed with a little chuckle. She playfully levelled a long and lovely finger at him. 'I'll arrange a dinner at the manor for tomorrow evening, and invite Ryan and Rita, together with Ryan's parents. That should give you something to work on.'

'Make it dress informal,' McCabe pleaded, conscious of having brought only one suit, a sweater, and a pair of jeans with him.

Beth had a disconcerting trick of looking away suddenly. She remarked, 'I could make it a pyjama party, but you'll have already enjoyed one of those with Sharee.'

'She doesn't wear pyjamas—' McCabe started to say, but clapped his hand over his mouth in pretence at having made a Freudian slip.

Beth laughed, before, 'Did you have any luck with John-John?'

'He wasn't at home.'

Sudden realization made Beth hit her forehead with the heel of her hand. 'Of course not! Can you spare an hour, Gerry?'

'Yes.'

'Then lock up your car and come with me,' she said, making for the parked Land-Rover.

They left the village to travel through scenic countryside. Familiarity with the roads allowed Beth to motor at speed, and her competent handling of the four-wheel-drive vehicle impressed McCabe. They topped a rise and negotiated a hairpin bend and McCabe, accustomed to grey and dingy streets, was mesmerized by the view. The ground in front of them swept down in a wooded slope to where a river rushed and foamed. An islet was like a verdant eel strung along the deep blue of the river. Far off in the west a snowfall of gulls wheeled against the back-drop of a dark-blue autumnal sky.

There was a quick change of scenery then as Beth confidently sent the Land-Rover hurtling down a narrow twisting road through some woods. She alarmed McCabe by taking one hand from the wheel to point to a flat picnic area. 'That place is a drive-in Sodom and Gomorrah at night,' she informed him, 'and that's not all that happens out here.' She leaned forward in her seat to point up at a towering viaduct. 'There's been three suicides from up there in recent times.'

'Lovers and losers,' McCabe commented wryly.

'They're one and the same thing,' Beth said cynically, in one of her swift changes of mood.

They rounded a bend and everything took on a fairy-tale aspect for McCabe. Facing them, totally unexpected in uninhabited countryside, was a church. It was an ancient building that McCabe guessed was Norman. Considerable restoration had been carried out.

'Surprised?' Beth asked, as she halted the Land-Rover. 'This was a monastery in medieval times. Lionel Blake, the vicar at Abbeyfield, raised funds to restore it. It's used for special occasions. Just about everyone in the district comes out here for a Christmas service. They have choir practice this afternoon.' Beth wound down her window. 'Listen.'

An excellent choir was singing a hymn. The sound seemed to have escaped from the church to float through the air unattached and eerie. McCabe was aware that Beth was studying him curiously.

'I'm Catholic,' McCabe excused himself.

Accepting this with a nod, she considerately enquired, 'Will that prevent you from going inside to meet John-John?'

'Lead on,' McCabe invited. 'I keep my work and my religion separate.'

'What about your women?' Beth enquired cheekily.

'Exactly the same principle, Beth.'

'I'll have to check that out with Sharee,' Beth giggled, reaching for the heavy iron ring of the door latch.

The latch made an unexpectedly loud clunk as Beth lifted it, making both of them uncomfortable. But the singing continued uninterrupted as they tiptoed inside and joined forces to close the door noiselessly.

Beth led him down a side aisle. An interior of carved Bath

stone imparted a yellow look to everything. A small man with wild grey hair conducted a choir of mixed sex. With a pulpit for a rostrum, the choirmaster's head jerked this way and that, pausing in a listening position occasionally, first to the left and then to the right, then nodding contentedly. It was as if he was carrying on a telepathic conversation with his singers.

Then the combined voices faded into a pregnant silence that was invaded by a solo male voice. Both hands raised, head thrown back, the choirmaster seemed to be coaxing out a truly wonderful voice that sang *Were You There When They Crucified Our Lord*?

The singer wore a monk's habit that was neither the traditional brown nor white. It was aquamarine blue, which complemented the shoulder-length golden hair of the man wearing it. McCabe couldn't understand why he felt deep disappointment on discovering that the singer was beardless.

Leaning close to McCabe, Beth whispered, 'That's John-John.'

The hymn ended in the usual way, but John-John's exquisite voice seemed to live on as a pleasing echo. Touching McCabe lightly on the arm, Beth told him, 'I won't be a minute,' and went over to speak to the choirmaster, who beckoned for John-John to come down from the gallery.

Coming back to McCabe, Beth reported, 'He can spare him for a few minutes.'

'I could use a few hours with him,' McCabe said.

'Then now's the time to arrange it,' Beth advised, as John-John came towards them, his aura of mysticism increased by his long blue robe that made it appear that he was drifting along rather than walking.

But the illusion of divinity receded rapidly when John-John stood before him. Though well past his half-century, his face was as unlined as that of a teenager, reinforcing McCabe's long held belief that the only true freedom came with insanity. John-John was so way out of the world that the cares of everyday life hadn't touched him for decades.

'Hello, Beth,' John-John politely acknowledged her, his eyes wonderingly on McCabe.

'This is Gerry McCabe, John-John,' Beth said. 'He wants to have a word with you.'

'"It is better to hear the rebuke of the wise, than for a man to hear the song of fools."' John-John treated McCabe to a Biblical quotation.

'Mr McCabe is a detective my father has engaged to find Katrina.'

Studying McCabe through over-bright, penetrating eyes, John-John spoke judgementally. 'You are a man who has known violence, Mr McCabe.'

'I've only ever defended myself,' McCabe explained.

'That means nothing.' John-John's long golden hair swung as he shook his head. 'The sword always defiles, regardless of whether you grasp the handle or are pierced by the tip.'

'I accept that,' McCabe said, eager to make constructive use of the short time John-John would be there. 'I would like to discuss the sixties with you, John-John.'

Face twisting in emotional agony, John-John cried out so loudly that the heads of the choir and choirmaster turned their way in alarm. Calming a little, somehow huddling down inside his habit, John-John wailed, 'What can I tell you? Only that we were lost in our wretchedness, disembodied by our imaginations. What gave us pleasure yesterday will give us tears tomorrow. I've counted the days, counted the hours, counted the long, aching minutes. We can't look back, that hurts too much. We can't look forward, it's a tall barrier we are unable to see over.'

Though forewarned by Solomon Quinn, McCabe hadn't anticipated John-John's rambling would be this nonsensical. McCabe would have left were it not for Beth's fingers digging hard into his bicep, staying him.

Moving closer to them, an anguished John-John spoke confidingly. 'It has to be in our power to reverse the slide into iniquity by performing an act of incarnation.'

Beth placed her hand gently on John-John's narrow chest in the region of his heart. She said calmly. '*Pax vobiscum*, brother. Will you walk outside with us for just a short while?'

A peaceful look crept slowly over John-John's face as he placed his hand on top of Beth's hand on his breast. He amazed McCabe by speaking rationally. 'Of course, Beth. It will please me to do so.'

Walking up the aisle between them, he spoke sympathetically to McCabe. 'I do appreciate your predicament, Mr McCabe, and will do everything possible to assist you in your quest. I was very fond of Katrina, and she has not been absent from my prayers for one single night since she went away. Your investigation may well bring about the end. The real end. Or maybe the real end was the day on which I last saw Katrina.'

Still staggered by the swift change that Beth had brought about in John-John, McCabe said, 'Thank you. I did try to call at your home, but was turned away.'

'That would be Abb,' John-John said with a fond smile. 'He is very protective of me, but he means well, Mr McCabe. You are an exception, of course, but were it not for Abb I would be plagued by unwelcome visitors, the majority of whom would probably wish to do me violence.'

'If possible, I would like to meet you for a long talk, John-John,' he said.

The sound of the church door opening made John-John turn to see the choirmaster's head come out, looking for him. He said quickly to McCabe. 'Then I will contact you as soon as possible.'

'Gerry is staying with Sharee Bucholtz, John-John,' Beth explained.

Bowing a sorrowful head, John-John intoned, 'Poor dear Sharee has suffered greatly. We all must pray that she does not find a supernatural remedy for her grief, but a supernatural use for it.'

McCabe anticipated more ranting. He got in quickly, 'Will you get in touch with me at the pub, John-John?'

'You can depend on me, Mr McCabe,' John-John assured him. 'I would like Beth to be there, too. It is indeed time that the unfinished affairs of days gone by were completed. There is much that I can't fit together inside of my head, Mr McCabe, but I will tell you things, name names, and your professional mind will produce order from the chaos and provide the answers.'

'I look forward to our next meeting, John-John,' McCabe said, as he got into the Land-Rover beside Beth.

Coming up to the side window, John-John mournfully said, 'They even killed the baby, thereby ending a life before it had really begun.'

Believing that he was again spouting nonsense, McCabe realized too late that he wasn't. But John-John was already walking away in the direction of the waiting choirmaster and the church.

'Nice seeing you, John-John,' Beth called, as she started up the engine, and he gave her a backward wave in reply.

Looking at the retreating figure, McCabe pondered on how the robed man could be close to certifiable one moment, and have the potential to be a valuable aide the next. Noticing his head turning to glance back at them, McCabe could see from his expression that something had occurred to him, and he stopped Beth from driving away. 'Hold it for a moment, Beth.'

An agitated John-John ran back to the Land-Rover. Opening the door, McCabe leaned out to ask, 'What's the matter?'

'What should we do, Mr McCabe, to make this world tolerable? Or rather, what do we have to stop doing?'

Not waiting for an answer, John-John turned on his heel and retraced his steps back to the church. McCabe closed the door of the Land-Rover and Beth drove away.

'What was that he said about killing the baby?' McCabe enquired, as Beth unexpectedly took a left turn.

'It meant nothing to me,' Beth replied with a shrug. 'We're taking a different route back to town, Gerry. I thought we could call in at Perham Farm and invite the Pavelys over to dinner tomorrow.'

Twenty minutes later, Beth turned into a field and drove on until they topped a rise. She parked the Land-Rover and they both got out.

A setting sun, anxious to be seen one more time that day, parted heavy curtains of cloud. In the dusk the expanse of dark green fields ahead of them seemed unnaturally close, as though they could have stretched out their hands and touched them.

'The wind has changed from a north-east round to a southwest, the rain bringer,' Beth reported, as they strolled away from the Land-Rover. She pointed to acres of flat land with a hedgerow for a perimeter. 'Even I find it difficult to imagine it now, Gerry, but there is where it all happened in the sixties. That field was a display of multi-coloured vehicles of all kinds, even gypsy-style horse-drawn caravans. It was alive with music, throbbing with passion, an exotic scene that I am sure will never again be seen. Standing here I feel really close to Katrina.'

She pointed to their left. 'Rita and Ryan live in the main farmhouse in that dip. Ryan's mum and dad moved into a shepherd's cottage about half a mile away when old Silas retired.'

'Do they own all this land?' an incredulous McCabe enquired.

'Every last acre, Gerry. The Pavelys are filthy rich,' she replied. Then she held both hands out at her sides, palms up, and announced, 'It's started to rain. Let's run back to the Land-Rover and drive on down to see them.'

Within a split second it was raining in torrents, soaking them to the skin before they had time to reach the vehicle. Both crouching to protect their faces from the stinging rain as they ran, they laughingly collided with the Land-Rover, and McCabe opened the driver's door for her.

Clambering in, she stumbled and fell against him. He caught the scent of her again. Coaxed out by the rain, it was even more stirring now. Having put an arm round her to steady her as she had lost her footing, he tightened it to pull her closer. McCabe felt the jarring impact of new emotions. Gently back brushing her hair, his fingers travelling lightly on Beth's face were suddenly fierce and demanding.

Tilting her head back, face very close to his, Beth's eyes narrowed so that they became smoky slits. Her lips were slackly apart, beckoning to him, begging him. Then her whole body stiffened and she thrust him away from her. In what was a half-shout, she said, 'No!'

Left outside alone in the rain as Beth got into the Land-Rover and closed the door, McCabe ran round to the passenger's side. Getting into the vehicle, he feared that Beth would be upset about him having made a pass at her. But she sat silent, staring straight ahead.

'Beth?' he said tentatively.

Her shoulders suddenly slumped. A kind of shrug in reverse. Then she said, 'Take no notice of my moods, Gerry. Give me two minutes alone with Coco the Clown and I'll turn him. I'd have him suicidal.'

Noticing him studying her, she made another joke. 'If you're trying to read my mind, Gerry, forget it. I haven't got past the first page myself.'

'I'm sorry if I upset you,' he apologized.

'Far from it. I've really enjoyed this afternoon.' She returned to being her old, flippant self. 'Listen, we can't very well call on the Pavelys in this state. Rita wouldn't appreciate us both dripping all over her Axminsters. I'll take you back to your car and telephone them with an invitation when I get home.'

When she pulled up beside his car, she said pensively, 'We've got along well together today, Gerry, but it will have to be different at the manor tomorrow night. You will find me cool towards you.'

'For the sake of your husband?' he asked, giving her an understanding smile.

'Partly, but principally for your sake and for mine.'

McCabe didn't fully grasp what Beth meant until she was driving away and he was unlocking his car. Then he understood. He thought back to how life had once been with his wife and daughter, putting fragments of memory into slots so well used that they were worn smooth at the edges. Not only did he understand what Beth had meant, but also he wholeheartedly agreed with her.

Illuminated subtly by flickering candles in antique candelabra on the dinner table, the dining-hall of Abbeyfield Manor had taken on an impressive atmosphere. Beth had prepared an excellent meal, and had skilfully recreated a grandeur that the manor would have possessed in ages past. The conversation over dinner had been lively and easy-going. Now, as the evening drew to a close and the guests were preparing to leave, Beth, in a last-minute attempt at fully involving McCabe, mentioned that he had spent the previous evening in the company of Detective Inspector Solomon Quinn.

'I've always been led to believe that there is no love lost between the police force and private detectives,' Silas Pavely commented. During the evening both he and his son had seemed to swell up, becoming big with their own importance.

The elder Pavely had a brown, strong-boned, tight-skinned

face, with heavy black eyebrows that contrasted with his iron-grey hair, black eyes, and a hawk-like nose. A frown laddered his brow as he awaited McCabe's response.

The evening McCabe had spent with Solomon Quinn had been enjoyable and informative. But over dinner this evening he had learned nothing. He sensed that the Pavelys had planned it that way. Only Mary Pavely, who was one of those lucky people who broke all the rules and got away with it, had defied the invisible censor.

'The police at Kilverham have been most co-operative, Mr Pavely,' McCabe said.

'They are not very responsive when someone from Abbeyfield reports a crime,' Ryan Pavely complained.

This stirred the detached Colonel Farquahar into commenting bitterly, 'The standard of service from all public institutions has declined deplorably. That damned fellow Wilson must shoulder the blame.'

Beth glanced at McCabe before saying to Ryan Pavely, 'You are being critical of the police as a ratepayer, Ryan, whereas Mr McCabe's viewpoint is that of a professional investigator.'

'How is your investigation progressing, Mr McCabe?' Rita Pavely enquired, her face remaining expressionless, but her undersized breasts rising and falling as though from an inner disturbance. 'Are you about to lay to rest the ghost of summers past?'

There was a dizzy silence before Mary Pavely, her hennaed hair flapping, peered over silver-rimmed glasses to level a warning finger at her daughter-in-law. 'That was most insensitive of you, Rita.'

'I am terribly sorry, Colonel Farquahar, Beth. It was thoughtless of me,' a blushing Rita apologized humbly.

The colonel, having faded completely into yesteryear, missed both Rita's unfortunate turn of phrase and her apology. Beth silently forgave her with a fleeting smile.

'I understand that you were Katrina's closest friend, Mrs Pavely,' McCabe said, tentatively.

'The pair of them were joined at the hip.' A smiling Silas came up with a cliché, his capped teeth gleaming in the candlelight. He turned to Beth's husband. 'The terrible twins at school, weren't they, Roland?'

'They had their moments,' Merrill agreed with a disarming smile at Rita, 'but they were ideal students compared to the majority.'

'It was an ideal world until those damn hippies invaded Abbeyfield,' Simon Farquahar said grumpily.

'I rather think that Beth, Rita and Ryan do not share your view on that, Colonel,' Mary Pavely disagreed. 'For the young people it was a wonderful time. They lived life to the full in an environment of colour, music, and friendship. I was no spring chicken when those gypsy rovers came over the hill, but I do remember that era as having put a blessing on everything.'

'A curse on everything, more like,' Colonel Farquahar remarked.

Rita spoke dubiously. 'It was enjoyable at the time, but in retrospect it is most unreal. Maybe it is just the passing of time, but I feel as if I dreamt that period rather than lived through it.'

'Well,' Beth sighed, pausing. 'That's because we were kids then, Rita. How could we have formed proper memories at a time when we used to jump to avoid the cracks in the pavement and make faces at the moon?'

'It was truly a great time as I recall, but it couldn't happen now,' Ryan declared. 'Today, with the Press, the radio, and television having everyone thinking alike and functioning alike, there is no place for the radical, or even the free-thinker.'

'Something that we should be thankful for,' Colonel Farquahar grunted.

'Amen to that,' Roland Merrill said fervently.

'And an end to this evening,' Silas Pavely said firmly. The vitality of the elderly that allows them to hide fatigue for long stretches had at last deserted him. 'Thank you, Colonel, for a most enjoyable time. And my thanks to you for a wonderful meal, a veritable feast, Beth.'

four

Though the others took their leave of McCabe in a detached, reserved way, Mary Pavely came forward to clasp his hand tightly. 'Good night, Mr McCabe, and good luck with your mission.'

Short and fat, with a huge bosom that she had to peer over, she hadn't worn as well as her husband. McCabe was mystified by the look in the elderly woman's eyes as they parted. He was pondering on this when Colonel Farquahar moved close to him while Beth and her husband were at the door doing the host and hostess thing.

'Bert wants to see you in the morning, McCabe,' the Colonel said in a hoarse whisper that had as much volume as a shout. 'You will find him in the hothouse to the right of the tennis courts.'

Beth coming back in through the door prevented McCabe from questioning the colonel. Car doors were slamming out in the night and Roland Merrill's voice could be heard calling after the departing guests.

'What are you two co-conspirators up to?' Beth's anxious tone belied her nonchalant manner. 'Are you keeping some secret from me?'

'I lack the inclination, and certainly the courage, to keep anything secret from you, Beth,' her father commented wryly.

'I would never question your courage, Father, but your inclinations are highly suspect,' Beth quipped, before turning to McCabe. She had a gleam in her eyes that was pure mischief. 'Will you stay and have a night-cap with us, Mr McCabe?'

'Yes, do so, my dear fellow,' her father urged.

'Thank you, but no,' McCabe replied, keenly aware of Beth's disappointment. 'I've got a full day tomorrow, so I want to get to bed as soon as I can.'

'That's understandable,' Beth remarked, brushing aside the soft curtain of blonde hair that had fallen over her cheek.

To her father and to her husband who had just come back into the manor, Beth's words would sound innocuous. But a tacit reference to Sharee Bucholz had put both innuendo and, McCabe was fairly certain, a touch of jealousy into her tone. That caused him concern.

Beth followed him to the door and stepped out into the silence of the night behind him. For some while they stood without speaking. The night birds swooping and diving around the huge house uttered no cries. The only sound in the darkness was the barely audible rippling of a stream that ran along the far edge of the lawn. Tilting her head back, Beth breathed in deeply. Her lips were parted, wet and full. Her exhalation was a sigh of satisfaction. Standing close, she spoke softly, making a little gesture with both hands as if trying to convey her words to him physically.

'I so much wanted you to stay a little longer, Gerry.'

'You shouldn't be here,' McCabe warned.

'It's risky,' Beth admitted. 'He'll be watching me from the shadows.'

'Then why take the risk, Beth?'

She shrugged. 'Why not? I live a humdrum life from which the only escape has been through fantasy. There is no taste in mental infidelity, Gerry. Dreaming impossible dreams is no longer enough.'

'You're still taking an awful chance by being out here.'

'I'll tell him that I wanted to ask if you have found out anything about Katrina. Lying to Roland enables me to keep my options open.'

What options? In the half-light an electric look zigzagged between them. Starkly aware of how dangerous was the situation, McCabe turned and walked to his car. He heard her call his name, low-voiced, but he kept on walking.

'Goodnight, Beth,' he said, without looking back.

Beth stayed silent. As McCabe drove away from the manor she was still standing where he had left her. A sad and forlorn figure in the gloom of night.

She was on his mind as he headed for the village. It would take a lifetime to know her, and even then some of the vague combinations of the countless facets that made up her personality would remain hidden. There was a depth to her that was beyond the senses.

He hoped that he wouldn't find Sharee Bucholz waiting up for him. Though tempted, he was determined to resist the landlady. A relationship with Sharee would be no more than a practised technique as well developed as a set of symmetrical muscles. McCabe was relieved to find the inn in darkness when he drove into the car-park. Switching off the engine, he sat for a moment, feeling relief and tension alternating in him like a cooling shower.

The question why the colonel's gardener wanted to see him disturbed his sleep, yet he still hadn't come up with an answer the next morning when he parked close to the tennis courts. An elderly man stood outside of a large greenhouse, pruning what the horticulturally ignorant McCabe guessed was a rose bush.

A small man with grey hair cut short back and sides military style, the gardener had the straight-backed stance of a long-serving soldier. Two collared doves sat protectively on a tree branch above the old man's head. They gazed with suspicion on McCabe as he approached.

'Mr Jakeman?'

'Bert will do, young fellow.'

'I'm Gerry McCabe.'

'I know who you are,' Jakeman responded with a nod. 'I've something in my shed that I think you should see.'

McCabe followed Jakeman along a trail that wound through trees. There were more trees now and the sounds of woodlife followed them along. They neared a small wooden hut. A few feet away from them a sparrow was teaching a youngster to fly while a small rabbit, totally entranced by the demonstration, tried it itself. The furred creature's noisy failure caused the fledgling to crash-dive. Screaming abuse, the mother sparrow chased the rabbit through hawthorn bushes. A lurking fox observed the little drama slyly from behind a clump of bright-pink valerian.

Unsettled by the Walt Disney scenario, McCabe waited outside the hut when the gardener went in. Reaching under a workbench Jakeman took out a small cardboard box. Opening the box he held it out to McCabe. Inside was a short, thin bone. About an inch in length, it lay on a folded piece of rag.

'Do you see what it is, McCabe?'

'It's a bone,' McCabe observed, 'What should it mean to me, Bert?'

'Maybe nothing, maybe everything. You see, I found it in the rockery, close to where I dug up the purse.'

Taking the box for a closer look, McCabe said, 'I'd say that it's more likely to be that of a bird rather than a human being.'

'Could well be that you're right,' Jakeman agreed. 'But you people have ways of finding out these days, haven't you?'

'It can be done. I'll see if I can get the police to take a look at it.'

Replacing the lid on the little box, Jakeman passed it to McCabe, saying, 'I'll leave it to you.' He paused for a moment, then went on in a confidential whisper, 'Remember that the colonel won't want Miss Beth to know about this, just like the handbag.'

'I won't say anything to her,' McCabe assured him.

'Ssshhh, keep your voice down,' Jakeman cautioned. 'She's coming.'

Unable to hear anyone approaching, a cold finger seemed to touch McCabe's spine as Beth stepped out of the trees beside them. Her unruly hair was semi-controlled by a blue Alice band, and she wore a simple linen dress that was flax-coloured and lower-calf-length. The moccasins that she wore explained the silence of her approach.

'Good morning, Bert,' she greeted the gardener, who appeared to struggle with an urge to salute smartly. Then Beth smiled at McCabe. 'Hello, Gerry.'

Her old flippancy had replaced her melancholy of the previous night. Falling into step beside McCabe as he walked to his car, she enquired with fake casualness, 'What brings you down into this neck of the woods, Gerry?'

'Just routine questioning, as the television cops say,' McCabe lied. 'The colonel mentioned that Bert Jakeman helped out up at Perham Farm when the hippies were there.'

'I'm surprised that no one warned you that old Bert spends a lot of his time on Planet Janet.'

'Sol Quinn did mention it,' McCabe acknowledged.

Beth then went on to defend the ageing gardener. 'Some very bad experiences in the Malayan jungle are responsible. Old Bert is as sharp as a tack most of the time, so take him seriously, Gerry.'

Beth's words gave the small box and its content in McCabe's pocket an importance. They paused beside the parked car in the shade of a yew tree. There was a challenge in her steady gaze as she asked, 'Where are we off to now?'

'*I'm* going into Kilverham,' he replied pointedly.

'I have all day free,' Beth said archly.

Opening the driver's door of his car, McCabe reminded her, 'You also have a jealous husband and a father who is paying me good money to find your sister.'

'You have a great talent when it comes to turning down a good offer, Gerry McCabe.'

'I don't even know what the offer is,' McCabe said with a grin, as he got into the car.

'There's one sure way of finding out, Gerry.'

He shook his head. 'My self-preservation instinct is too strong.'

She came to bend a little to look in at him, her face very close. 'Isn't there an old maxim, related to boxing I think, about being able to run but not hide?'

'I'm not hiding from you, Beth.'

'Perhaps not,' she half-agreed, 'but you can't deny that you're running.'

She was right. McCabe accepted this with a nod, saying, 'I'll be calling at the manor this evening to report to the colonel. I'll see you then.'

Starting the engine of the car, he drove off.

'You appreciate, Mr McCabe, that you have put me in a difficult position?'

Detective Superintendent Peter Rendall wore rimless spectacles like those of a preacher that made him look bland. But McCabe wasn't fooled. Rendall had the Establishment stamp of one who enjoyed the warm security of knowing that something incredibly powerful in secret ways watched over him. The superintendent had been trained to clothe vitally important questions in innocuity.

It was oppressively hot in the office and an ill-at-ease Sol Quinn took off his jacket and draped it over the back of his chair. He had called McCabe earlier on his mobile to report that forensics had come up with something on the tiny bone he had left at the police station that morning.

McCabe responded cagily. 'I'm familiar with police procedure, Superintendent. I spent twelve years in the Met.'

'I know.' Rendall's brow creasing into a dubious frown that revealed he had checked McCabe out and wasn't impressed. 'But now you are a member of the public – nothing more, nothing less.'

'But a member of the public who may have brought a serious crime to our attention, guv,' Inspector Quinn said in support of McCabe.

'Sol tells me that you are of the opinion that Katrina Farquahar is buried in the grounds of Abbeyfield Manor, Mr McCabe,' Rendall said.

'The gardener found her handbag in the rockery there, Superintendent.'

'If she is,' Rendall said, 'then it will be doubly bad news for Colonel Farquahar.'

'I don't understand,' a mystified McCabe said.

Sol Quinn enlightened him. 'You brought us a finger bone belonging to a foetus, Gerry.'

'So, it would seem that Katrina was pregnant,' McCabe said in surprise.

'We don't know if the Farquahar girl, or anyone else, is buried at the manor,' Rendall cautioned.

'With respect, Superintendent,' McCabe said, 'surely the handbag and the bone call for the possibility to be explored.'

Rendall lit a cigarette, drawing on it deeply. He let his professional air seep back into his face before responding. 'I agree, but the decision to go ahead is not mine: I have a meeting with the chief constable late this afternoon.'

'I'll ring you as soon as there is any news, Gerry,' Sol Quinn promised, as he showed McCabe out of the office and walked with him to the front door of the police station.

'Thanks, Sol,' McCabe said.

Checking that Rendall was out of earshot, Quinn spoke in a confidential half-whisper. 'My guv'nor is a sound copper, Gerry, and that dig will happen.'

'But?' McCabe asked in doubtful expectation.

'Rendall's one of the in-crowd, a few influential local businessmen and public officials who owe each other favours. It isn't a particularly erudite circle, but in an insular district such as this the group holds power. The super's being leant on not to assist you in any way. You've made someone nervous, Gerry.'

'Who is that someone, Sol?'

The detective inspector shrugged. 'I'd tell you if I knew, but I don't know. An educated guess would be the Pavely family. You won't get anywhere with either Silas or Ryan, but Rita could prove useful.'

'She was the only one of the Pavelys who didn't seem to have something to hide at dinner last night,' McCabe agreed. 'Apart from Mary, that is.'

With a wry smile, Quinn said, 'The old girl is a bit of a loose cannon, but she's a loyal wife and a doting mother. With no blood tie, Rita is your best chance. Have you an excuse for having a word with her?'

'I'll come up with something,' McCabe replied, as he went down the steps of the police station with a backward wave of thanks to Quinn.

The slender figure of Rita Pavely came out of the farmhouse door as McCabe approached. A bucket carried in her right hand dragged down one of her narrow shoulders. It was a sight that encouraged him. Women were at their most unguarded when doing familiar chores. The skin-tight jeans that she wore emphasized the thinness of her legs.

'Why, it's Mr McCabe,' she exclaimed.

'Hello, Mrs Pavely,' he greeted her.

'Rita, please,' she corrected him. 'We dined together at Abbeyfield Manor, something that locally makes us both members of an exclusive club. Can I help you in some way? Neither Ryan nor his father is here at the moment.'

'I was hoping that I might have a few words with you, Rita.'

With a sideways bend she reached for the bucket. The movement was delayed as though a shyness that had lain dormant in her made her uncertain what to say. Then she murmured an answer. 'I'm on my way to the paddock.'

'I'll walk with you if I may?' McCabe asked a question rather than made a statement.

'It's quite a way,' she warned, picking up the bucket.

'The exercise will do me good,' McCabe said with a smile, taking the bucket from her.

She led the way up a sharp rise. It was difficult underfoot now. For a short distance they picked their uneven way over stones and through wizened thorn bushes that plucked at the legs of McCabe's trousers. Small stones slipped out from under their feet; gathering speed, they were joined by other loose stones and began to rumble like a miniature avalanche.

'Are you adapting to living in the countryside, Gerry?' she enquired.

'No, this is still an alien world to me. I was with Bert Jakeman this morning, and I was expecting that any minute he'd start talking to the animals.'

Rita grinned happily. Her small, even teeth flashed, her dimples dimpled. Her face then serious, she changed the conversation to advise, 'Don't be taken off guard. For all its appearance of serenity, there is far more violence in the countryside than in the streets of any big city.'

Seeming to regret having spoken, she moved off a little ahead of him. McCabe asked. 'Was that just an idle observation, or a warning?'

Using levity to avoid giving a straight answer, she said. 'An idle observation. I don't think the Green Wellie Mafia has a contract out on you.'

'I'm relieved to hear that,' said a mock-serious McCabe.

'But now you're wishing that you hadn't volunteered to carry that heavy bucket,' she guessed, as they made their way carefully down a slope to where a horse moved wildly in a head-swinging way in excited anticipation of being fed.

'I'm a bit worried,' McCabe confessed. 'This is the first time that I've been this close to a horse.'

'Royal's an old softy,' Rita assured him, patting the neck of the animal.

McCabe tentatively placed the bucket on the ground in front of the horse and it lowered its head and started to feed.

'I suppose you want to ask me some questions about Katrina,' she remarked absently.

'Would that bother you, Rita?'

'No, not in any real sense. It was so long ago, so distant now.'

'I expect that you knew her boyfriend fairly well.'

'Andy Fairview? Yes, he worked and lodged here at the farm.'

'A nice lad?'

Rita said wistfully, 'He was a nice enough chap, yes. Katrina was crazy about him.'

Phrasing his next question delicately, McCabe asked, 'This is difficult, Rita, but have you any idea how serious the relationship was between Katrina and this boy?'

'Are you asking what I think you're asking?'

'Probably. Is it possible that Katrina was pregnant when she disappeared?'

Rita Pavely's grey eyes steadily returned his gaze with an instant, wary unfriendliness. Then she made a pretence of studying the horse before saying, tight-lipped, 'I wouldn't know.'

Ashen-faced, her lower lip was trembling and she had to lock her fingers together to keep her hands from shaking. Puzzled by her reaction, McCabe was trying to think of a way of rescuing the situation when a four-wheel drive pick-up came over a rise. His movements made jerky by annoyance, Ryan Pavely got out of the truck before it had come to a halt.

'Can I help you with something, McCabe?' he asked. He sounded almost affable, but the angle of the weak sunlight made his eyes horrible little beads.

Wrapping both arms tightly around him in greeting, Rita explained tremulously, 'Mr McCabe was just asking about Katrina, Ryan.'

'I thought you had asked all of your questions over dinner last night, McCabe,' Pavely said guardedly.

'I thought the same,' McCabe conceded, puzzled as to why Pavely had become defensive so quickly. 'But something I learned this morning opened up a lot of possibilities.'

Pavely gave a disbelieving shake of his head. 'You have to earn a living, McCabe, the same as the rest of us, but in the end Katrina's family and you will have to accept the truth about her disappearance.'

'Which is?'

'The girl eloped with Andy Fairview because her old man disapproved of their relationship,' Ryan Pavely said emphatically, as he slipped an arm around the waist of his wife and turned away to walk back to his vehicle.

'It's likely that Katrina Farquahar was pregnant,' McCabe called after him.

Stopping, shoulders hunching, his body going rigid, Pavely then did a slow, robotic turn. Glaring at McCabe, his lips formed silent words. But when he regained control of himself, all he said was, 'All the more reason for the two of them to run away.'

'Maybe you're right,' McCabe shrugged.

'There's no maybe about it, McCabe,' Pavely said gruffly. 'Get in, Rita, and I'll drive you back to the house.'

Deep in thought, McCabe watched the vehicle until it vanished over the low hill. Why had Rita Pavely over-reacted to his theory that Katrina Farquahar may have been pregnant? He was searching his mind for a possible answer when the horse nudged him with its head. Startled out of his reverie, McCabe bade the animal farewell and started to walk back to where he had left his car outside of the farmhouse.

About to leave for Abbeyfield Manor, McCabe paused at the door when Sharee Bucholz called to say that he was wanted on the telephone.

'Who is it?' he enquired.

'A lady, Gerry. She didn't give her name.'

It had to be Beth. She was the only woman who knew that he was staying at the Fox and Hounds. Despite himself he felt a thrill as he picked up the receiver.

'Hello.'

'Is that Mr McCabe?'

It was a voice that McCabe didn't recognize. He replied, 'It is.'

'This is somewhat awkward for me, Mr McCabe. I am Maria Farquahar.'

This put McCabe off mental balance for a moment. Then he enquired, 'How do you know about me, and how to reach me, Mrs Farquahar?'

'Before answering that question I need your promise to keep what I tell you secret, Mr McCabe.'

'You have my promise.'

There was a long pause at the other end, then. 'Thank you. You see, Mary Pavely and I were always good friends and, unbeknown to her family, we have kept in touch ever since I left.'

'I see,' McCabe commented in a calm voice, although excitement was erupting in him. This explained Mary Pavely's peculiar manner when taking leave of him after dinner the previous evening.

'Are you planning to return to London at any time in the near future?'

This was an entirely unexpected lead for McCabe, who offered eagerly, 'I can be there tomorrow if that is convenient for you, Mrs Farquahar.'

'That will be fine. I'll look forward to meeting you, Mr McCabe. Have you a pencil there to jot down my address?'

With a pencil already in his hand and his notebook on the telephone stand, McCabe said, 'Go ahead, Mrs Farquahar.'

Having left Abbeyfield early, McCabe reached London just as the rush hour traffic was easing. After his few days spent in the countryside the tall buildings on each side of him were slightly claustrophobic. Maria Farquahar had to be his priority, but in the past hour his need to see his wife and daughter had taken precedence. Even logic didn't offer a solution. Carol didn't know that he was in London, so it made sense to telephone her first then call on Mrs Farquahar. That would give his wife time to prepare for his visit, and Cindy would be due home from school by then.

On his way to Maria Farquahar's home in Ladbroke Grove, his mobile phone rang. There was a cacophony of horn blaring as he indicated left and swung over to park at the kerb. The call was from Solomon Quinn.

'What's happened, Sol?'

'I thought that you'd like to know they'll start digging at Abbeyfield Manor tomorrow morning, Gerry. I need you to get Colonel Farquahar's agreement.'

'That will be easy.'

'How soon can you get to him?'

'This evening.'

'That's a bit late, Gerry.' The policeman sounded uneasy. 'Could do it this afternoon?'

'Impossible. I'm in London right now, Sol.'

'London!' Quinn croaked. 'What are you doing in London?'

'I'll explain when I get back. Don't worry, Sol. Trust me.'

'I always worry when someone says trust me,' Quinn groaned, before switching off.

McCabe tapped in his wife's number. There was dread in his veins while he waited. It was toxic and deadening. When Carol answered she sounded nervous, then became remote, distant on finding that it was him calling. People who were once close find it difficult to communicate on the telephone where their facial expressions and body language can't be observed. He asked after her and Cindy before saying that he was in Town and would like to visit. Carol reminded him that she worked in the mornings. She would be at home later in the day. They agreed a time, each of them a little wary of the other.

When the call ended, he sat for a moment to allow the emotions stirred by Carol's voice to subside. Then he prepared himself for his purpose in coming to London. Starting the car, he pulled away and turned left into Ladbroke Grove. He drove slowly, reading house numbers. Maria Farquahar's home was a small house squeezed between two decaying tenements. Time had washed over the cramped building leaving the scars of fading paint and crumbling brickwork.

McCabe rang the doorbell twice, looking up at the grimy brickwork and dirt-streaked windows. Coming out to stand on the top step, Maria Farquahar rested one hand high on the door-jamb in an unconsciously elegant pose. Though she could be only a few years younger than the colonel, she had an effect that took McCabe back instantly to the thrilling moment when Beth had first opened the door of Abbeyfield Manor to him.

'Mr McCabe,' she said with a smile. 'How nice of you to call.'

'My pleasure, Mrs Farquahar,' he responded.

The grip of her slim, cool hand was firm. With the eyes of a thinker, faded, with distance in them, she was a woman made for dignity, even for a sort of magnificence. She had short silver-grey hair, slender shoulders, slender arms, and long slender legs.

McCabe followed Maria Farquahar into a nicely decorated living-room. Wearing a charcoal grey trouser suit, she moved well. Despite her age, each curve of her body complemented the other, a study in perfect symmetry. The furniture was ageing and the carpet was showing wear, but everything in the room was clean and tidy. A faint reflection of Abbeyfield Manor was evident in the exquisitely shaped lampshades, the heavy curtains at the windows and the pictures on the wall.

Maria Farquahar sat in a comfortable chair and studied McCabe comfortably. With elbows resting on the chair arms, slim hands linked on her lap, her nervousness was betrayed by the restless little movements of her fingers. Standing on a sideboard were framed photographs of Beth and Katrina as schoolgirls. For a woman apart from her family for so long, they must have been harrowing reminders of passing time, the milestones of mortality. Otherwise the room was bare of the souvenirs of life. McCabe was struck by how little she had accumulated in what should have been the most important and comfortable years of her life.

'Tell me, Mr McCabe, how are the colonel and Elizabeth?' Her face wore a pensive expression.

'They are fine, Mrs Farquahar,' McCabe replied. They both recognized this as a lie, but they let it ride because they were more comfortable with it than they would have been with the truth.

'Mary Pavely keeps me up to date with everything at home.' She nodded. The light in her eyes that had made her special had gone out. 'It's been a terrible time for us all. Everything went so wrong after Katrina left us, Mr McCabe. I'd dearly love to be back at Abbeyfield, away from all the malice and greed and competition and anger of the outer world. To have no thought beyond the growing of roses and the leisurely, lovely rhythm of the seasons.' She gave a deep sigh. 'But I made my bed, as they say, and I must lie on it.'

'We all make mistakes, Mrs Farquahar.'

'All of us, Mr McCabe?' She looked at him keenly. 'You immediately struck me as a man completely in control of himself and his life.'

'That is proof that first impressions are far from reliable; believe me,' McCabe said.

'You surprise me. No, I can understand. There are times in life when gales of malevolent forces batter us from all directions so that we are not really aware of what we are doing. When it is over all we have left are memories and regrets. Life has a way of imprinting the bad times deeply on the memory. I suppose you have been acquainted with my stupid involvement with Sylvester Hartley.'

'Yes,' McCabe answered truthfully. 'That came up naturally when I was being briefed. Apart from the fact that you are the missing girl's mother, it is no business of mine.'

'I appreciate that. Somehow I've learned in a kind of way to live with my foolishness. My punishment is in being alone all these years.' Then she brightened. 'But you didn't come here to hear me whinge.'

'You have something to tell me,' McCabe prompted.

'I have, yes. However, I am wondering why you have been asked to investigate after such a long time.'

'There has been a development that may well turn out to be nothing, Mrs Farquahar.'

'I take it that you can't tell me what it is.'

'I'm sorry,' he said, to confirm that she had it right. 'What is it that you want to tell me?

Suddenly embarrassed, she said, 'I feel foolish because after

I'd telephoned you it didn't seem so important. It isn't what I suppose you would term as evidence, but would be better described as an old woman's intuition. I pray that you won't consider me to be a time-waster.'

'Not at all,' McCabe assured her.

Thanking him with a sweet smile, she asked, 'Have you come to know, or know of, Dr Ralph Ronan a physician in Abbeyfield, Mr McCabe?'

'No.' He surfed his memory and came up with a blank. 'Does he play a part in this, Mrs Farquahar?'

'I believe so, but, as I warned, it is pure conjecture, if you like. Ralph Ronan is retired now, but it was always rumoured that he carried out illegal abortions in the flower people era.'

'And you think that maybe…?' McCabe coaxed her apprehensively.

Swallowing hard and looking away from him, gazing out sightlessly through the window, her voice faltered as she replied. 'It keeps occurring to me, persistently, night and day, that Katrina might have been pregnant, and Doctor Ronan botched an illegal operation.'

'During which she died?'

Not having intended to speak so harshly, McCabe heard his words echoing hollowly around the room. This fitted in with the find of Katrina's handbag and the tiny bone. It would explain everything. Everything, except for how or why the doctor would have buried the girl in the grounds of Abbeyfield Manor. Unsure of what to say next, he looked at Maria Farquahar. Head bowed, she was quietly weeping.

'That is what I fear,' she replied.

'But Katrina's boyfriend disappeared at the same time, Mrs Farquahar.'

She looked up, bravely, dabbing at her eyes with a handkerchief. 'That did, of course, occur to me, Mr McCabe. Andrew was a nice lad and I know that he really cared for Katrina. But if he was responsible for my daughter's condition, then surely it would have been instinctive for him to flee in the face of such a tragedy?'

That was a logical conclusion to reach, and McCabe agreed with her. 'I will certainly pay the doctor a visit, Mrs Farquahar.'

'And you will keep me informed?' she asked worriedly.

'Every step of the way,' McCabe promised.

'Thank you, Mr McCabe. Now, I must atone for my lack of manners. Which would you prefer, tea or coffee?'

Standing, ready to leave, McCabe replied, 'That is kind of you, Mrs Farquahar, but I have further business here in town, and it is necessary for me to be back in Abbeyfield early this evening.'

'I understand.' Disappointed, she stood and walked to the door with him. Hesitating for a moment, she asked. 'Will you tell the colonel and Elizabeth that you have spoken to me?'

'That is your choice, Mrs Farquahar.'

Deep in contemplation for a long moment, she then said, 'I think it best not to mention it.'

'I will telephone you regularly,' McCabe promised. 'I would like to call on you again if that is all right.'

'I will be delighted to see you. I have enjoyed your company today.'

Reaching the bottom of the steps, he turned. 'Are you sure there is no message you would wish me to give either to your husband or daughter, Mrs Farquahar?'

'No, there is no message,' she replied unhappily. 'Goodbye, Mr McCabe, and thank you.'

five

'Am I welcome?'

That was all that McCabe could think of saying, and it sounded pretty trite. This wasn't a joyful homecoming. Standing, supported by one hand clutching the edge of a table, Carol's lips struggled with a tentative smile. With tinted blonde hair that shimmered in soft waves to her shoulders, she was beautiful. It was a beauty that McCabe noticed still seemed repressed by a crippling shyness.

There was no place for small talk between them. No neutral ground for conversation. The spotlessly clean room had a fresh, scented air. Kylie Minogue sang at low volume from a portable radio. McCabe waited expectantly.

'I'm sorry,' Carol apologized for no reason. 'I'm just a bit surprised by you turning up like this, Gerry. What brought you back?'

'I had to come to London on business.'

'I didn't mean that exactly, not what brought you to London,' Carol explained awkwardly.

It was McCabe's turn to feel uncomfortable. 'I was hoping that maybe we could talk. Perhaps we could even find a way back for us.'

She glanced at him thoughtfully for a moment, as if she had made some sort of decision, then sucked in her breath, shook her head and turned away again.

After long minutes had passed, Carol glanced at her watch. 'It's time to meet Cindy from school. Why don't you come with me?'

Spirits lifted by this, McCabe hesitated. So much time had gone by that Cindy wouldn't recognize him. It would depress him terribly to have to be introduced to his own daughter as her father.

'I'll drive you there,' he offered.

Carol shook her head. 'It's only a short walk.'

She put on her coat and they went out into the drab streets of Kennington together. They walked side-by-side, both of them careful to avoid touching. Carol's stiff, strained attitude in the flat had faded. They spoke little and she was still reserved, but McCabe noticed that the animosity was no longer there. He also was very aware that the wraith of the offbeat and enigmatic Beth Merrill was no longer haunting him.

Soon after they joined other parents waiting at the school gate, a bell rang inside the building. When the school doors opened and children erupted noisily and excitedly, a worried McCabe feared that he would be unable to pick his own child out from among them. But then there was no mistaking Cindy as she spotted Carol and ran towards them. Her pretty little face wore a frown of puzzlement as she looked at him.

'Daddy!'

Unable to believe his ears, McCabe bent to scoop his little girl up into his arms. As he held her tightly, she turned her curly head to Carol to ask, 'Is Daddy back with us now, Mummy?'

'No,' Carol told her gently. She gave McCabe a pseudo-sly glance. 'Daddy is working away, out of London. But he will be staying to have tea with us.'

'Goody,' Cindy squealed.

Delighted by Carol's oblique message, McCabe insisted on carrying his daughter home. They had walked only a few yards when he felt Carol take his arm. She smiled when he turned his head to look at her. Then she spoke softly. 'Don't read too much into this, Gerry. It's only an invitation to tea. I have a lot of thinking to do before it can be anything else, if it ever can be.'

Acknowledging the warning, McCabe was nevertheless convinced that they had made great progress towards becoming a family again.

*

Keeping his promise to Quinn, McCabe was back in Abbeyfield that evening and at the manor to bring Colonel Farquahar up to speed.

Elbows resting on the desk in his study, the colonel's chin was in his cupped hands. After McCabe had told the old man about the bone of a foetus and the dig that would begin in the morning, a long silence followed. Then the colonel raised his head to look beseechingly at McCabe.

'Then my daughter was with child, McCabe.'

'We can't be certain of anything at this stage, Colonel,' McCabe advised. 'We don't even know if someone is buried there, and if that is the case, it might well not be Katrina.'

Reaching out a bony hand and placing it on McCabe's arm, the colonel said, 'You are attempting to spare my feelings, McCabe, and that is kind of you. But you and I both know that if there is a body lying under that rockery, then it is ninety-nine point nine per cent certain to be that of my elder daughter.'

'I prefer to keep an open mind.'

'I only wish that I could do the same, son,' the colonel murmured. Then a sudden realization caused him to groan. 'Beth has to know about the excavation and why it is taking place. How are we going to tell her?'

The old man was trembling visibly, and McCabe said, 'It is not something that I would welcome doing, Colonel, but, with your permission, I will explain the situation to Mrs Merrill.'

'By God, you are a true gentleman, McCabe.' Relief raised the colonel's voice an octave. 'If you are sure, I would be terribly grateful. Beth is on her own in the drawing-room at the moment. Will you have a drink with me before you go to see her?'

'I need more than Dutch courage, Colonel,' McCabe politely refused.

He found Beth half sitting on the edge of a table flicking through the pages of a magazine. She smiled. 'I didn't expect you back so soon. I thought you would make an occasion of it: take in a show; call to see the wife.'

Aware that she was probing, McCabe let it go by. The time spent with Carol was still warmly pleasant in his mind. 'My trip to London was business not pleasure, Beth.'

'Did you learn anything about Katrina?'

McCabe shrugged in reply. 'Possibly another clue.' He gestured for her to sit in a chair.

'I'm quite comfortable here, thank you, Gerry.'

'What I have to tell you will be upsetting,' McCabe explained.

Beth looked him straight in the eyes. She was clever, worldly, and blessed with a whole lot of native intelligence. 'I don't do upset; I'm too tough now.'

'I still want to spare you,' McCabe explained.

'Spare me from what?'

'A short while ago, Bert Jakeman found Katrina's handbag buried in the rockery.'

'Here at the manor?'

McCabe was relieved that Beth was taking the news well. She was her usual stoic self. He answered her with a nod.

'Are you sure that it was my sister's handbag?'

'Yes. It held her driving licence and exactly three shillings and ninepence in coins, Beth.'

Beth was shaken by this news, but only momentarily. She returned to being her old self in a fraction of a second. 'Why are you telling me this now, Gerry, after keeping it from me for days?'

'The colonel didn't want you to know.'

'But there's something else, isn't there?' Beth guessed astutely.

'There are two other things,' McCabe told her gently. 'The police forensic people are going to examine the rockery tomorrow morning.'

'Searching for a body.'

'That's right.'

'You said two things,' Beth reminded him. 'What's the second?'

'Jakeman has also found what has since been identified as the finger bone of a foetus.'

'Which suggests to you and my father that Katrina was pregnant?'

'That is a possibility.'

With a vigorous shake of her head, Beth objected. 'Certainly not.'

'You don't believe that Katrina could have been pregnant?'

'The two of us were that close, Gerry, that I'd have known even if her period had been a few days late.' Beth made an exasperated signal with both hands. 'You say that a finger bone has been found. That would mean that Katrina would have been around six months' gone.'

McCabe was convinced, but it demolished all of his theories. He said, 'I believe you, Beth, of course. But how did Katrina's handbag come to be buried there?'

'That puzzles me,' Beth conceded. 'But my sister was not pregnant. If, heaven forbid, a body is found there, then it won't be Katrina. That is definite.'

'I hope that you are right.'

'We'll know in the morning, won't we?' she said, with a wan smile, walking to the far side of the table.

'I have to go back to the colonel, Beth,' McCabe said. 'Will you join us for a drink?'

'I'll be along in a little while,' she assured him in a subdued tone.

Lingering for a moment, McCabe was reluctant to leave her. Beth had turned her back to him, seating herself on the edge of the table again. Seeing her shoulders shaking, McCabe quietly left the room. First lying to himself that she would want to be alone to grieve over her sister, he then admitted that he lacked the courage to remain with her.

Through a wide window, McCabe could see a late evening sun filtering through the smoke-laden air. Pressuring its red-tinged rays on Abbeyfield, the half-light filled the bar of the Fox and Hounds with a stale gloom. Trying desperately to recall the time he had spent with his wife and daughter earlier that day, he failed, because Beth's sorrow haunted his mind. He stood alone at the bar, watchful in a practised, covert way. All the regulars were there.

'Time really does fly, doesn't it?'

Sharee had asked the question, having come up without him noticing.

'How do you mean?' McCabe asked, frowning.

'Happy Hour must be over,' she said with a laugh. 'Is life with the Farquahars getting you down?'

McCabe shook his head. 'Just life itself. Do you know a Dr Ralph Ronan, Sharee?'

'Know him!' Sharee took his hand as if it was the most natural thing to do. Sexual chemistry threatened to overcome McCabe's resolve. 'I'm probably his chief creditor here in Abbeyfield.' She pointed with her free hand. 'That's the doc sitting over there by the window.'

McCabe looked to where an elderly man, grey hair clustered in natural curls on his long, aristocratic head, sat alone at a small table.

'Is he approachable?' McCabe enquired.

Reaching for a glass, Sharee held it up to an optic. 'Take this single malt over and he'll welcome you like a brother.'

'Put it on my bill,' McCabe said, picking up the glass.

Ronan was older than McCabe had estimated from a distance. Head down, he was studying ice cubes melting in his empty glass. He looked up as McCabe placed the large whisky on the table, and asked, 'Doctor Ronan?'

'If you didn't know that already, young man,' Ronan responded, with a sardonic smile, 'you wouldn't have bought me a drink.' Pushing his empty glass away, he slid the one brought by McCabe in front of him. 'Now you want me to sing for my supper, as it were.'

The doctor looked terminally tired, so weary that his courtesies were reduced to the barest necessities. McCabe guessed that after years of hard drinking, the booze had stopped working as well as it once had. His lightweight fawn-coloured suit was well cut but had a creased, slept-in look. An amber tie enhanced a grey flannel shirt that had a frayed collar. Doctor Ralph Ronan had clearly known better things. Sharee walked over carrying a Guinness for him, and McCabe thanked her before getting down to business.

Pointing to a spare chair, he asked, 'Do you mind if I join you, Doctor Ronan?'

'You have invested in me, young man,' Ronan said, holding up the whisky before putting the glass to his mouth. Then he said. 'So you might as well have your pound of flesh.'

'I'm Gerry McCabe,' McCabe introduced himself as he sat.

'Ralph Ronan,' the doctor said, offering a long-fingered hand. 'That's Ralph, not Rafe, as they say these days. Like "maudlin" instead of Magdalen for the Oxford college. Utter piffle.'

'I'm a private investigator, Doctor Ronan.'

'I had reached that conclusion,' Ronan said. 'You must be the chap I heard was here to investigate the disappearance of the colonel's daughter. Bit late in the day, what!'

'Not really,' McCabe replied. 'This is confidential at the moment, Doctor, but there is good reason to believe that there is a body, possibly that of Katrina Farquahar, buried at the manor. The police are to start digging tomorrow morning.'

Ralph Ronan took time to absorb this. There was a tremor to his rich tones as he lowered his voice to ask, 'And you've heard malicious gossip that I performed illegal operations at the time Abbeyfield became a latter-day Babylon?'

'The person who suggested this to me didn't do so maliciously, Doctor Ronan, and neither was it anyone here in Abbeyfield,' McCabe assured the old man. 'If you tell me it is nothing but gossip, then I will accept your word and apologize for troubling you.'

Draining his glass, Ronan remained silent as an observant Sharee brought him another single malt and a bottle of Guinness that she placed beside McCabe's still two-thirds full glass.

'I'll pay for these, McCabe,' the doctor said, putting his hand inside his jacket. It jammed against something in his pocket and he kept his hand in there.

Sharee stood close to McCabe, a thigh pressing against his upper arm. The warm intimacy of this contact caused him fleeting fantasies that he found difficult to banish.

'No need, Doctor Ronan. Mr McCabe has taken care of it.'

'Most kind,' the doctor murmured, waiting until Sharee had left the table before going on. 'I believe I can guess the source of your information, McCabe, and I would be lying if I claimed it was mere gossip. Forewarned is forearmed, as the old adage tells us, and I should be grateful to you. The rumours were very strong at the time.'

'If they were nothing more than rumours,' an uncomfortable McCabe was ready to call a halt.

Taking off his rimless glasses with a gentlemanly gesture, Dr Ralph Ronan looked directly at Gerry through sunken eyes. 'There is little point in me denying you an explanation, McCabe. I was middle-aged then and I, like all others of my generation, was shocked by what was a totally unanticipated eruption of immorality. I remember that some families moved away because they couldn't stand the shame that a pregnant, unmarried daughter was in those days. When begged for help I weakened only once. My lame excuse is that I saved two very close friends of mine from torment, but what I did has been on my conscience day and night ever since. I disgraced an honourable profession.'

Moved by the old man's distress, though desperately wanting to hear more, McCabe said reassuringly, 'I won't pry, Doctor.'

'But you seek the name of the girl involved, McCabe?'

'Not at the expense of causing you pain, Doctor Ronan.'

'It may well prove therapeutic to talk about it,' Ronan pondered. He continued. 'The girl concerned is a respectable married woman now, living here in Abbeyfield. Her husband knows nothing of this. Only the girl, her parents, and I know the terrible secret.'

McCabe lifted his glass to drink in the hope of covering the sudden dread that shot coldly through his whole body. They were not talking about Katrina, so it could well have been Beth Farquahar who'd had the abortion. Yet he had to know for sure, because if it wasn't Beth the woman concerned would have had a connection, everything in common, with a girl who was pregnant around the same time and in similar circumstances to her. She would likely be able at least to guess who was carrying the foetus that was buried in the rockery at the manor.

'Do you think that this girl would be willing to speak to me, Doctor?' he asked.

With a shake of his head, Ronan answered. 'No; that would be difficult for her after so much time has passed. Is it important to your investigation, McCabe?'

'It would help immeasurably, Doctor.'

'Hmm,' Ronan mused, then remained silent for some time. Then he added. 'The parents are still my very good friends, McCabe. Perhaps I could persuade them to speak with you.'

'I'd be very grateful,' McCabe said. 'I am staying here at the pub.'

'Leave it with me and I will contact you,' Ronan promised.

'Thank you, Doctor Ronan,' McCabe said, as he signalled to Sharee. 'I'll get you another drink.'

'I couldn't possibly allow that, McCabe,' the doctor said in feeble protest.

A dawn made dark by thick fog added to the gloom of that morning. Two policemen wearing overalls and wellington boots knelt beside the rockery. They carefully removed stones and earth with gloved hands. Hovering over them in white plastic suits, like creatures from outer space, were a man and a woman, a two-person forensic team. Detective Superintendent Peter Rendall and Detective Inspector Solomon Quinn stood with McCabe some distance away.

Using a brilliantly white handkerchief to clear the mist from the lens of his glasses, Rendall spoke to McCabe. 'I take it that we won't have any hysterics from the father and daughter if anything is found, Mr McCabe?'

'Neither the colonel nor Mrs Merrill is the hysterical type, Superintendent,' McCabe answered.

'Good,' Rendall nodded.

'Something's happened, guv,' Quinn warned, as the male in the white suit suddenly dropped to his knees and the woman called to them.

Replacing his glasses hurriedly, Rendall said, 'You remain here please, Mr McCabe.'

Left alone, McCabe wondered anxiously what the find might be. A black dread was creeping through him at the thought of having to report whatever it was to Beth and her father.

'Both my father and I have convinced ourselves that it is Katrina,' Beth declared solemnly.

She and McCabe walked side-by-side through the walled grounds of the estate. McCabe found being with her added something holy to the tranquillity that was night. He had agreed when Beth had suggested that they take a stroll, because she was so emotionally upset. Her husband was busy marking school papers. Though she struggled to conceal it, she was agonizing over the likelihood that the human remains found that morning were those of her sister.

The moon that had risen in the past half-hour was hidden behind trees, but it was a full moon and there was plenty of light for them to find their way. Now, as the footpath became a series of steps leading up a grassy rise, Beth had broached the subject that was on the minds of both of them.

'The only thing we know for sure right now is that the girl was pregnant,' McCabe said. 'You were adamant that your sister could not have been in that condition.'

'I know,' Beth humbly admitted. 'But at times like this you doubt even your own firm convictions.'

'It could be that your accepting that it is Katrina is some kind of emotional defence.'

'Possibly,' she admitted. 'There is an inexplicable comfort in mourning in advance.'

'But it's causing you unnecessary suffering if it is not your sister, Beth.'

'You don't really believe that it isn't, do you?' she challenged quietly him.

'I have an open mind,' McCabe replied. 'But that's possible only because I am not closely involved.'

'I thought that the passing of more than three decades would have us ready for bad news, but it hasn't,' she said. The tendons in her neck were taut against the skin.

They moved into the velvety shadows of some pine trees before starting down a slope. McCabe clasped her hand when she missed her step. The mournful cry of a curlew added tension to the suddenly fraught atmosphere. Far down below, the blue and white police barrier tape constructed around the rockery moved in a light breeze. Beth caught sight of a movement there at the same time as he did. A shadow split away from a hedge to become a blurred, moving silhouette of a human figure.

Beth gripped his arm with both hands now, the fingers digging in hard as she howled, 'Oh God!' Moving into a clearing, the figure took shape as a cowled monk. Beth croaked fearfully. 'It's a monk, Gerry, There was an abbey here hundreds of years ago.'

The truth suddenly dawned on McCabe. He identified the figure. 'That's John-John.'

'What's John-John doing here on the estate at this time of night?' Beth wondered.

'He's heard what's happened,' McCabe suggested. 'He was fond of Katrina, wasn't he?'

'He liked her, but fond is probably too strong a word, Gerry.'

This set McCabe thinking. What had drawn the eccentric man this far from his caravan home? Did John-John know something about the remains unearthed that day?

'John-John has never frightened me before,' Beth said speculatively as the robed figure drifted along to disappear into a wall of shadow beyond the rockery. 'Why is he here, Gerry?'

McCabe shrugged, but that simple gesture implied much. 'Who knows! Don't forget that his mind doesn't work properly, Beth.'

'That's what worries me,' Beth said in a fearful, quiet voice.

'We had better be getting back,' McCabe advised.

A sad Beth reluctantly agreed. 'Back to what is certain to be a sleepless night. How long before we know?'

'I can't answer that, Beth. It depends on too many factors.'

Walking among the morning shoppers in Kilverham, McCabe was distracted by memories of his time with Beth the previous evening, and the puzzling sight of John-John Menson at the makeshift grave. The yet to come identification of the human remains also preyed on his mind. He was passing a quaint-looking old public house when a clergyman came out at speed. A small man with nervous mannerisms, he puffed animatedly on a cigarette. He could have been anything between fifty and ninety years of age, and had all the grooves and wrinkles to keep McCabe guessing. He had close-cropped grey hair, grey eyes, a grey face, and was dressed in a grey suit. A chameleon able to blend with any background.

'Good morning,' the clergyman said, pointing over his shoulder at the public house behind him and giving McCabe a face-splitting grin. 'Don't get the wrong impression. I was calling on a parishioner, not imbibing, although I do confess to the odd tipple.'

'Your secret is safe with me,' McCabe promised wryly.

'You are a true gentleman, sir.' The clergyman waved his cigarette hand from side to side. 'Tell me, am I right? Would you be Mr McCabe?'

'That's me,' McCabe confirmed.

The cleric chuckled. 'Don't be alarmed, I am not psychic. You are simply a victim of small town syndrome, Mr McCabe, which makes a stranger stand out like the proverbial sore digit. Allow me to introduce myself. I am Peter Pulman, the Methodist Minister here at Kilverham. I must say that Ralph's description of you was most accurate.'

Frowning, McCabe questioned, 'Ralph?'

'Ralph Ronan, Mr McCabe, Doctor Ronan.'

'Doctor Ronan,' McCabe nodded. 'I have a feeling that I know what this is about.'

'With all due respect, Mr McCabe, I don't put much stock in feelings,' Pulman advised. 'Intuition always has a shadow, and it is too easy to mistake the shadow for the real message.'

McCabe was impatient. He asked, more abruptly than he had intended, 'Could you pin it down, Mr Pulman?'

'Of course. I'm a little olde worlde and haven't yet caught up with the rush and tear of modern life,' the clergyman apologized wordily. 'The fact is, Mr McCabe, that two of my flock, as it were, are friends of Ralph Ronan. Ralph has been in touch with them, and they have agreed to have a private word with you. For some reason they were hesitant about ringing you, so I made a note to look you up. Bumping into you like this is jolly convenient.' Reaching into his jacket for a wallet, he removed a slip of paper and read it before passing it to McCabe. 'Thomas and Beryl Jenkins. They live at Morlton. It's all written down here, their address and everything.'

McCabe regretted his earlier sharpness with the minister. In an age when the world seemed to like being ruled and regimented by tyrants, Peter Pulman possessed an old-fashioned gentleness.

Thanking the clergyman who moved off with a cheerful wave

of farewell, McCabe revised his itinerary. The pathologist's report would have to wait. It was probably too early for any result, anyway. He would first pay a visit to Doctor Ronan's friends.

Walking to his car he didn't see Sharee Bucholz approaching until she was just a yard or two away.

'Well, hello,' she said, stopping, standing close. She looked as if she were cross with him. But as he watched the hostility melted and she appeared pleased with herself as she continued, 'Funny, isn't it? You can avoid me back at the pub, but there's no escape for you out here in the street.'

'I haven't been avoiding you, or trying to escape, Sharee,' he protested unconvincingly.

'You could have fooled me. When was the last time you risked being alone with me?'

'It isn't like that,' he tried to assure her.

'Nice try, Gerry,' she giggled, 'but I still prefer the one about the Three Bears. Now,' – she raised the heavy bag of shopping she was carrying – 'what are the chances of a lift home?'

'I'm sorry, Sharee. This isn't just an excuse: I really do have to see someone.'

Disappointed, she managed to smile. 'I'll believe you, though thousands wouldn't.'

'I'd like your help, though. How do I get to a place called Morlton?' McCabe enquired.

Her smile faded fast. 'Forget Morlton, Gerry. I can guess why you're going there and, believe me, that is one hornets' nest you shouldn't stir up.'

'What do you mean?'

'I've said enough,' she said gravely. 'This is just work to you and if you go ahead then maybe you won't regret it, but an awful lot of nice people around here will suffer.'

'I don't understand,' McCabe pleaded as, with a little peck of farewell on his cheek, she left him.

The sun was still low enough in the sky to produce a strobe lighting effect through the trees that lined the road. Slightly mesmerized, McCabe took a while to notice the blue flashing light of a police car on his tail. It took him a few minutes longer to connect the police car with himself. He pulled into a lay-by, and the police car followed.

A young uniformed constable came to him with an officially polite, 'Good morning, sir.'

'Good morning, Officer,' McCabe said. 'Is there something wrong.'

'Not at all, sir. I have a message from Detective Inspector Quinn. He would like to see you back at the station.'

'Is it urgent?' McCabe enquired, hoping to get to see the Jenkinses before returning to town.

'I believe so, sir.'

'OK, please tell DI Quinn that I'm on my way.'

Postponing his visit, McCabe wondered why Sol Quinn hadn't telephoned him. Picking up his mobile he saw that the battery was flat. He hadn't charged it since arriving in Abbeyfield.

The normally calm, self-possessed Sol Quinn was pacing about his office when McCabe entered. He fixed him with a steady stare before speaking. 'This is strictly off the record, Gerry.'

'Whatever you say, Sol,' a puzzled McCabe said with a shrug.

'Katrina Farquahar.'

The autopsy result had arrived. The blood in McCabe's veins went icy. 'It was Katrina?'

'No.' Quinn shook his head. 'I'm sorry, Gerry, I put that badly. They are still no closer to identifying the remains. What I'm saying, Gerry, is that I might well have found Katrina. I did a bit of probing on your behalf.'

'This is good of you, Sol,' McCabe said appreciatively, as he sat down.

'I just hope that it leads to something.' Resting his elbows on the desk, Quinn was his old self once more, bland and composed. 'As I said, I *might* have found Katrina. I have definitely located Andrew Fairview. He's the manager of a farm in Gloucestershire. It's about fifteen miles out of Stroud. I've got the address.'

'Is Katrina with him?' McCabe asked.

'That I don't know. But I did get the impression that he is married.'

McCabe checked his watch. It was 12.25, still early in the day. If he set off now he should be in Gloucester at around four o'clock.

'I'll find out when I get there,' he told Quinn, getting to his feet.

'I wish you luck, Gerry,' Quinn said, as he also stood. 'When you walk out of that door you are on your own. Whatever you find out, don't telephone me here at the station. You can buy me a pint in the pub tonight and tell me about it. But you didn't get this Fairview guy's address from me, right?'

'Don't worry, Sol, and thanks again,' McCabe said, as he made his way out of the office.

The farm was situated on the top of a hill in surroundings that had even more rural beauty than the countryside around Abbeyfield. Getting out of his car, McCabe paused for a moment, breathing in deeply. Reluctant to move, he forced himself to walk over to the house where a farm labourer had told him he would find the manager.

Andrew Fairview was outside the house repairing a fence. He did not in any way resemble McCabe's preconception of what a farmer should look like. Lean to the point of thinness, Fairview had the body of an office worker and the face of an artist. Within minutes of meeting him, McCabe decided that Andrew Fairview was a straightforward, honest person.

'I'm quite happy to tell you all I knew about Katrina,' Fairview had said, when McCabe had introduced himself. 'I was just about to go in for my tea, and you are welcome to join us. Elise, my wife, does, of course, know that Katrina was once my girlfriend.'

With the possibility in mind that Katrina had changed her name, McCabe went into the house. Meeting Elise Fairview had a disconcerting effect on him. She bore no resemblance to the photograph of Katrina that Beth had shown him. Elise had long, straight golden hair that framed a schoolgirl's face. Her slender build added to the pre-pubescent illusion, and her long-lashed eyes had an engaging frankness.

'This is Mr McCabe, Elise,' a smiling Fairview introduced the visitor to his wife. 'He's a private detective hired by Katrina's father.'

'Has something happened to her?' Elise enquired anxiously.

'That's what her family has hired me to find out,' McCabe replied. 'She left Abbeyfield at the same time as your husband, Mrs Fairview, and she hasn't been seen or heard of since.'

Fairview said wonderingly. 'That's odd.'

'Why do you say that?' McCabe asked.

'It's a long story, Mr McCabe.'

'I would like to hear it if you have the time to tell me. Let's make it less formal by you calling me Gerry.'

SIX

'That's fine. This is Elise, and I'm Andy,' Fairview said in response. 'I said it was odd because I wasn't aware that Katrina had not stayed in touch with her family. We didn't stay together long after leaving Abbeyfield. I suppose the dream ended when reality kicked in and we found ourselves penniless and homeless. We'd visited London together a few times in the past, and Katrina wanted to go there. London held no appeal for me, so we split up.'

'Did you keep in touch?'

'For a while. Though Katrina never sent the "Wish you were here" kind of message. Then she got married, and I only heard from her once or twice afterwards.'

'Do you know who she married?' McCabe asked hopefully.

Fairview shook his head. 'No. It was a long time ago. Elise and I were married then. I remember that Katrina's husband had a shop somewhere outside London.'

'It was in Staines,' Elise volunteered, rolling her eyes heaven-wards in exaggerated despair at her husband's lack of recall. 'I've a better memory than Andy.'

'If you are that good, remember her married name then,' Fairview challenged his wife playfully.

Elise Fairview searched her memory for the name. 'It began with L, I'm sure of that. Ley ... Leyton ... No, that isn't it. Leyland!' she said loudly. 'That's it – Leyland.'

Delighted with this information, McCabe wanted to leave the Fairviews as swiftly as he could without being thought of as rude. When they offered to share with him the tea Elise was cooking for them, he thanked them but declined. Excusing himself by saying he had to return for an appointment with the police in Kilverham that evening, he paved the way for a quick exit that would give no offence.

At the door, he turned to ask, 'Would you like me to contact you when I have news of Katrina?'

Andy and Elise looked questioningly at each other, and came to an agreement telepathically.

Placing an arm around his wife, who cuddled contentedly against him, Andrew Fairview replied, 'Thanks for the offer, Gerry, but no. All that belongs in the past, and there is no place for it in our present.'

'So, she's alive and well and living in Staines as they say,' Sol Quinn mused, as he idly rotated his glass on a table in the Fox and Hounds.

McCabe cautioned, 'All we can know is that Katrina was alive for some time after she left Abbeyfield.'

'We now also know that the remains we found are not those of Katrina Farquahar, Gerry.'

'That's right.'

'Which complicates identification,' Quinn remarked. 'Have you told the colonel and Beth about this?'

'No.' McCabe shook his head vigorously. 'I'll tell them if and when I find Katrina alive.'

'I suppose you are off to Staines at sun-up, as they say in the cowboy movies.'

Sharee Bucholz stopped as she was passing their table to complain jocularly, 'You boys are ruining my trade. People feel uneasy having a policeman and a private detective around.'

'Only those with a guilty conscience need worry,' Quinn told her.

'Have you ever met anyone who doesn't have a guilty conscience, Detective Inspector?' Sharee asked as she moved away, giving McCabe a special smile.

Sol Quinn grinned slyly at McCabe. 'I doubt very much if you'll be in any condition to leave early in the morning.'

'I'll make it,' McCabe assured him. 'But there's something here that I have to deal with before I head for Staines.'

Something had been increasingly pressing him to speak to the Jenkinses. He planned to go to Morlton first, then drive up to Staines. He would then stay in London overnight. Perhaps suggest to Carol that if she could get someone to babysit Cindy they could take in a theatre or a club together.

Standing up from the table, he said to Quinn, 'I have to make a telephone call.'

At the bar, McCabe asked Sharee, 'Can I use the phone, Sharee? I forgot to charge my mobile.'

'It'll cost you,' she warned, giggling.

'I'm sure that you'll be rewarded in Heaven,' he told her.

Her eyes danced a little solo as she countered with, 'I'd prefer to be rewarded in bed.'

About to reply, McCabe spotted John-John Menson beckoning to him from the shadowy doorway. Manoeuvring his way through the crowded bar, McCabe reached the door to find that John-John had gone. Outside, the air of a late autumn evening was chilled by dampness. He found a robed and cowled John-John sitting on an iron bench in the pub's small garden.

'Did you want to speak to me about something?' McCabe enquired.

'Yes, Mr McCabe, it was good of you to come out here.'

Relieved that Menson was in a rational state of mind, McCabe asked, 'Would you like to come inside? If you don't drink alcohol, you could have an orange juice or something.'

Turning his head to look through the brightly lit windows at the drinkers moving about, John-John, his voice shaking, said, 'Oh no, I couldn't do that. Can't you sense the presence in there of people from the past as well as the present?'

'I don't understand,' McCabe said, shattered by John-John's rapid shift of consciousness.

'You should have no trouble comprehending, Mr McCabe, as you are a time-traveller yourself. Tomorrow you intend to return to 1969. By doing so you will bring a tragedy of yesteryear into the present, and thereby ruin the future.'

'I'm sorry, John-John,' McCabe said, starting to walk away.

'Mr McCabe,' John-John called. 'You have learned that it was not Katrina buried at the manor.'

Astounded, McCabe came back to the robed figure's side. John-John was tranquil now, but very depressed.

McCabe asked. 'How could you possibly know that? I only found out myself this afternoon.'

'You people with your silly notions of what time is,' John-John said despairingly. 'I could teach you so much, Mr McCabe. For instance, how well did you know your father before he met your mother?'

This nonsense had McCabe ready to leave once more. But he was stayed by a sudden realization that just about everything Menson said, no matter how bizarre, carried a message.

'What were you saying with regard to my intentions for tomorrow, John-John?' he asked.

John-John spoke in a grave tone. 'I implore you, Mr McCabe, not to go to Morlton.'

This was a repeat of the plea Sharee's had made in Kilverham that morning. But how could he know of his intention to visit Morlton? McCabe enquired, 'What are you trying to tell me?'

'I am saying that to reopen old wounds at Morlton will have consequences so terrible that the human mind is not capable of contemplating them in advance.'

Disturbed but not deterred by this, McCabe said, 'I'll think about it, John-John.'

'That is all that I ask, Mr McCabe.'

Having said that, John-John stood and walked off. McCabe watched him go, gliding like a ghost in the night until the growing darkness swallowed him up. It was a fitting exit. It seemed that the night was the only thing that John-John had left, and even that wasn't doing much for him.

McCabe stopped at the bar on his return, to order drinks for Sol Quinn and himself. Carol had been as reserved as ever on the telephone. Though agreeing that he could stay over for one night, she had not been enthusiastic about an evening on the town. He suspected that she would use failure to find a babysitter as an excuse. They ended by declaring another truce in a seemingly unending cold war. One side of McCabe knew that he had lost Carol forever, while another side denied it.

Pouring the drinks, the normally cheerful Sharee was intense as she asked, 'Did you find your way to Morlton this morning, Gerry?'

McCabe sensed acute anxiety behind the question. He could think of no reason why his projected visit to an elderly couple should cause both Sharee and John-John Menson so much concern.

'I got side-tracked,' he told her. 'If everything goes according to plan, I should get there tomorrow morning. Are you still advising against it, Sharee?'

'What I said this morning was just a friendly hint, Gerry,' she answered evasively. 'I wouldn't dream of interfering in your business.'

'But you would still prefer me not to go to Morlton.'

'Like I said, it's up to you.' She looked to where Roland and Beth Merrill had just entered the bar, and Beth raised a hand to McCabe in remote greeting. Sharee remarked, 'You sure are in demand this evening, Gerry.'

Eyes seeking a clue in his face as he approached, Beth asked her question as soon as he was in earshot. 'Have you heard anything, Mr McCabe?'

Disturbed by the involuntary but massive thrill her presence caused, he rebuked himself. This time tomorrow evening he would be with Carol. Beth would then be so distant that she might as well not exist. That was the way it should be, the way it must be, both then and now, he told himself.

'Nothing yet, I'm afraid,' he told her. Taking an index finger from the full glass he held in his right hand he pointed it to where Sol Quinn sat. 'I'm with Detective Inspector Quinn. Forensics would ring him here if an identification had been made.'

'Thank you,' a sad and disappointed Beth said quietly.

'We mustn't keep you from your friend, Mr McCabe,' Merrill said. His eyes were neither friendly nor unfriendly. That perturbed McCabe.

'Of course not,' Beth agreed with her husband.

'I'll let you know the moment that I hear anything,' McCabe promised.

Turning away to rejoin Quinn, McCabe found that he was now

reluctant to leave the Merrills. Beth drew and held him with a terrifically powerful magnet.

The grey sky was greasy with leftover night when McCabe stopped his car outside a red brick council house in the hamlet of Morlton. Walking up the front garden path, he heard the clucking of chickens coming from behind the house as he knocked on the door.

A grey-haired man came shuffle-footed round the corner from the side of the house. The answer to the question he asked was already in his tired eyes. 'Mr McCabe?'

'Mr Jenkins,' McCabe responded as they shook hands. 'I hope I'm not too early.'

'Not at all. Come round the back if you don't mind. I've sealed the front door up for the coming winter. An easterly wind blows straight in here.'

In the sitting-room, Jenkins introduced McCabe to his wife. The elderly Beryl Jenkins was painfully thin and as flat chested as a surfboard. Her gold-rimmed, flat-lens glasses made it seem that she never looked at you directly. Instead, she took you in with a series of quick peripheral glances. She looked as tired as her husband did. McCabe guessed that anxious anticipation of his visit had caused the couple a sleepless night.

'It is good of you to see me,' McCabe said as he took a proffered seat.

'Doctor Ronan vouched for you,' Beryl Jenkins explained. 'Ralph has been a close friend for many years.'

'Nevertheless, we do not wish to relive old sorrows,' her husband warned.

'I understand that,' McCabe assured him. 'I take it that Doctor Ronan told you that I am working for Colonel Farquahar.'

'To discover what happened to Katrina,' Jenkins said.

'That poor girl,' Beryl Jenkins whispered sadly. 'We never cease to worry about our children regardless of what age they are. It is impossible to imagine what torment Colonel Farquahar has endured these many years.'

'There has recently been a development that complicates everything,' McCabe informed the elderly couple. 'The police have found the remains of a girl buried in the grounds of Abbeyfield Manor.'

'Good heavens!' Thomas Jenkins exclaimed.

'Katrina?' Beryl Jenkins questioned breathlessly.

'We don't think so, Mrs Jenkins,' McCabe answered. 'The remains were those of a pregnant female. As part of my investigation I am attempting to discover the identity of any local girl who was pregnant in the late 1960s, and Doctor Ronan suggested that you may be able to assist me.'

The Jenkinses looked at each other through a minute or more of silence, and then Thomas Jenkins faced McCabe. 'Ralph had our daughter in mind. But she is alive and well today.'

'So I was given to understand, sir. I was hoping that she might be able to tell me of any other girl in the same condition in that era.'

Again they remained silent for a time. Then Beryl sobbed a little as she protested, 'We would like to help, Mr McCabe, but Rita has suffered enough in the past. We simply can't ruin her life now.'

Understanding hit McCabe suddenly and hard. 'Rita' had to be Rita Pavely, Ryan's wife. Now he could grasp why both Sharee Bucholz and John-John Menson had tried to dissuade him from contacting the Jenkinses, who, aware of Beryl's mistake, were looking at him aghast.

Arriving in Staines, McCabe found Katrina's home address in the area's telephone directory under 'Leyland, K'. McCabe drove to one of a terrace of tiny houses in a narrow back street. There was a small gate and a walk-up, and one of those doorbells that rang somewhere so deep inside the house that a caller is convinced that it doesn't work.

There was no one at home, but a nosy next-door neighbour had accepted his lie that he was a close friend. She told him that Katrina was a secretary employed by a firm of solicitors. The firm had a modest suite of first-floor offices above a car showroom. A woman sitting at a computer keyboard took off her headphones and smiled a welcome as McCabe entered. Though her auburn hair was neat and tidy, she patted it unnecessarily.

'Can I help you?

'I am looking for Mrs Katrina Leyland,' McCabe explained.

'That's me,' the secretary replied, looking puzzled rather than worried.

The image that McCabe had of her disintegrated in his head. Katrina was overweight, and the plainness of her round face was accentuated by an unimaginative hairstyle. There was no hint of the attractive girl in the old photograph. She had none of the vivacious sexuality that her sister possessed.

'There is nothing for you to worry about,' McCabe hastened to assure her. 'My name is Gerard McCabe. I am a private detective.'

'I suspect this has something to do with my father,' she stated rather than asked.

'Colonel Farquahar engaged me to find you.'

Katrina forced politeness to the fore. 'Why now? I haven't had any contact with my family since 1969.'

McCabe was nonplussed. To handle the matter objectively was to run the risk of being cruel. He decided he needed more thinking time. 'There is a reason, Mrs Leyland, but I'd rather explain it somewhere other than here. Perhaps I could take you to lunch?'

'Not today, I'm afraid. Mr Smythe, my boss, is due in court in half an hour, and I have to go with him. It's an important case.'

Doing a swift mental rearrangement of his itinerary, McCabe suggested, 'Tomorrow then?'

Top teeth lightly nipping her bottom lip as she concentrated, a trace of Beth showed through for a fleeting moment. 'I can make it tomorrow. My lunch break is at twelve.'

'Then I will call for you here at noon,' McCabe said, uncomfortable on noticing that her eyes were swimming with unshed tears.

Knuckling at her eyes in a childish way, Katrina murmured, 'I am so ashamed of myself. The first thing I should have asked you was how my family is keeping.'

'The colonel is well, although somewhat frail due to his age, and your sister is fine.'

'My mother?' Katrina looked at McCabe steadily, before questioning him apprehensively.

'Mrs Farquahar left home soon after you. She is living in London now.'

'Alone?'

'Yes, she lives alone,' McCabe replied. 'I'll leave you to get on with your work now, Mrs Leyland, and look forward to us having lunch together tomorrow.'

He was at the door when Katrina called to him.

'Mr McCabe.'

'Yes?'

'What if I don't want to be found?'

'Then I won't have found you,' McCabe answered.

'Thank you,' she said. An easy smile lightened her face and the trouble lines were gone.

'This time I get to play the hostess,' Maria Farquahar said with a gentle smile, as she placed a tea tray on the table between her and McCabe.

With an afternoon unexpectedly spare, McCabe had called to keep the colonel's estranged wife informed as he had promised. An ulterior motive was to learn how much she knew about Rita Pavely, or Jenkins as she then was, in the 1960s.

Taking a sip of tea, Maria Farquahar looked at him over the rim of a delicate china cup. 'Well, Mr McCabe, I just can't wait to hear the latest from Abbeyfield. I still have a need to be free of the prison that I find this ridiculously self-important city to be.'

'That's understandable,' McCabe concurred. 'First, you have no reason to worry about Katrina. She is alive and well, but at this stage I am unable to tell you any more. However, the remains of a girl and a foetus have been found buried in the grounds of Abbeyfield Manor. There is nothing to link this with Doctor Ronan, Mrs Farquahar. It would seem he only performed one illegal operation, and that was on the daughter of close friends of his.'

'Do you know who the girl buried in the manor grounds is, Mr McCabe?'

'No,' McCabe said with a shake of his head. 'The police have yet to establish her identity.'

'Then this girl who had the abortion is still alive,' Maria

Farquahar mused. 'Abbeyfield has experienced more than its share of human lapses since the 1960s.'

'Do you know the maiden name of Rita Pavely, Mrs Farquahar?' McCabe enquired.

'Of course. She is Tom and Beryl Jenkinses' only child,' she replied; then understanding dawned on her and she covered her mouth with her hand. 'Was it Rita who...?'

Giving a confirming nod, McCabe asked, 'Have you any idea who the father might have been?'

'None at all, I'm afraid.'

'Katrina was her friend I believe,' McCabe said. 'She never mentioned to you that Rita was in trouble?'

'Good heavens no! It would have been as much a shock to Katrina as it would have been to me,' Maria Farquahar answered adamantly. 'Please take great care with Rita, Mr McCabe. Though Mary is a lovely person, the Pavelys are not liberally minded people. I shudder to imagine the distress it would cause Rita if they were to discover her secret.'

'I will tread carefully,' McCabe promised. Draining his cup, he placed it back on the tray.

Apparently wondering whether or not to tell him something, Maria Farquahar finally made up her mind. 'I've learned that Sylvester Hartley is in business back in the Kilverham area.'

'I thought that he was struck off as a solicitor,' McCabe protested.

'He isn't practising as a solicitor,' Maria Farquahar explained. 'I didn't get the full story, but I gather that he has set up a few companies and has a different name now.'

'Did you get his new name, Mrs Farquahar?'

'No, I'm afraid I didn't.'

In McCabe's mind, Hartley's liking for women made him a suspect for the pregnancy and possibly the murder of the dead girl. Maybe he had also seduced Rita Jenkins. But conjecture wasn't fact. McCabe got to his feet. 'I'll see what I can find out about Hartley, Mrs Farquahar. I'd best be on my way now.'

'Of course. But you will call again?'

'I will.'

*

The Blue Oasis smelled of cigars, expensive women and cheap aftershave. Yet it was the best of a mediocre group of clubs all located within a square mile close to Carol's home. Strobe lighting reflected garishly off a chromium-trimmed bar, and tatty tables and chairs were placed around a dance floor. They had come here only because the babysitter could not stay past midnight. He'd had tea with his wife and daughter, and had spent a great hour with Cindy, who had showed him all her new toys while chattering on in her delightful way.

Now McCabe doubted that their short time together that evening could bring about a change in Carol. This was McCabe's home turf, his stamping ground, and the ease with which he had slipped back into it proved that the outback that was Abbeyfield had only a surface effect on him.

'Lighten up, Gerry,' Carol said, her mouth struggling with a smile. She looked as if she didn't want to be there.

'I'm worried that you are thinking this evening is a mistake, Carol.'

'The night is yet young, as they say,' she observed neutrally. In the subdued lighting her face had a mature, unselfconscious kind of beauty.

'But we aren't,' McCabe said. 'What are we doing here, Carol?'

'Trying to pick up the pieces,' she suggested with a small shrug.

'Maybe that's what I'm doing. But what about you?'

'I would like to,' she answered earnestly, 'but I'm just not sure that I can.'

On a bandstand at the rear of the room, a drummer was warming up his traps while two teenage girls wriggled to his jungle beat and a cluster of gay men swayed to the rhythm with their arms around each other's waists.

'Is this job of yours out of town coming to an end?' Carol asked, as she sipped white wine.

'It's showing no sign of doing so right now, Carol,' McCabe replied. 'An old guy hired me to find his daughter, and I've just found her. I'm meeting her for lunch tomorrow.'

'Then it sounds to me like you have done what you are being paid to do.'

Shaking his head sadly, McCabe said, 'Not only does the

daughter not want to be found, but also when I began looking for her I turned up the remains of a pregnant girl buried in the grounds of the manor of the man who's paying me. That meant involving the police.'

'Which means that the girl who was missing—'

'A woman now,' McCabe explained. 'It was in 1969 that she disappeared.'

'Blimey,' Carol exclaimed. 'So she might have had something to do with the death of the other girl.'

'She might at least know her identity. That's why I am having lunch with her tomorrow.'

A spotlight was playing over a black girl singer up on the stage. At a microphone, she wore a silky red gown that clung tightly enough to prove that she was going commando, and was cut low enough to expose a lot of bosom. Singing Whitney Houston's *I Will Always Love You*, she was making more music with her hips than she was her voice. Her lack of talent was in keeping with the Blue Oasis standard.

With a sideways glance at him, Carol joked, 'That singer is a threat to our endeavours to kiss and make up, Gerry.'

'I'm a reformed character,' he pledged, doing an exaggerated crossing of his heart.

'Gerry,' she said, her face very serious, 'hearing about this family that you are involved with has set me thinking. Would you say the father is trying to get everything back to how it was in 1969?'

'Most definitely.'

'How do you rate his chances?'

'Somewhere way below zero.'

'Exactly,' she agreed with an emphatic nod. 'There is a lesson for us in that, Gerry. Both of us are trying to recreate what we once had. It isn't possible to recreate the past. What we should be concentrating on is our future together.'

'You are right, Carol.' McCabe readily agreed. 'Would you like to dance?'

'I would love to,' she said, standing and holding out her hand to him. 'This may be a new start, but you will still be sleeping on the settee.'

McCabe shrugged. 'At least I'll be getting my mobile charged overnight.'

'That's all that will happen overnight,' she quipped, and they both laughed.

Body fragrances were mixed into a pot pourri of heady smells that had no individual identity as they moved on to the packed dance floor. McCabe was thrilled as she moved into his arms. He regretted having to return to Abbeyfield the next day.

The small restaurant where they had lunch had been too crowded to permit conversation of a personal nature. Katrina was pleasant company, and they were now on first name terms. McCabe had told Katrina of the remains of a pregnant girl being exhumed. Terribly shocked, she had been unable to make even an educated guess as to the dead girl's identity. Now, they strolled in through the gates of a park.

Stepping off the tarmac path on to the grass, enjoying its softness and resilience underfoot, McCabe said, 'Your sister told me that she lent you three shillings and ninepence on the day you left Abbeyfield.'

'Beth did give me some money,' Katrina said slowly. 'But I couldn't say the exact amount.'

'The colonel's gardener found your purse with exactly three shillings and ninepence in it.'

'My purse?' Katrina queried, in what McCabe sensed was mock disbelief.

They took a seat on a wooden bench close to the water. Katrina smiled as a mallard duck waddled up awkwardly to stand beside her, expecting to be fed titbits.

'We should have brought a doggy bag from the restaurant,' she said.

Taking a seat beside her, McCabe continued where he had left off. 'It was your purse, Katrina. Your driving licence was in it.'

'Oh.' She blushed a deep scarlet. 'I suppose that I have long tried, unsuccessfully, to block that day from my mind, Gerry.'

'It was that bad?'

'Worse,' Katrina said in solemn recall. 'We, Andy and I, were two silly, romantic kids who believed ourselves to be madly in love. My father was totally averse to the new age culture that had virtually taken over Abbeyfield. Daddy wanted the best for Beth and me. There was no way that he would have accepted Andy, a farm labourer, so we eloped.'

Her expression was so sad that McCabe asked gently, 'Which was something you soon came to regret?'

'Perhaps, I don't know. I'm not sure what Abbeyfield, my family, or my life was like then. I suppose it's like the way you see places that you once knew in a dream, different in some odd way to how your memory has stored them.'

Katrina's dabbling into philosophy brought Beth to McCabe's mind. He felt guilty to discover that this was the first time he had thought of her since meeting his wife and daughter yesterday. Forcing himself back to his work, he prompted Katrina. 'We were discussing your purse.'

She sat with her hands together as a steeple pointing skywards, chin resting on her fingertips. 'That's right. I don't know how it ended up in the manor grounds. A lot of the flower people were about to move off that day, and we sort of got together in the Fox and Hounds at lunchtime. That was when my purse was stolen.'

'Do you know who took it?'

'Not really,' Katrina replied. 'I have my suspicions. But the only person who went anywhere near my coat that day was a good friend of mine.'

'Would you say that he or she was desperately in need of money at the time?'

'Suzi,' Katrina replied, 'had a lot of problems, but I don't think she would steal from me.'

'I take it that Suzi is Suzi Duoard?'

'That's right.' Katrina stopped talking. Her finger-steeple parted. Her hands lay twitching slightly in her lap. 'If Suzi did take my purse, then it could be Suzi who was buried there.'

'Was she expecting?'

'Not that I know of. But everyone was stressed around then. We were all so happy for so long, Gerry, but then, for no apparent reason, the whole hippie community suddenly fell apart.'

'So it is possible that she was pregnant and you wouldn't know about it?'

'Oh my God! I hope not.'

Katrina had become terribly upset. McCabe suspected a whiff of a real scandal that could devastate Abbeyfield. He asked, 'Do you know who could be responsible if Suzi was pregnant?'

John-John Menson's rambling words ran through McCabe's head. *They even killed the baby, thereby ending a life before it had really begun.* Had Menson been speaking of the baby that he had given Suzi Duoard?

Looking uncomfortable, Katrina answered stiffly, 'I don't want to talk about this. Look,' – she stood up from the bench, turning to face him – 'we have to agree that there is nothing that will induce me to return to Abbeyfield.'

'It would make several people very happy if you did,' McCabe advised.

'It wouldn't make me happy; far from it,' Katrina countered, her fists wrapped into hard knots.

'I'm probably speaking out of turn, Katrina, but I believe it would be wrong to permit your father and your sister to go on believing that you are dead.'

Giving this a lot of thought, Katrina seemed to realize the awesome power that she held. She spoke calmly and resolutely. 'I agree with you that it would be wrong to cause the colonel and Beth further trauma. If I say that you can tell them that you've found me, can I have your promise that you won't tell them where I am?'

'If that is your wish, you have my promise.'

seven

When he was still some forty miles from Abbeyfield, McCabe's mobile rang.

It was Sol Quinn. *'I've got some big news for you, Gerry.'*

'The remains are those of a hippie girl named Suzi Duoard,' McCabe predicted, enjoying the moment while hating himself for stealing his friend's thunder.

'What did you do in London, visit a fortune-teller?' a disgruntled Quinn asked.

'No, I've had a long talk to Katrina Farquahar, and have since put two and two together.'

'Did she tell you who the father of the unborn child was, Gerry?'

'No,' McCabe admitted. *'Who was it?'*

'I was asking you, not telling you,' an annoyed Quinn explained. *'Maybe we'll know soon. The girl was strangled, so it's murder.'*

'The killer is probably still strolling the lanes of Abbeyfield.'

'We can always arrest John-John,' Quinn said drily. *'I take it that you'll be going straight to the manor when you get back.'*

'Yes. I'm not far from Abbeyfield now.'

'You didn't bring Katrina back with you?

'She didn't want to come home,' McCabe reported. *'The idea terrifies her.'*

'How are you going to tell the colonel that the prodigal daughter won't be returning to the fold?'

'I've got the next hour or so to think about it,' McCabe answered unhappily.

Arriving at the manor to find that the Pavelys were there for dinner eased McCabe's worry. Beth invited him to stay, but he politely turned the offer down with the half-lie that he had arranged to meet Solomon Quinn. Telling Beth that he would like to speak to her in private for a few minutes, he led the way out into the hall. The fact that Beth's husband followed them caused McCabe consternation. With a difficult subject to broach, he felt restricted by the presence of Roland Merrill.

'I was going to tell both you and the colonel this,' McCabe began. 'But I'll have to leave it to you to pass it on to your father.'

'You've found something out,' Beth guessed, then asked anxiously. 'Is it bad news?'

Someone in the dining-room must have said something amusing. There was a roar of laughter from the diners. McCabe waited so as not to have to raise his voice when he spoke. When the raucous laughter subsided into giggling, he answered her.

'Not in the sense that I expect you mean,' McCabe said. 'The remains in the rockery are not those of Katrina.'

'Thank the Lord.' Beth, her eyes closed, breathed the words like a prayer. 'This will mean so much to my father. Do you know where she is, Mr McCabe?'

'Yes, but I'm not at liberty to say.'

'What nonsense is this, McCabe?' Roland Merrill protested. 'Colonel Farquahar will be paying you good money to find his daughter.'

'I've found his daughter, Merrill,' McCabe said flatly.

'Something that we have only your word for,' Merrill retorted.

'Please, Roland,' a distressed Beth pleaded, then questioned McCabe. 'I don't understand. Is she with Andy?'

'No. They split up and went their different ways soon after leaving here. Andrew Fairview is married now.'

'And Katrina?' Beth enquired breathlessly.

'Katrina was married, but she's divorced,' McCabe replied. 'She has no children and lives alone. She's comfortably off and has a well-paid job.'

'Then why won't she come home?'

'Too guilty,' Merrill volunteered bitterly. 'Guilty about the shame she brought on both our families, Beth.'

'I am certain there is nothing in what you say, Merrill,' McCabe said.

'Then why won't she show her face here, McCabe?'

'I don't know, but she has her reasons not to return, and I have to respect that.'

'I appreciate that, Mr McCabe,' Beth said softly, close to tears. 'Possibly things will change in the near future.'

'They probably will, Mrs Merrill. Katrina knows how to get in touch with me. I will come back tomorrow when you have no guests, and explain things more fully.'

'Thank you.'

Roland Merrill stood watching as Beth showed McCabe to the door. She bade him 'Good night', but her husband uttered not a word.

Hi-jacked by Sharee Bucholz, a bored McCabe stood watching the judging of the floats and presentation of prizes by an announcer from the local television nightly news programme, who was acutely aware of his status as a non-celebrity. The Abbeyfield Bonfire Night Carnival was a diversion that McCabe didn't welcome. Forming up in the Fox and Hounds car-park at six o'clock in the evening, the convoy of ten trashy floats, led by the Kilverham Brass Band, had done a full tour of the village before returning to a field at the rear of the pub. Here a travelling funfair provided a brightly lit, gaudily coloured, noisy centre for the continuing festivities.

Then Sharee was steering McCabe by the arm towards a sedately whirling old-fashioned set of galloping horses. Groups of people stood eagerly waiting for the ride to stop. At his side, Sharee was buzzing in excited anticipation as the roundabout slowed.

'This has been coming to Abbeyfield for donkey's years. I absolutely loved it as a kid,' she said, shouting above the thump-thump of organ music from the centre of the ride. 'Come on, Gerry. This will be great training for you to join the Abbeyfield Hunt.'

Unable to resist her bubbling enthusiasm, McCabe climbed up on a carved, brilliantly coloured horse given majesty by inlaid gold leaf. Feeling foolish, he had to grasp the twisted brass rod with both hands as his horse moved forwards and upwards at the same time. Sharee laughed at his predicament, and then he was laughing with her as they moved sedately in a circle, both of them level at one moment then finding themselves either looking up or down at the other the next. The organ was playing *The Blue Danube*, and Sharee swayed happily to the waltz-time rhythm.

The magical ride ended all too soon. A laughing Sharee challenged him. 'Come on, let's see how good you are at hoopla.'

He won her a prize, a bright blue teddy bear, at the hoopla stall. Hugging the cuddly soft toy to her, she deliberately stood close to McCabe. Thinking of Carol and the evening they had enjoyed at the club in London, he wondered why he didn't instinctively draw away from Sharee.

'Have you a cigarette, Gerry?' Sharee asked.

Taking a packet of cigarettes from his pocket, he opened it and held it out to her. When his lighter flared modestly, the little glow revealed and accentuated her features in close-up, the yellow flame lighting her face dramatically. Breath quickening, McCabe knew that he had to be careful. He needed to shield himself from her magnetism. Head back, she blew smoke out, saying, 'There's Beth and Roland over there by the dodgems. We'd better go over to say a few words.'

Embarrassed by the way she was clinging to his arm, he walked with her to where Beth and her husband stood together but as remote as two strangers.

'Enjoying yourselves?' Sharee enquired.

Thankfully for McCabe, conversation was difficult. The blaring of modern music deepened the grinding of dodgem car wheels on metal plates and the crash of collisions.

'We've only just arrived,' Roland Merrill answered woodenly.

'I don't expect that we will stay very long,' Beth said. She went on, 'I'm surprised to see you enjoying all the fun of the fair, Mr McCabe.'

Releasing McCabe's arm, Sharee pushed him a little way towards the Merrills. 'You'll be here long enough to chaperon Gerry. I'd better go and open up or my regulars will lynch me.'

Bidding them all a cheery farewell, Sharee moved off out of the fairground lights into the surrounding darkness. Left in an uncomfortable atmosphere with Beth and her husband, McCabe said, 'I have to be off, too, so I won't spoil your evening.'

'Still investigating although there is nothing left to investigate, McCabe?' Merrill remarked.

McCabe had decided what he must do. Suzi Duoard had been murdered and buried in the grounds of Abbeyfield Manor, which meant that he owed a duty to Colonel Farquahar to clear the whole matter up before leaving. Then Katrina might well return to her family. That was the only conclusion to the case that would allow McCabe to accept his fee with a clear conscience.

'I still have things to do,' he told Merrill. 'Have either of you heard anything about Sylvester Hartley being back in the district?'

Startled, Beth exclaimed, 'What on earth makes you ask that?'

'A rumour I heard yesterday,' McCabe replied.

'Do you think he might be mixed up in what has happened here?' Beth enquired, a tremor in her voice.

'There may be some connection.'

Merrill seemed about to argue when Ryan Pavely called to him from a little distance away.

Without excusing himself, Merrill turned away from Beth and McCabe to join Ryan and Rita Pavely. When he was out of earshot, Beth questioned McCabe. 'What's been happening, Gerry?'

'I got held up everywhere that I went today, Beth. I'm sorry that I didn't get to call on you and the colonel,' McCabe apologized.

'That wasn't what I was asking about,' she said, keeping a close eye on her husband. 'You and Sharee Bucholz looked like you're an item.'

'I was an innocent bystander until Sharee insisted that I join her at the carnival,' McCabe, unnerved by the memory of Sharee's possessiveness and Beth's jealousy, defended himself.

'It must have been awful for you,' Beth began cynically, but said no more as her husband returned.

'Ryan and Rita are planning a candle-lit carol service out at the old monastery this Christmas,' Merrill reported. 'He asked if I can get the school to join in.'

'That will be nice,' Beth commented, her total lack of interest obvious.

'I told him I'll be delighted to have the school take part,' Merrill said.

There were concerted 'Oooooohs' and 'Aaaaaaahs' from the crowd as rockets whooshed up into the night to explode and drop back to earth as masses of varicoloured sparks. The Merrills were now watching the fireworks intently, which presented McCabe with the opportunity to make his excuses and leave them.

He was rounding the corner of a huge fairground lorry when Rita Pavely suddenly appeared in front of him. She became brilliantly illuminated as a massive rocket exploded in the sky. Then the light in the sky went out and the two of them were alone in the night.

'I've been waiting to see you, Gerry,' Rita said, her voice a thin, reedy sound.

Having learned fast the hazards of village life, McCabe asked, 'Where's your husband?'

'He's busy with the pig roasting.'

She seemed to consider that to be an answer, but McCabe hadn't a clue as to what she was talking about.

'Perhaps we should go back out into the fairground,' he suggested.

'No,' she said quickly. 'My parents said that you've been to see them.'

'I did speak to them, yes.'

'And you know all about what happened to me,' she said, her bottom lip visibly trembling.

'You have no need to worry. I'll make sure it remains confidential.'

'But it will lead you to make further enquiries?' she asked plaintively.

'Possibly,' he admitted. 'If it does you won't be mentioned at any time.'

'That doesn't reassure me. Everyone in Abbeyfield puts two and two together. I beg you to drop this part of your investigation.'

Though moved by her dread, McCabe could only say, 'I'm sorry, Rita.'

She looked off into the night as she said, 'I'm sure that we can reach agreement on this. Ryan is at Kilverham market tomorrow. Could you come over to the house in the morning?'

Awareness of what she was offering told McCabe how utterly desperate the woman was. He felt disgust, but pity welled up in him to defeat it. When he spoke it was in a kindly way. 'Apart from Doctor Ronan and your parents, Rita, I am the only one who knows about your problem in the past. I have given you my word that I won't reveal it to anyone.'

In the half-light her eyes were a blank dark blue as she slanted a look at him. Then she turned and was gone into the darkness from which she had appeared.

'Sylvester Hartley?' Sol Quinn said the name slowly and thoughtfully. 'He's a possibility, certainly, Gerry.'

They were sitting in Quinn's office, where the scent of furniture polish had the acrid quality of incense. The two of them were drinking coffee while McCabe gave an account of the time he had spent with Katrina and with her mother. His thoughts occasionally wandered to Rita Pavely, who would right then be keeping her morning vigil. Detective Superintendent Peter Rendall, as bland and composed as ever, entered the room and brought McCabe's mind back to current matters.

'Good morning, Mr McCabe,' Rendall said. 'Anything new, Sol?'

'One thing that will interest you, guv: Gerry heard in London that Sylvester Hartley is back in this area.'

Not responding for a short while, Rendall picked up some papers from Quinn's desk and pretended to read them. Then, peering over silver-rimmed glasses, imprisoning McCabe with a peripheral glance, he said, 'I hope this information is reliable, Mr McCabe. Hartley isn't a man to fool with.'

'He's wanted for fraud, guv,' Quinn reminded his superior.

'I'm well aware of that, Sol.'

'I think this is worth following up, guv,' Quinn said, with a meaningful glance at McCabe. 'He might even be linked to Suzi Duoard's murder.'

'As I said, Hartley is an eggshell job,' Rendall said. 'We have to tread carefully.'

McCabe felt dislike of the Rendall prickling under his skin. It had to be something either intuitive or instinctive, as it defied analysis. Rendall didn't look like anyone else, senior policemen never did; you don't see them driving trucks or climbing ladders on building sites.

'Gerry doesn't have to worry about local politics, guv.'

'If Hartley is at the centre of things everyone has to worry, Mr McCabe.'

Letting this pass without comment, McCabe declared, 'If Hartley does tie in with the murder, then I want to find out.'

Getting up from his chair, Quinn picked up a file. 'I've an idea that I might find a lead for you, Gerry.' Lips pursed, he read for a while, then jabbed at a page with a forefinger. 'Ah, here we are. Ali Westwood. It says here that she was close to Hartley. She must have been a stunner, as she won a quite a few beauty contests.'

'Is she still around here, Sol?'

Rendall answered for Quinn. 'Westwood is here in Kilverham, Mr McCabe. She's over the hill now. She runs a seedy B&B place in Wesley Street. You know the sort of place, caters mainly for those on the social.'

'Thanks for the advice,' McCabe said. 'When I told Katrina that her mother had left Abbeyfield shortly after she did, it struck me that she suspected she had left here with someone.'

'Possibly she thought it was Hartley,' Rendall acknowledged.

'So, what are we going to do about Hartley, guv?' Quinn asked.

'Let Mr McCabe probe around for a few days. You will keep us up to speed?'

'I will,' McCabe promised.

'Thank you,' Rendall said. His smile was very condescending. 'But watch yourself.'

'I'll be watching my back, Superintendent.'

'If anything goes wrong, you are on your own,' Rendall warned. 'Understood?'

'Understood, Superintendent.'

It was dark by the time McCabe located Wesley Street. But he was in no hurry. Not wanting the embarrassment of facing Rita in the

Fox and Hounds, he didn't intend to return until after closing time. He brought his car to a halt beside a half-illuminated sign that read Stratford Hotel. Hotel? That was a misnomer. The dingy building was reminiscent of the many horrible places in London that made a cardboard box under Waterloo Bridge preferable.

As he went in through the open front door he was knocked back momentarily by a dull, heavy smell overlaid by a reek of fried onions. The garbled sound of raised-voiced conversation came from a room to his right, where men and women sat eating around a large table. Their laughter was constant. But it was not the joyous laughter of people enjoying themselves. It had a hollow cadence.

A dishevelled, pouting girl came out of a room at the end of the passageway, closing the door behind her. Eyeing him suspiciously, she then sullenly announced, 'We ain't got no vacancies, mister.'

'I'm not looking for a room,' McCabe told her, counting his blessings. 'I wonder if I could have a word with Ali Westwood?'

'What do you want with Miss Westwood?' the girl asked belligerently.

A woman came out of the same door at the end of the passage and called to the girl, 'It's all right, Letitia.'

Doing an about turn, the girl walked away. The door slammed behind her angrily, causing the woman to wince as she came towards McCabe. She was an attractive redhead whose beauty was but a shadow left behind by that which is gone. She had on an iridescent pale-green robe that ended less than halfway down her chunky thighs. A delicate hand, long slim fingers tipped with dark-purple nails perfectly kept, held the top of the robe closed.

'Forgive Letitia her rudeness,' she said. 'A visitor wearing a good suit invariably means trouble in a place like this.'

'All is forgiven. My name is McCabe.'

She didn't offer her hand. 'You already know my name, which worries me. I hope I'm mistaken.'

'Mistaken in what way, Miss Westwood?'

'In thinking that you are a policeman.'

She had the brittle arrogance of a woman who had suffered hardships from birth, and had survived them by sheer animal instinct. It was McCabe's guess that she had whored her way through a seedy life.

'I was in the police a long time ago. I'm a private detective now.'

'I hope you don't think that I find that reassuring, Mr McCabe,' she said.

'I'm not investigating you, Miss Westwood. I believe that you might be able to help me with some information.'

Reaching out sideways she found the door handle of the dining-room by instinct, and pulled the door closed. She gave McCabe a tight-lipped smile. 'I do hear things from time to time. But my memory needs jogging, if you get my meaning.'

'I never expect something for nothing. You name your price,' McCabe invited.

A cool Ali Westwood said, 'If I can help you, then I'll assess the worth of the information when you say what it is you want.'

McCabe came to the point. 'I am told that you know a man named Sylvester Hartley.'

Ali Westwood's half-smiling face instantly switched to an expression of anger. Her pale brow creased and her eyes had hardened. 'You have been misinformed, Mr McCabe.'

'But I—' McCabe started to say, but she cut him short.

'I believe that our conversation is at an end. Good evening, Mr McCabe.'

Accepting that it would be pointless to argue, McCabe said, 'Good evening, Miss Westwood,' and left.

As he drove through moonlit countryside towards Abbeyfield, McCabe pondered on Ali Westwood's reaction to his enquiry about Hartley. Fear is often the base of anger, and he guessed that he had frightened her badly. Passing a line of dark shops snuggling beside a brightly lighted pub that a litter of parked cars suckled around, McCabe slowed as the surface beneath his tyres became rough. As the road curved and dropped and rose again, his interior mirror reflected a pair of headlights that were gaining on him fast. Then the headlights started to flash as the vehicle came up tight behind.

When the lights of his own car picked out a lay-by ahead,

McCabe pulled off the road. Passing him, the vehicle that had been on his tail, an ancient Land-Rover, swung in across his bow and came to a halt, police style.

Leaving his headlights switched on, McCabe opened the door of the car and stepped out. In the glare of the headlights the hulking figure of Abb Perkins was walking menacingly towards him. At Perkins's side was an older, rough-looking man.

'What's this about?' McCabe asked.

Not replying, Perkins suddenly kicked McCabe's open car door hard. The top edge of the door caught McCabe under the chin, breaking the skin. Knocked dizzy by the impact, McCabe was in no condition to resist when Perkins pulled the car door wide open and reached out a huge hand to grab him by the front of his jacket. In a swift, trained movement, Perkins threw a right-hand punch with his spare hand. Able to see it coming, but held so tightly that he had no opportunity to evade it, McCabe felt the fist connect with the side of his head. There was no pain; just a disabling disorientation as the world around him swayed about at strange angles.

The second man came round behind McCabe to hold both his arms, pulling him clear of the car as Perkins drove a twisting left hook into his midriff. McCabe's body twisted in pain, an agony so intense that it cleared his mind. Reaching for Perkins's head with both hands, he gouged at his eyes with his thumbs. When the big man pulled away from him, McCabe kicked with his right leg straight from the hip to the heel, catching Perkins in the groin with the flat of his shoe. The recoil of the kick sent McCabe's body backwards, slamming the man holding him against the car. Driving his elbow back at full force into the man's stomach, McCabe then launched himself at a half-blinded, bent double Perkins. Instinctively, the big man stretched out his right arm in an attempt at grabbing McCabe.

Catching the big fist in a two-handed grip, McCabe pulled Perkins's arm up over the top edge of his car's door. In an expert move he yanked down hard on the hand to inflict a clean break that snapped the bone like a carrot. Using the palm of his left hand to push the man's prominent chin up, McCabe drove his right elbow hard into the throat. Coughing and wheezing as he struggled to breathe through his damaged throat, but managing a howl of pain for his broken wrist, Perkins slumped to the ground. He lay quivering, with blood trickling from his mouth.

Spinning round to face Perkins's companion, McCabe found the other man coming at him fast and low, arms high. He was showing yellow teeth in a grin that wasn't human. It broke his face up into a bunch of hard, ugly knots as McCabe stepped quickly forward. Taking him by surprise, he moved in between the older man's arms. Left arm raised to protect himself, McCabe cut his opponent across the bridge of the nose with the hard edge of his right hand. With the bone between his eyes smashed, the man crashed against the side of McCabe's car and clung to it, his face leaving a thick zigzag smear of blood on the bodywork.

A quick check proved to McCabe that Abb Perkins was still unconscious. A noisy eruption of vomit from the man who still clung to the car, hopelessly trying to focus as he collapsed to the ground, drew McCabe's attention. Reaching down he grasped the man by the lapels of his jacket and pulled him up roughly. Peering into the man's shattered face, McCabe harshly questioned him. 'Who hired Perkins to get me?'

Mashed face oozing dark blood, the man couldn't answer. His eyes rolled up in their sockets, only the whites showing as he passed out. Laying the man on his back on the ground, McCabe waited. Within a minute or two his patience was rewarded as the supine man began to choke on his own blood, and rolled on to his side to clear his nose, mouth and throat. Showing no mercy, McCabe used a foot on the injured man's shoulder to press him on to his back once more, then transferred the sole of his shoe to the man's throat.

Applying steady pressure, McCabe asked once more, 'Who hired Perkins to get me?'

Lifting his foot a little to permit the man to answer, McCabe applied pressure again as he reiterated his question. 'Who hired Perkins to get me?'

'Oh God,' the stricken man moaned, blood gurgling in his throat.

'Speak up,' McCabe ordered.

He raised his foot again, but only in threat as the injured man shrieked beseechingly, 'Please! No!'

'Who paid you and Perkins to come after me?' McCabe asked.

The man croaked what sounded like a name, but McCabe couldn't catch it. When he asked for it to be repeated, the man said. 'Piers Heaney.'

With the name meaning nothing to him, McCabe took stock of the situation he was in. He would have no need to shift the men, one unconscious and the other semi-conscious, in order to drive his car out of the lay-by. But, as he went to get into his car, the beating he had taken before overpowering his attackers caught up with him. Sick and dizzy, he staggered against the side of his car and slid down on to his knees.

Barely in touch with the world, he was aware of two hands in his armpits, pulling him up to his feet. Certain that either Perkins or his accomplice had recovered sufficiently to tackle him again, McCabe tried to get together enough to defend himself. But it was no use. He was too far out of it. Everything went black for him.

He was pulled upright as a voice spoke close to his ear. 'You cut down the tree to make a cross that you must now carry by day and by night.'

Blinking to clear his blurred vision, McCabe realized that it was John-John Menson who had lifted him to his feet. The cowl of his monk's outfit up over his head, Menson was looking down sadly at the two unconscious men lying on the ground.

'I was just on my way home when I heard the commotion,' John-John told McCabe as he propped him against the car and did a test to see if he could remain upright unaided. McCabe passed the test. 'I would beseech thee, Mr McCabe, strive to become such that thou are able to become non-violent.'

'These two guys jumped me,' McCabe explained to exonerate himself. He swung the driver's door open wide. 'I have to be on my way.'

Taking McCabe by one arm, a surprisingly strong Menson dragged him round to the other side of the car and opened the front passenger door. Pushing McCabe into the seat, he said, 'You are in no fit condition to drive, Mr McCabe.'

Slamming the door, John-John hurried around the front of the car to get into the driver's seat. He held the door open so as to use the courtesy light to search for the controls.

McCabe asked nervously. 'Can you drive, John-John?'

'I used to own a Bedford Dormobile,' Menson replied. 'Light blue, it was. I even had my initials on both of the doors – JM in gold italic letters.'

'That must have been a long time ago,' McCabe remarked diplomatically.

Frowning, peering at him, Menson objected, 'That's not so. We're talking 1978–79.'

As he finished speaking, Menson put the car in gear and released the clutch. The vehicle took a violent leap out into the road and then stalled. McCabe was about to insist that he take over the driving as it was plain that Menson had not driven for some thirty-five years, but John-John tried the manoeuvre once more, and got it right. Moving the car off, he steered it to the correct side of the road and carried on.

Moving into second gear, Menson left it there and they travelled through the night at no more than fifteen miles per hour, with the engine roaring. Expecting to see headlights loom up behind at any moment, McCabe worried over the very real possibility of being stopped by the police. If he was discovered being chauffeured by a mad monk in a blue habit it would take more than Detective Inspector Solomon Quinn's high intellect to save him.

But they remained alone in the darkness. Encouraged to believe that they might reach the Fox and Hounds without incident, McCabe decided to do some probing. 'The police have identified the remains found in the manor estate, John-John.'

'Suzi Duoard.'

'What are you, John-John?' McCabe enquired fearfully.

'I am other than what I imagine myself to be,' Menson replied enigmatically. 'By discovering that I also found forgiveness.'

McCabe asked, 'Do you know who fathered the child that Suzi was carrying?'

'A child that never cried,' Menson said sorrowfully.

The sorrow reinforced McCabe's notion that the baby Suzi Duoard had carried was Menson's. Did that mean that Menson had murdered her? Though he found this difficult to believe, he had to accept that a killer might well be driving him through the night.

Slowing the car to a crawl as they reached the pub, Menson steered it awkwardly into the car-park. It pleased McCabe that the place was in darkness. The left side of his face felt badly swollen, and he knew that there was much blood on his clothing.

When the car stopped he wondered how Menson would make it all the way back to the scrapyard on foot. John-John enlightened him by saying matter-of-factly, 'I will return your car first thing in the morning, Mr McCabe. I am mindful that there are two men lying injured in the dark night.'

Face hurting and his battered body causing him trouble, McCabe didn't protest. He said, 'You are a Good Samaritan, John-John.'

'No, Mr McCabe,' Menson said, argumentatively. 'The only good that does not happen by chance comes from outside our material world.'

With that he drove off jerkily. Standing bewildered, watching the rear lights of his car dimmed by distance, McCabe had a name running continuously through his head: the name was Piers Heaney.

eight

Sol Quinn grinned after glancing quickly at McCabe's face. 'Ali Westwood sure packs a mean right hand these days.'

McCabe stifled his annoyance. The day had started badly for him. Sharee had tried to mother him at breakfast, and Beth had been overly concerned about his injuries after he had telephoned her to drive him to the police station at Kilverham. John-John had not returned his car, and on the drive to Kilverham, Beth had joined him in his own fear that he would never see the vehicle again.

'What does the other guy look like?' Beth had asked cheekily, and when McCabe had held up two fingers in reply, she had giggled. 'There's no need to be rude about it.'

'Two guys,' McCabe had explained.

'And one of them was Abb Perkins. I am impressed,' she had remarked seriously.

Now, as Quinn drove McCabe to the scrap-yard in the hope that John-John had his car there in one piece, the detective took up the same theme by suggesting, 'If you downed Abb Perkins, Gerry, you must have done him some serious damage. He sure is a big guy. Maybe John the Baptist has spent all night burying the bodies of Perkins and the other bozo, whoever he is.'

'Then you'll have to do your duty by digging them up and arresting me.'

'I'd give John-John a hand to bury them deeper.' Quinn grinned.

'You wouldn't be able to do that, Sol,' McCabe predicted. 'You and I have reached the time of life when the capacity to be moulded into new forms has been lost. That's a serious handicap in a fast-changing world. John-John Menson is probably luckier than both of us are. He lives life as an emotional freelance, never encountering the sort of things that cause us stress.'

'You're saying once a copper always a copper?' Quinn said, as he turned off the road to drive slowly through the deserted scrap-yard.

'Something like that.'

'What about you, Gerry? You once were a copper. What are you now?'

'I wish that I knew the answer to that,' was McCabe's heartfelt reply.

Heading for Menson's caravan, they saw McCabe's car parked outside. To McCabe's relief it looked intact. As they got out of Quinn's car, Menson opened the door of his caravan and leaned out, his neck and head forward in an eagle-like pose.

'He doesn't look good,' Quinn warned McCabe, out of the side of his mouth.

Coming down the steps, tying the rope sash around the waist of his robe, Menson glanced suspiciously at Quinn before pointing to McCabe's car, saying, 'Ready and waiting for you, Mr McCabe.'

'Where's Perkins, John-John?' McCabe enquired.

Menson's precise reply proved Quinn's prognosis wrong. 'In hospital I presume, together with Mr Carver. When I arrived back there last night someone had called the police and an ambulance. Several cars had stopped, so I drove on past and returned when everyone had gone.'

'Mr Carver, John-John,' Quinn said. 'Is this Billy Carver?'

'It is.'

'Billy Carver's known to us, Gerry,' Quinn informed McCabe. 'He's an old lag who's done stretches for GBH.'

'I'm not surprised,' McCabe said, adding, 'I want to ask Menson if he knows who Piers Heaney is.'

Taking a look at Menson, a cynical Quinn said, 'You're wasting your time.'

'I don't think so,' McCabe countered confidently. 'John-John, does the name Piers Heaney mean anything to you?'

'We only fully recognize the existence of those we love, Mr McCabe,' Menson replied.

Proved right, Quinn grinned crookedly. 'What did I tell you, Gerry?'

'Piers Heaney?' McCabe repeated the name to Menson.

Doing a circular walk in the wreck-confined space outside his caravan, hands behind his back, head drooping in thought, Menson replied, 'We have defiled and emptied the whole earthly sphere. You ask from whence renewal will come to us. It can come from the past alone, but only through love.'

'Get your car, Gerry,' a chuckling Quinn advised. 'I'll run a check on Heaney for you when I get back to the station.'

'Another time slip,' McCabe exclaimed as Beth slowed her Land-Rover Discovery outside Kilverham Primary School. The old-fashioned stonework, the archaic tower and the high windows were a reminder of Dickensian school buildings.

Beth parked the Land-Rover. It eased McCabe not to be in a moving vehicle. His body was still painful from the beating it had received the previous night. On his return to Abbeyfield Manor after collecting his car from Menson, McCabe had told Beth that the remains found in the manor grounds were those of a pregnant Suzi Duoard.

'You didn't know that the Duoard girl was pregnant?' McCabe had asked her.

'I had no idea. Though I was younger than most of them at the time, I thought I knew all about sex.'

'So you don't know who might have been responsible for Suzi's condition?'

Beth had shaken her head, and he'd said, 'I think I might get Katrina to come home if the murder is solved.'

Beth had sat down, holding her head in trembling fingers, deep in thought. When she looked up, McCabe had taken hope from the expression on her face. 'I have an idea, Gerry. Suzi had no one around here, but there was a local girl who fell for a baby; everyone knew about it at the time. Gail, the girl I'm talking about, knew Suzi well. They may have confided in each other.'

'It's worth a go, Beth. Is this Gail still around here?'

Beth's reply had been disappointing. 'No. As soon as they knew she was expecting, her parents sent her off to stay with an aunt. Gail never returned, and soon afterwards her mum and dad sold up and moved away. I suppose that they went to wherever it was they had sent Gail.'

This had McCabe thinking they had reached a dead-end, until Beth said that Elsa Langley, the head teacher at Kilverham Primary School, would most likely know the whereabouts of the disgraced local girl.

'Miss Langley was Gail's teacher at that time,' Beth had told him.

A problem had occurred immediately to McCabe, and he had shared it with Beth. 'If we question your Miss Langley, Beth, surely she will tell your husband?'

'Highly unlikely,' Beth had responded with a harsh little laugh. 'Miss Langley was deputy head at the senior school in Kilverham, but when the head retired, she was bypassed and Roland was given the position. Miss Langley protested, and the county council made her head of the primary school. I don't think Miss Langley has spoken to Roland since.'

'Can you come to the school with me?' McCabe had asked.

'I'll drive you there.'

Now McCabe got out of the Land-Rover and followed her into the school. The place had the unmistakable collective aroma of schoolchildren. Elsa Langley, sixtyish, rose from behind her office desk to greet them. Beth introduced him.

The head teacher smiled at Beth. 'How can I help you, Mrs Merrill? I must say that you sounded quite James Bondish on the telephone.'

Beth and McCabe both gave the smile expected by an intellectual who has wittily shown a knowledge of lesser things. Then Beth followed up with, 'I was hoping that you could give Mr McCabe some information.'

'Personal information regarding a pupil?' Miss Langley queried cautiously.

McCabe watched the teacher pick up a gold ball-pen and fiddle idly with the calibrated rings that made it a calculator. She carried out a lengthy and obviously unnecessary calculation.

'Yes,' Beth nodded, before quickly qualifying the intended enquiry by saying, 'but a pupil of long ago.'

'In what capacity are you here, Mr McCabe?'

'I am a private detective, Miss Langley,' McCabe answered. 'Helping the local police.'

'With a murder enquiry,' Beth added supportively. 'You had a pupil back in the 1960s, Miss Langley. Her first name was Gail, and I think her surname was Potter.'

'Patten, Gail Patten,' Elsa Langley said. 'No doubt you remember Gail's circumstances?'

Beth gave an affirmative nod. 'You have no doubt heard of the human remains found in the manor grounds.'

'I read of it in the paper. What a tragedy. It wasn't a local girl, I understand.'

'No, she came here with the flower people. But we think that Gail might know something useful about her. Do you know where Gail and her parents moved to, Miss Langley?'

'They went to Worcester. I had their address, but they have since moved, and I have no idea where they are now.'

A disappointed McCabe said, 'I am sorry to have troubled you, Miss Langley.'

'Wait a moment, Mr McCabe.' The head teacher held up a hand. 'Gail has a cousin living on the other side of Abbeyfield, in that pretty little village, Morlton. I believe that they kept in touch. The cousin was Muriel Grainger, but she is married now and has a young son going to Middleway School, where my colleague is head. Would you like me to telephone my colleague?'

'Thank you for offering, Miss Langley, but I think we will have to be very discreet,' McCabe said.

'I agree, Mr McCabe. It would be so easy to cause offence.'

'Do you know the cousin's married name, Miss Langley?' Beth asked.

'Oh yes, it's Philpott. Her husband is Bertrand Philpott, a parish councillor.'

Thanking the head teacher, Beth and McCabe left the school. When they were in the Land-Rover, Beth seemed a little unsure of herself for a moment. She pulled the jacket she wore tighter round her, as if it was some kind of shield to keep them separated. McCabe was striving to remain remote, distant, when his mobile rang. It was Solomon Quinn calling with news of Piers Heaney.

Heaney owned a club in Fenton, about thirty miles north of Kilverham, as well as being the proprietor of Perkins's scrapyard. Quinn agreed with McCabe that Heaney might well be Sylvester Hartley, who had heard that McCabe had been making enquiries, hence the assault by Abb Perkins.

'*Are you doing anything this evening, Sol?*' McCabe enquired.

'*What I'm not doing is going to Fenton, Gerry. It's a gay club.*'

Faltering only briefly, McCabe said, '*We'll survive. It could be well worth a visit.*'

'*Well ...*' Quinn began hesitantly before deciding. '*You're right. I'd like to nail Hartley, if it is he. What if I pick you up around nine o'clock?*'

'*I'll be ready,*' McCabe promised, before he switched off.

'I heard most of that,' Beth told him. 'You think this Heaney might be Sylvester Hartley?'

'It's a possibility,' McCabe admitted. 'No more than that.'

Beth started the Land-Rover's engine. 'I take it we are going to see this Philpott woman?'

Muriel Philpott's house stood two storeys tall and offered good views of both a river and the countryside. The carefully tended gardens at the front of the house had artistically designed flowerbeds that stretched to a river-bank. Where the bank curved into a little cove, stood a small boathouse. Pretty in a delicate way, she invited Beth and McCabe into a large square room with an oriental theme for its décor.

'Wow!' Beth exclaimed after introducing herself and McCabe. 'I envy you both your skill and your taste, Mrs Philpott.'

'I can't take the credit,' Muriel Philpott confessed. 'We had it designed.'

She gestured for them to be seated. McCabe said apologetically, 'We don't want to take up your time, Mrs Philpott.'

'If I can help you in any way, then I will,' she said, looking from him to Beth.

Beth said, 'I remember your cousin, Gail, when she lived at Abbeyfield.'

'Poor Gail.' Muriel Philpott smiled wistfully. 'Gail was little more than a child when life went wrong for her. What has interested you in her, Mrs Merrill?'

'Call me Beth, please. I should have explained that Mr McCabe is a private detective hired by my father on a family matter. Mr McCabe's investigation has had a nasty side effect. The remains of a pregnant hippie girl from the sixties were discovered buried in the grounds of my father's estate.'

Clapping a hand over her mouth, Muriel Philpott moaned, 'How awful.'

'It gets worse. The girl was murdered,' McCabe said, anxious to get to the point, 'most probably by the man or boy responsible for her pregnancy.'

'Poor girl. This is terrible, Beth, but I fail to see how I can help.'

Beth took care explaining. 'The dead girl's name was Suzi Duoard. She was a singer and very popular, so Gail would have known her.'

'And it's possible ... as both she and Gail were, er ... pregnant around the same time, they ...' Muriel Philpott mused.

'That they might have shared their troubles,' McCabe filled in 'We wouldn't make a direct approach to your cousin on so delicate a matter.'

'So we were hoping ...' Beth started to say, but their hostess interrupted her.

'That I might make the approach to Gail?'

'Exactly.' McCabe nodded.

Expelling a sighing breath, Muriel Philpott said wonderingly, 'Gail has been married for a long time, and she and her husband have children of their own. Her husband does, of course, know about her son, Edward, who is a pilot with British Airways. Ed is married with a family of his own. As far as Gail is concerned, her early life is a closed book.'

'We don't wish to open up old wounds,' McCabe assured her.

'I appreciate that, Mr McCabe. But Gail, is, I wouldn't go so far as to say unstable, but she is, shall we say, highly strung.'

'It is our problem, not yours,' Beth told her kindly, as she and McCabe prepared to leave.

A chagrined, obstinate silence pervaded the room for a while. Then Muriel Philpott broke it. 'I would be a coward if I let fear of some mild repercussion deter me from helping people like yourselves with major difficulties.'

'We don't want you to feel obligated,' Beth promised.

Muriel Philpott's shoulders made a faint gesture of resignation. 'I won't make any promises, but I will telephone Gail this evening and try to broach the subject circumspectly. How can I get in touch with you?'

'The Abbeyfield area isn't one of the best for mobile phone reception,' Beth replied, 'so I'll give you my number, and I will pass any message on to Mr McCabe.'

'As I said, no promises,' Muriel Philpott reiterated, as she came to the front door to wave them off. She was closing the door before Beth had completed the first manoeuvre of a three-point turn.

'A nice woman,' Beth commented as they drove past the house. 'Comfortably off, a nice, uneventful life, and then we arrive to unload a nasty big skeleton from the family cupboard.'

'I don't need you to make me feel uncomfortable about what we've just done,' McCabe said mildly.

Changing the subject, Beth said, 'I should be going with you to that club tonight, Gerry. Neither you nor Sol Quinn knows what Sylvester Hartley looks like.'

'And, hopefully, he doesn't know what Sol Quinn and I look like. But he would know you, Beth, so I can't risk taking you with us.'

'Spoilsport,' Beth muttered, putting her foot down hard on the accelerator.

When they reached the manor and McCabe got out of the Land-Rover, Beth made a kiss at him through the window. Walking to his car, McCabe reminded himself that Beth was nothing more than an interlude in his life, a hyphen between past and future. He didn't succeed.

Getting out of Quinn's car, McCabe glanced up at the green canopy above the shabby entrance to the Starland Club. Quinn led the way in. From behind a desk in reception a pretty Asian girl smiled at them with a wide mouth and good teeth. They went up a wide stairway to the second floor. As they entered a spacious room they had to step gingerly over a young man with spiky blond hair who lay peacefully asleep on the floor.

The lighting was dim and the air was stuffy with perfume and body heat. But the music was not the harsh stuff of discothèques, but soft, romantic ballads and instrumentals. It was still early and most of the pairing up and departing had yet to be done. Same-sex couples were dancing together, but separated by modern dance. Their movements were oddly convulsive, very sexual, but at the same time impersonal.

As he ordered drinks, a relaxed Sol Quinn advised, 'Try to look as if you want to be here, Gerry.'

When they were seated at a table, Quinn took a photograph from his jacket pocket. 'It's an old picture, but we should be able to recognize Hartley.'

Handsome, young and sophisticated, the man in the photograph had an air of supreme confidence.

'I was expecting a mug shot,' McCabe remarked.

'Hartley hasn't had a mug shot taken – yet,' Quinn said. 'Poor old Colonel Farquahar found this in his wife's room after she'd left him.'

McCabe had noticed that two young men seated on barstools had been slyly watching Quinn and him since they had arrived. Now the two of them walked over and placed their glasses on the table.

One, of medium height and slim build, was at his handsome, sartorial best, wearing a silk shirt the colour of Marsala wine, with fawn-coloured trousers and chalk-white sneakers. The second man was taller and his body was running to fat. His black hair had been permed. Looking deeply at McCabe, he asked, 'Mind if we join you?'

'Why would you want to do that?' McCabe asked.

'Just so's you know that you have friends that you don't know about.'

'We don't even want the friends we do know about,' McCabe replied bluntly.

Quinn shot McCabe a warning look, then invited them to sit by gesturing to two empty chairs. They sat, the slim one close to McCabe. He slid dark, liquid eyes towards Quinn.

'We haven't seen you guys here before.' His accent was bored, authoritative, and petulant.

'No, we're from out of town,' Quinn replied. 'A friend of Piers Heaney suggested we come to the club and introduce ourselves to Piers.'

'Heaney's as straight as a plumb-line,' the slim young man gave a disdainful flick of his head.

'That's just as well with his looks,' the guy with the curly dark hair commented. 'By the way, I'm Gaz and this is Del.'

'We wouldn't know Piers Heaney if we tripped over him, Gaz,' Quinn said.

'You probably won't want to know him when you see him,' Del said. 'Cast your eyes over there, boys. That's Heaney doing his *Casablanca* act. Humphrey Bogart he is not. More's the pity.'

Looking to where a distinguished-looking man resplendent in a velvet tuxedo, a lace shirt, and a drooping bow tie, was playing the host to an adoring group, McCabe exchanged glances with Quinn. There could be no doubt that he was Sylvester Hartley.

Gaz indicated a line of unaccompanied young men, some of them not so young, sitting at small oak tables along a wall. 'That lot are the house whores, Heaney's rent boys. Strictly speaking that's not quite true. Piers Heaney neither pimps for them nor had any personal connection with them, but they all pay him a nightly fee in advance for permission to work out of his club.'

Del sniffed. 'Heaney's on the make all round.'

'Good luck to him, I say,' Gaz said.

The music started up again. McCabe's hand was resting on the table and Del placed his hand lightly over it. It was a delicate hand; long slim fingers perfectly manicured. 'Our dance, I believe.'

Eyes widening in shock, McCabe's angry reaction was stopped by Quinn kicking his ankle. The policeman told Del, 'It's a bit early for us to let our hair down, so to speak, Del. We need to get into the mood, if you know what I mean.'

'I understand,' Del smiled. 'Strangers in a strange town, and all that sort of thing. Well, you've got us, so you don't have to find your way around. Do you see that guy standing over there?'

McCabe and Quinn saw a tall man of mixed race, with a heavy musculature and a lean, intelligent face. With a house muscleman at his side, he was studying a laughing, shouting group of men at the bar. Half-drunk, they were disturbing others with their horseplay, and the tall man looked ready to intervene.

'That's Max Kronin.' Del leaned close to McCabe to inform him confidentially, 'He's the manager here at Starland.'

'Max will fix you up.' Gaz took over from Del. 'He's mainly into crack and heroin.'

'He's a dealer?' Quinn queried.

'Max is a licensed dealer,' Del said with a knowing grin.

Unconsciously slipping back into policeman mode, Quinn said, 'There's no such thing as a licensed dealer, son.'

'That's what you think,' Del, not noticing Quinn's gaff, scoffed. 'Max is licensed by Heaney to deal here in the club.'

'You're kidding. They wouldn't take a chance on keeping a stash here in the club,' Quinn said, with a shake of his head. 'What if the filth raided the place?'

Laughing at the older man's naïvety, Gaz said, 'The pigs aren't bright enough to find Heaney's stash.'

'I don't know,' Quinn mused doubtfully. 'A friend of mine who ran a pub thought that. But he was wrong.'

'That won't happen here, because —' Del started to say, but Gaz said his name sharply to stop him.

'I hear that they take the floorboards up, and that sort of thing,' Quinn said.

'They could rip this whole place apart and find nothing,' Gaz assured Quinn.

Dismissing Gaz's claim with a wave of his hand, Quinn protested, 'I can't buy that.'

'Your friend should have had a big safe in his office with a false back,' Del boasted of his knowledge of the Starland drugs set-up, before an alarmed Gaz pulled him roughly to his feet.

'Let's dance,' Gaz said tersely to his friend.

Reaching out to run a finger down McCabe's jawline, Del said, 'Don't go away, sweetie.'

Then he was dragged off to the dance floor by Gaz. A happy, smiling Quinn turned to McCabe. 'We've got Sylvester Hartley, Gerry.'

'I don't follow you, Sol,' McCabe confessed his ignorance.

'Only the local force can do a drugs bust in Fenton.'

Quinn chuckled. 'I have a buddy here in Fenton, DI Mike Sterne, who can. Once Mike has arrested Heaney, I can set the ball rolling to prove that he is Hartley.'

'I like it,' McCabe nodding to indicate Del and Gaz who were dancing together. 'But how do we shake off that pair of prats?'

'Not by going to the GENTS, that's for sure,' Quinn grinned. 'Let's sneak away.'

Emptying his glass, McCabe agreed. 'That suits me fine.'

Keeping a wary eye on their two new unwanted friends, they beat a hasty retreat from the Starland Club.

On an unusually warm late autumn morning, McCabe was eating breakfast in the kitchen of the pub. The doors leading on to a small terrace were open, and with the sun as yet just above the horizon there was a deliciously cool breeze winging itself in from the distant river. In the middle distance, the black-green bristles of pine trees marked the edge of a wood. For Londoner McCabe there was something magic but subliminally savage in these surroundings.

The telephone on the wall opposite to him gave its discreet buzz. McCabe returned Sharee's quick smile as she hurried into the kitchen to answer the phone. Her eyes turned towards McCabe as she listened, a signal that the call was for him.

'It's Beth Merrill for you, Gerry,' Sharee said.

Thanking her, McCabe took the phone. 'It's me, Beth.'

'We have a problem; a big one, Gerry.' Beth sounded far from her usual laid-back self. 'Gail must be more of a fruitcake than Muriel hinted that she was. Rita Pavely rang me a few minutes ago in a hysterical state, gabbling on about Gail having telephoned old Doctor Ronan, who rang Rita's mum and dad, who then got in touch with Rita. I can't make head or tale of it. Anyway, you will be able to solve the mystery this morning, as Rita wants to see you.'

'Why me?'

'Rita wants to meet you out at that place I showed you on the way to see John-John at the church that day, the place where the locals do naughty things in their cars. But I'm sure that Rita doesn't have a lovers' tryst in mind, Gerry.'

'Did she give a time?'

'Ten-thirty.'

'I'll be there,' McCabe promised.

'You'll let me know what you find out, Gerry?'

Promising that he would, McCabe replaced the telephone and sat down at the table. Having lost his appetite, he was pushing the part-eaten meal away from him when Sharee returned to the kitchen.

Glancing at the plate, she raised her eyes to study him. 'Trouble?'

'Probably,' McCabe replied with a doleful nod.

'I did warn you when you got here, Gerry,' Sharee sympathized, reaching out to give his right hand a gentle squeeze. 'You've remained in Abbeyfield too long.'

Getting up from the table, he apologized for not eating his breakfast. 'It was a great breakfast, as always. I just lost my appetite.'

'Make sure that's all you lose,' Sharee cautioned him.

At first judging this to be one of her jokes, it dawned on McCabe as he left the kitchen that she had been deadly serious.

McCabe rounded a hairpin bend and felt a slight recognition of the wooded slope that swept down to a river. Driving cautiously through the woods, he came suddenly on the flat area to his left that Beth had previously pointed out to him. The towering viaduct just up ahead confirmed that he was in the right place.

A sleek grey Mercedes saloon was parked close to the edge of the woods. It was the only vehicle there, so he parked his car beside it. He was stretching, breathing in deeply the pure air of the countryside, when he saw Rita Pavely.

Wearing skin-tight jeans as she had when he'd met her on the farm, and a bright orange top, she stood leaning with her back against a tree, speaking meditatively. 'Each time I stand here I have an almost eerie feeling that I am passing through time. I can sense that the people of a long-gone age still live here among the trees. They laugh, love and drink mead, arguing the questions of all eras and all times. I wonder what beliefs and what credo and what desires they had? What were their moral codes and moral attitudes? It is an experience that I wouldn't miss for the world,

Gerry, but in a way it depresses me with its evidence of the uselessness of the struggles of mankind. To realize that they have gone, taking all their hopes and their pains with them. It has all ended in this, a forest that holds no record of them ever having existed.'

This unexpectedly profound observation coming from a countrywoman unsettled him. He could tell that in spite of her venture into philosophy, Rita was in emotional turmoil. There were plainly things that she needed to say.

He tentatively encouraged her by saying, 'Beth said you needed to see me. Is it about this girl named Gail?'

A bird that had been singing in the middle distance suddenly stopped. The tension in the air was increased by this new and unexpected silence. An occasional rustling in the undergrowth seemed to crackle loudly.

'Yes.' She reached out to pull a shaft of wild wheat from its coarse scabbard, then chewed on the sweet end. 'Please believe that I don't blame you. I don't suppose any of us can expect a lie to live forever, no matter how much we wish it would endure. How did you find Gail Patten, or whatever her name is now?'

'I didn't find her, Rita, I found her cousin. She promised to have a quiet word with Gail.'

'Some quiet word,' Rita said despondently. 'The fright of what's happened could be the death of poor old Doctor Ronan, and from a selfish viewpoint my marriage is about to explode, or implode, whatever marriages do in times of crisis.'

The bird recommenced singing as suddenly as it had stopped. But its sweet and delightful melody went unnoticed by its human audience of two.

'I don't quite follow you,' McCabe told her gently.

'I'm sorry,' she apologized with a small, forced smile. 'Gail Patten fell for a baby around the same time that I did. Her parents were every bit as upset as mine were, but it was just our two families who knew of Gail's condition and mine. You know that Doctor Ronan helped me out. Gail's mum and dad knew of my parents' close friendship with the doctor, and they made an approach through my dad, but Doctor Ronan refused.

My mum and dad tried to convince Gail and her parents that I'd had a miscarriage. Soon after that, talk of Gail's pregnancy began to spread. She moved away, then shame made her parents follow her.'

'But you think that Gail and her family must have known about your abortion?'

Rita blew out her thin lips with a little fluttering sound. She looked at her hands. They were shaking. 'I'm sure that they did, and they resented the fact that Gail had to face the disgrace while I "got away with it". Our two families were always quite friendly, but that changed. By the time the Pattens left Abbeyfield they weren't speaking to us. Gail always had a volatile temper. She rang Doctor Ronan this morning in an awful mood, complaining that someone is telling tales about her, raking over the distant past. She says that she doesn't intend to be the talk of the village while she wasn't the only one to be in trouble at that time. Gail even mentioned me by name, and came close to threatening Doctor Ronan.'

'I'm so sorry, Rita,' a saddened McCabe said. 'Why would she believe that you would want to bring up her past over thirty years later?'

'Perhaps Gail has borne a grudge all this time.'

'I'll do everything I can to stop it from going any further,' McCabe avowed.

'What can you do, Gerry?'

'I'll get back to Gail's cousin this morning and hopefully arrange to meet Gail. If I explain the facts about Suzi Duoard, then Gail will understand that she has no cause to worry. I will assure her that not one word about her or her past will ever be spoken in Abbeyfield.'

Immensely relieved, Rita asked, 'Will you do that right away?'

'I need to go back into Abbeyfield to collect any mail there may be for me,' McCabe explained, 'then I'll get straight to it.'

'Would you ring me as soon as you know that everything will be all right, Gerry?'

Aware of how worried she was, he promised, 'Of course I will.'

'What time do you think that will be?'

'Well ...' he said, doing some rapid mental calculations, 'it will be before two o'clock this afternoon at the very latest.'

Raising her tiny body on tiptoe, she kissed him quickly on the cheek. 'Thank you. Thank you so much.'

nine

On the return journey to the Fox and Hounds, McCabe made a detour to take in the manor. He glimpsed Beth looking out from an upstairs window. She came to meet him. Her hair was loosely arranged as ever and its fairness flamed as she passed through arrows of sunlight. A little breathless from having run down a long flight of stairs, she came to stand close to him. The yellow, flowered dress she wore boosted the impact she made on McCabe. Her stance was provocative, hips thrust forward.

One hand up to shield her eyes from a bright morning sun, she asked, 'To what do I owe this unexpected pleasure?'

McCabe explained the Rita Pavely situation to her. As honest and straightforward as ever, she was dubious about his rescue mission.

'If Muriel Philpott sent Gail off on a rampage, Gerry,' she reasoned, 'how do you expect the same woman to calm her down?'

With serious doubts having crept into his own mind, McCabe was in danger of being completely demoralized. 'It's the only chance that I have, Beth.'

They stood together with the morning going on around them and mysterious communications going on between them. Bending his arm to check his watch as a ploy, McCabe didn't fool Beth. She stretched out a hand to clasp his. 'I know that, Gerry, and I wish you success.'

'Thanks,' he said, getting into his car, giving her a wave and driving away.

There was no mail waiting for him at the pub. That disappointed him. Not wanting to jeopardize his incipient relationship with Carol by moving too fast, he had, while in London, given her his temporary address in the hope that she would take the initiative. Each day he dared to expect a letter from her. Each day he became more disappointed.

'I'm about to make coffee,' Sharee called an invitation to him.

'I'm in a hurry, but thank you, Sharee,' he called back, as he went out of the door in a rush.

In the car-park his steps faltered when he saw two uniformed policemen intently studying his car. There was a kind of inverted violence in the stiff-legged way they circled the vehicle.

Walking towards them he asked, 'Is there some kind of problem?'

'Is this your car, sir?' the younger of the two officers enquired with an impersonal air.

'Yes.'

'You are Mr Gerard McCabe, 39 Thornton Street, London SW19?'

'I am.'

The older policeman closed his notebook and made a ritual of replacing it in his breast pocket before speaking. 'This vehicle has been reported as being at the scene of a serious assault on two men on the Kilverham road two nights ago.'

'Sorry, but I can't help you on that,' McCabe said, ready to unlock the driver's door.

The older constable said in an official tone, 'There are certain procedures to be followed, and we must ask you to accompany us to the station at Kilverham.'

'Look,' McCabe said, keenly aware that the morning was fast disappearing. 'I'm not trying to be awkward, but I do have pressing business. Could you contact a friend of mine at the station, DI Quinn? He'll vouch for me.'

The two policemen looked at each other questioningly. The younger one shrugged. The older one bit his fingernails. Then the younger one walked a few yards away, bent his head downward and a little sideways, and his radio crackled. There was an indecipherable exchange of conversation. Then the constable walked back to his colleague and McCabe.

'Detective Inspector Quinn is out of the area today, Mr

McCabe,' he reported. 'But Detective Superintendent Rendall says that I can accept you word if your agree to call at the station this afternoon, sir.'

'You have my word that I will be there, Constable,' McCabe said thankfully.

An hour later, having broken the speed limit throughout the journey, McCabe was seated in the Philpott sitting-room opposite to an extremely nervous and apologetic Muriel.

'I was really careful when speaking to Gail. She has always been a little unpredictable, but she seemed to jump to the wrong conclusion, thinking that someone was out to drag her name through the mud. She just wouldn't listen when I told her that wasn't the case. I find it difficult to understand her. After all, I would imagine just about everyone in Abbeyfield has forgotten Gail after all these years.'

'Does Gail remember Beth?' McCabe asked.

'Yes. Beth is younger than she is, but Gail really liked her,' Muriel answered.

'So she wouldn't resent Beth asking questions?'

Shaking her head, Muriel Philpott said, 'No, I sensed that she believes someone else is out to cause her trouble.'

'Does Gail remember Suzi Duoard?'

'I'm so sorry,' Muriel apologized. 'We only spoke on the telephone, and she flew into a temper immediately, so I didn't get the opportunity to ask her.'

'What is my chance of talking to Gail?'

'That so much depends on Gail, I can't make any promises,' Muriel replied. 'But I'm willing to redeem myself, as it were, by trying to help you put things right. Gail doesn't go out to work, so there is every chance of catching her at home.'

'Does she live far away?'

'In Cheltenham. That's a good hour's drive.'

McCabe's spirit took a nosedive. If they found Gail at home when they arrived, then less than half an hour of his promised deadline for telephoning Rita Pavely would remain. He asked. 'Could you come with me right now, Mrs Philpott?'

'I'll get my coat,' she told him unenthusiastically.

They spoke little on the journey that got them to Cheltenham ten minutes ahead of Muriel Philpott's predicted one hour. Following her instructions, he turned into an estate of houses constructed of yellow stone from local quarries.

'That's Gail's place,' Muriel said, pointing to a house with an estate agent's FOR SALE sign on a post in the garden.

Pulling his car into the kerb, McCabe looked to Muriel for guidance. 'Do we both go to the door, or you first?'

'With Gail everything has to be played by ear. Come on, we'll both go.'

The woman who answered Muriel's knock on the door was wearing horn-rimmed glasses that made her already severe face daunting. McCabe tried to imagine this staid creature cavorting in a hippie camp, but quickly conceded defeat. Gail greeted Muriel warmly but swept a suspicious, non-welcoming glance over McCabe.

Muriel Philpott launched straight into the introductions. 'Gail, this is Mr McCabe, the man I mentioned when we talked on the telephone.'

'Pleased to meet you, Mrs Wilson,' McCabe said, as she shook his hand limply.

His politeness wasn't reciprocated. Admitting them to her house with obvious reluctance, Gail Wilson opened the door of a lounge, saying listlessly. 'If you'd like to sit down I'll make us some tea.'

She returned with a tray with three cups of tea and a bowl of sugar lumps on it. In a strained silence, McCabe could hear the clock ticking, and it sounded too noisy. Looking out of the window at the estate agent's sign, he remarked conversationally. 'Are you planning on moving out of this area, Mrs Wilson?'

'I don't wish to be rude,' she replied, glaring angrily at him, 'but are you expecting me to believe that you don't know?'

'I'm sorry?' McCabe looked at the woman blankly.

'I can assure you that neither I nor Mr McCabe knew that you were selling your house until we saw the sign when we drove up,' Muriel told her.

Looking from one to the other of them, Gail asked shakily, 'Isn't that what this is all about? Hasn't Rita Pavely somehow learned that we are moving back to Abbeyfield once we sell up here?'

'I can promise you that Mrs Pavely has not the faintest notion of your plan, Mrs Wilson,' McCabe said firmly.

'But ... but ...' Gail faltered. 'There was a good deal of acrimony between our families back in the sixties, and I naturally assumed that Rita, now ultra-respectable, wouldn't want someone back in the village who knows her past as intimately as I do.'

'Oh dear, Gail,' Muriel sucked air deep into her lungs in a reverse sigh as she exclaimed. 'You have got hold of the wrong end of the stick.'

'I am a private detective hired by Colonel Farquahar, Mrs Wilson,' McCabe said firmly. 'The only reason we are here is to ask you if you knew a girl named Suzi Duoard.'

Gail nodded. 'Suzi, yes. She wasn't from Abbeyfield, but turned up with the rest of the hippies. She was a real fun person.'

'Did you know that Suzi was pregnant?' McCabe enquired.

'No ... well ... yes,' Gail replied guardedly.

'There is no comfortable way to tell you this, Mrs Wilson. Suzi's remains have been discovered buried in the grounds of Abbeyfield Manor. The remains of a foetus were also unearthed.'

'Heavens above!' Gail was mentally knocked sideways for a few moments. Useless tears brimmed her eyes. Recovering slightly, she said in a croaky voice, 'I see. You believe it possible that Suzi and I might have discussed our pregnancies.'

'Yes. That perhaps you would know the father of the child.'

'I'm afraid that I don't have a clue. Suzi was an extrovert, which gained her a reputation she didn't deserve. I would be willing to swear that, like myself, Suzi Duoard made a one-off mistake.'

McCabe took a gamble. Intuitions and hunches are either misunderstood or unappreciated. Guess wrong and it will be forgotten; get it right and you're under suspicion. 'I have John Menson down as the favourite to have been responsible for her pregnancy, Mrs Wilson.'

'John Menson?' Gail enquired awkwardly. 'No, you may have the right man, but you have the wrong woman.' Then she blushed a bright red before saying quickly, 'No, that wasn't a Freudian slip, I wasn't referring to myself.'

'Your personal history is your business, not mine.' McCabe assured her. It dawned on him that John-John's rambling reference to them having 'killed a baby' was nothing to do with Suzi Duoard. He said aloud, 'Rita Pavely!'

'You decided that yourself; I didn't tell you,' Gail Wilson pointed out defensively.

'Everything we have discussed will remain confidential, Mrs Wilson. Would you feel that Suzi Duoard's lover was a hippie?' McCabe asked.

'I wouldn't like to say.'

Gail had answered so guiltily, so evasively, that McCabe came to the conclusion that Gail either knew or strongly suspected who had made the Duoard girl pregnant. But she wouldn't say.

'You have been most helpful, Mrs Wilson,' he said gratefully. 'There is just one thing: you have both Rita Pavely and Doctor Ronan in something of a frantic state.'

'I know that I must have,' Gail admitted ashamedly. 'Now I bitterly regret what I did. Could I ask you to tell Rita that I will cause her no further trouble, Mr McCabe? And perhaps you would call on Doctor Ronan and Rita's parents?'

'You can rely on me,' McCabe promised her.

'And we'll see more of each other, Gail,' Muriel said, as she parted from her cousin on the doorstep.

Both Muriel and McCabe waved as they drove away from the house. He checked his wristwatch. It was twenty minutes past two o'clock. His Rita Pavely deadline had passed, and that worried him. At the end of Gail Wilson's road he pulled into the kerb and reached for his mobile.

'I promised to let Rita Pavely know how we got on,' he told Muriel Philpott as he tapped in Rita's number.

'Thank God that it's good news,' Muriel said.

But there was no reply. All he heard was Rita's recorded voice saying. *'I am sorry that I am unable to answer at the moment. Please leave your name and number and I will get back to you as soon as possible.'*

Switching off his phone, McCabe somehow managed to drive

even faster on the return journey than he had on the way out. When he stopped outside of her house, Muriel Philpott said nothing other than a polite goodbye, but McCabe had the impression that she was mightily relieved to get out of his car.

He tried Rita's number again on the way back to Kilverham. It was now past three o'clock, and once again he got the answering service. Needing to report to the police station, and aware that he would cause Rita more trouble if he drove to Perham Farm to speak to her, he left a message.

He said. *'This is McCabe. I know you are interested in how my investigation is going, and just wanted to say that all is well. Everything turned out fine today.'*

Satisfied that he had said enough to make Rita cease worrying, he drove on to Kilverham. Parking in the only vacant space outside of the police station, he was walking towards the building when Sol Quinn came out through the door at a half run.

Pointing to McCabe's car, the detective called, 'Leave it there, Gerry. We'll go in my car.'

'Go where?'

'I'll explain along the way.'

'I have to report inside,' McCabe explained.

'Forget it. I've fixed that. You are in the clear where the Perkins's thing is concerned.' Quinn then continued urgently, 'Come on, we've got a jumper.'

Quinn's 'we' didn't settle easily on McCabe's ears.

'Count me out, Sol,' he said, making no move to get into the car. 'I was involved with two suicides when I was in the job, and, believe me, that's not how I want to spend the remainder of this afternoon.'

Already in the driver's seat, Quinn leaned across and opened the passenger door, swinging it wide. Fixing McCabe with a steady look, he said, 'Get in, Gerry. You'll want to be in on this one. It's Rita Pavely.'

Shocked to the core, McCabe got into the into the passenger seat. The fact that Rita hadn't answered her mobile had worried him greatly, but he had not anticipated anything as drastic as this. Reversing the car, Quinn swung it fast out on to the road. He turned his head to left and right, studying the traffic before speaking again. 'From the reports I've had she's up on Hendly Valley viaduct, determined to jump.'

A small group of people had gathered when Quinn drove across grass to where the lofty viaduct rose to form a close horizon that McCabe couldn't see beyond. He had brought Quinn up to speed on Rita Pavely's predicament. Now the detective lowered the window to speak to a uniformed constable.'What's happening, Joe?'

'She's been up there for about half an hour, sir, threatening to jump.'

'When they spend a long time threatening to top themselves,' Quinn observed, 'it often means they have no intention of doing so.'

'I think this amounts to more than a cry for help, sir,' the constable differed respectfully.

Quinn accepted this with a nod. 'Then you had better call an ambulance.'

'I've done that, sir, and ...' The uniformed officer pointed skyward as the unmistakable staccato sound of a helicopter reached them.

'Good man,' Quinn said. Easing his head out through the car window, he looked upwards. 'She's not up there now, Joe.'

'She is, sir,' the constable said, 'She's stepped back a little, out of sight.'

A worried Quinn talked himself through the situation. 'The nearest trained negotiator is sixty miles away in Gloucester, and he's a specialist in persuading armed offenders to give up their hostages. Have you informed anyone, Joe?'

'I've radioed in, and her husband is on his way.'

The helicopter hovered high and to one side, awaiting instructions. Quinn had to raise his voice to be heard. 'How did these people come to be here, Joe?'

Following the uniformed officer's pointing finger, McCabe was surprised to see Doctor Ronan standing with his neck craned, looking up at the viaduct. The constable reported, 'It seems she telephoned that old guy to tell him that she intended to take her life, sir. It was him who rang the station. That monk, or whatever he is, just appeared from nowhere, and I think the woman and the other two men were just passing by.'

Doctor Ronan recognized McCabe and walked over to him. The elderly physician looked totally shattered. He was dressed untidily and even his spiky white hair didn't seem to fit his head.

'A bad business this, McCabe,' Ronan said, lighting a cigarette and waving the match around long after the flame had died.

McCabe agreed, as John-John strode up. Robe flowing, he jabbed an accusing finger at McCabe. 'I pleaded with you, Mr McCabe, but you paid no heed. You unleashed a force akin to gravity; a force from which deliverance is impossible. Now she stands at the final gateway, through which she will pass into eternity in an instant.'

McCabe didn't respond. Rita Pavely suddenly appeared up on the viaduct, wearing the same orange top and jeans as earlier. At the sight of her, John-John sat on the grass and pulled his legs underneath him like a child. He began a low-toned chanting.

Unable to watch Rita teetering on the edge of the viaduct, McCabe asked, 'Can I try something, Sol?'

'Nothing heroic,' Quinn cautioned. 'It's a long climb, Gerry, and she's likely to be down here before you get halfway up.'

'There's no way of reaching her at this stage, but I think I can change her mind, Sol.'

'Then give it a go, Gerry,' Quinn said.

Cupping his hands, McCabe shouted, 'Have you got your mobile up there with you, Rita?'

Her thin right arm moving jerkily, Rita reached behind her to the back pocket of her jeans. When she brought the arm forward and raised it, a relieved McCabe could see that she was holding a mobile phone.

'I have left a message for you, Rita, play it back,' McCabe shouted.

Holding her phone with both hands, Rita fiddled clumsily with it. There was a concerted groan from the watching group, and a dryness in McCabe's throat and fear in his heart as the tiny instrument escaped from Rita's fumbling grasp. She released a shriek of utter despair as the mobile phone dropped. Falling unbelievably slowly, it collided with a projection on the viaduct as it came down, and was already in pieces when it hit the ground.

'Tell her the good news now,' Quinn urged McCabe.

Cupping his hands once more, McCabe yelled up at Rita. 'I was able to settle everything today. There will be no more—' He broke off as a Land-Rover noisily pulled up and Ryan Pavely leapt out.

Looking up at his wife with wild eyes, Pavely ran up to Quinn and McCabe, calling out a question as he came, 'What's going on.'

Neither Quinn nor McCabe had time to give an answer. The woman in the little group screamed and John-John Menson rolled on to his knees, praying loud and beseechingly. McCabe looked up to see the tiny figure of Rita Pavely topple from the viaduct and plummet earthwards. Ashamed that he had to look away cowardly before Rita smashed into the ground, he saw that Solomon Quinn was doing the same. But neither of them could escape the awesome sound of a body splattering on jagged rocks.

Both McCabe and Quinn tried but failed to stop Ryan Pavely from running to the shattered body. Then the air was rent by a terrible and unearthly howl as a distraught Pavely fell to his knees beside what was left of his wife.

Sharee Bucholz closed the Fox and Hounds early on the night of the catastrophe. Only a few customers had been in. Rita Pavely's vacant chair disturbed McCabe greatly. He kept remembering the woman he chatted with up in the woods that morning. Her pleasant, wistful little smile, and the snatch of philosophy with which she had surprised him. She had been so alive, so vital then that it was difficult to accept that now she was no more.

A concerned Sharee sat across the table from him in the pub's private quarters. Though physically close, they were set mentally far apart by McCabe's recent stark and personal encounter with mortality. Inappropriately but unintentionally, Sharee had on the tight yellow woollen dress that she had been wearing the first night they had met, and the rising carnal interest that he felt made him ashamed. The double brandy that she had poured him earlier was in front of him, untouched.

McCabe's head had been numb since he had forced himself to look at Rita's body. Ralph Ronan had managed to drag an inconsolable Ryan Pavely away from his dead wife. The three uninvolved onlookers had backed away to distance themselves from the horrific scene. The two paramedics from the ambulance had maintained a professional stoicism throughout, but McCabe could tell that they had done so with difficulty. Though harrowing sights would be a part of their daily routine, it had to be rare for them to face something so terrible. Quinn's reactions to the tragedy had betrayed his hard man image as just an act. As a good copper of the sort McCabe had once been, Quinn lived life in the world as if it were a jungle. Even so, the feeling side of a sensitive person always remained intact. That was something that McCabe had learned many times over.

The most astonishing direct response to the young woman's suicide was that of John-John Menson. Walking over to McCabe as he was about to get into Quinn's car, John-John had spoken clearly and precisely. 'Possibly this is the wrong time to say this, Mr McCabe, as we are all understandably most terribly upset. Nevertheless, what has happened here has impressed upon me the importance of getting this whole matter resolved as swiftly as possible. Would it be possible for me to talk to you at some length. Shall we say tomorrow morning?'

'I would welcome the opportunity to speak with you,' McCabe had replied. 'I'll drive over to fetch you, and we'll find somewhere quiet to have a chat.'

Shaking his head, John-John had said, 'That won't be necessary. You see, unless you have any objections, I would like Beth to be present. I can make my own way to Abbeyfield Manor by ten o'clock, if that will suit you.'

'I'll see you there at ten, John-John,' McCabe said.

'Every day I spend in this job reminds me how little we can ever know about the human mind, Gerry,' Quinn had remarked wonderingly about Menson.

'Obviously the change in him today was brought about by

shock,' McCabe remarked, adding dubiously, 'But I fear it is too much to hope for that he will stay the same until tomorrow.'

Now Sharee tried to end a silence between them by commenting, 'They say that it's good to talk, Gerry.'

'I don't feel much like talking, Sharee.'

'It worries me that you could be blaming yourself,' she said, looking directly into his eyes.

McCabe was wary of her. Strong emotion such as he was suffering tended to blur judgement. He felt that Sharee was able to see inside his head. She regarded him with an eye that weighed, measured, and evaluated the thoughts that at that moment were mercilessly tormenting him. He corrected her miserably. 'I am to blame, Sharee.'

'I know you better than to believe that, Gerry.'

'I've known me longer than you have, and I'm still not sure about myself.'

Sharee argued, 'You have to look at it logically, Gerry. In an insular community such as this, it would be impossible to do work like yours without causing side effects. Drastic though they may be.'

'You'd make an excellent counsellor, Sharee.'

'I doubt it,' she said, permitting herself a small smile that said she was pleased. She looked down at his glass. Hesitating for a moment, she then pushed it towards him. 'But I'm advising you to drink that up and I'll pour you another.'

Taking a sip of his drink, McCabe shook his head. 'No more, thanks. Alcohol doesn't dim my problems, it makes them clearer.'

'That's me finished as a counsellor,' Sharee laughed softly. 'I confess that I don't have an answer.'

'I'm not even sure what the question is, Sharee.'

'Personal experience has taught me one thing.'

'What's that?'

'That you shouldn't be on your own tonight,' she answered. Her voice was thick and sexy. 'Come on.'

Apart from being captivated by his charming hostess, McCabe discovered that despite being in the grip of despondency, he had been excitedly wondering where their conversation was leading. He watched Sharee move as gracefully as a bright yellow flower blown in the wind as she walked to open the door leading to the stairs. Standing in the doorway she stood looking at him, waiting.

Gaining time by slowly emptying his glass, McCabe was aware that she had left the decision to him. An image of Carol formed in his mind, tacitly reminding him that the next few minutes could determine his future.

There was too much to lose he decided. His chest seemed pushed down by a great weight. Dragging air into his lungs, he mentally commanded them to fill up. Getting up from the table he could tell from Sharee's look of disappointment that she had read the expression on his face. She turned to walk away.

'Wait.'

His own voice uttering the one-word command surprised him. There was no way that he could be alone that night. She turned to look at him through half-closed, heavy-lidded, deliciously dangerous eyes.

McCabe went slowly to her.

'It is so long ago that I socialized that I feel really gauche,' an embarrassed John-John Menson remarked as he sipped coffee.

Beth had invited McCabe and Menson into the parlour at Abbeyfield Manor. She now sat avidly waiting for John-John to impart the expected information. Menson seemed most reticent, despite remaining clear headed and articulate.

McCabe was ill at ease. He could still find Sharee's perfume about him, hours after leaving her bed and having showered. With his conscience battered by his betrayal of Carol, the eagerly anticipated letter from her had arrived that morning. As shy with a pen as she was with the spoken word, she had nevertheless written from the heart. She was willing to consider them getting back together. On any other morning he would have been ecstatic.

He had slept little. Awaking at dawn, Sharee had turned her head on the pillow to face him. Her eyes had been strikingly brilliant in the half-light. McCabe had sensed the tension in her. It had been odd to find a woman with such a vivacious personality as Sharee to be so subdued.

She had asked in a small voice, 'Do you think that you can forgive me?'

'What is there to forgive?' he had questioned. 'There were two of us involved.'

'I took advantage of your distress, Gerry,' she had murmured.

'That's not true. But I have commitments back home.'

She had reached out to stroke his face. 'I suspected something like that. Don't worry, Gerry. I am no threat to you. I will have to be content with the memory of last night that I will forever cherish.'

McCabe had since been wrestling with his own guilt. Forcing his mind back to the present, he asked, 'What was it that you wanted to talk about, John-John?'

'It is a most delicate matter,' Menson replied hesitantly. 'The subject is one that it would be deceitful of me to broach without Beth being present. By the same token, it is something that I have difficulty mentioning in front of her.'

'Don't let me worry you, John-John, I'm broadminded,' Beth said in her flippant mode. 'Are you going to tell us who fathered the child the Duoard girl had been carrying, John-John?'

Eyes turning evasively away from McCabe and Beth, Menson spoke guardedly. 'That was my intention, but I now discover myself incapable of inflicting the extreme distress that such a disclosure would cause.'

Noticing that Beth's face had been drained of colour and her body had gone rigid, McCabe was mystified. An electric bell mounted high on the wall rang loudly. Beth became animated. 'My father must have fallen again. It is often difficult to lift him back up. I hate to ask, Gerry, but could you come with me?'

'Of course,' McCabe said.

A worried Beth had already left by the time he had got to his feet. Menson called after him, 'Mr McCabe, I have let you down, but I will make amends if you could make some excuse to Beth so as to return alone.'

Accepting this with a nod, McCabe went off in the wake of Beth. While delighted that he would know the identity of Suzi Duoard's murderer within a very short while, he was worried as to how he could get back to Menson alone without offending Beth.

Providence solved the problem for him. When they reached

Colonel Farquahar's bedroom they found that the old man had managed to pull himself up from the floor. He half lay, half sat, clinging to an arm of a chair. The colonel's breathing sounded loudly in room that had old-fashioned and simple furnishings, mahogany panelling, a grandfather clock, and a shining brass barometer with an inscribed plate.

'My dear fellow,' the colonel greeted McCabe gaspingly. 'It is so embarrassing to have you see me in this deplorable state.'

'Don't worry, Colonel.' McCabe placed a hand on a bony shoulder. 'Nothing could affect the admiration and respect I have for you.'

'Most gracious of you, McCabe,' the colonel grunted, as Beth and McCabe helped him straight into the chair.'

'I can manage, thank you,' she smiled gratefully at McCabe. 'You go back to John-John; I will be with you as quickly as I can.'

Gladly taking her advice, McCabe bade Colonel Farquahar farewell. He hurried expectantly along a lengthy corridor, restarting the conversation with Menson on entering the parlour.

'Right, John-John, you were about to tell me something.'

Standing with his back to McCabe, Menson was studying a portrait in oils of Queen Victoria. At the sound of McCabe's voice, he turned to inform him, 'The prince of this world did not enter either the vegetative or the social realms. Christ did not pray for the world, and He redeemed only the vegetative, not the social.'

John-John had slipped back into what the locals termed his John the Baptist role. The rapt expression on his face confirmed for McCabe that he would remain irrational indefinitely.

ten

Nevertheless, he tried. 'Can we talk of Suzi Duoard, John-John?'
'The cry of suffering rings throughout the land,' Menson
continued.

'I need to know who Suzi Duoard was involved with, John-
John,' McCabe said sharply.

'They ask - what is the power of attention? It is nothing more
nor less than the virtue of humility in the intellectual order. Soon
we shall gather together to exalt the birth of Christ in joyous
song, yet already we see the sinner voluntarily indulging in
pride.'

Entering the room, Beth was startled by the change in Menson.
She shivered slightly. Her eyes danced a little solo as she looked
at McCabe and asked, 'What brought this on?'

'I don't know.' McCabe drew a long, shaken breath. 'Whatever
it was happened while we were out of the room.'

Not speaking now, John-John had sweat standing out in great
beads on his not unhandsome face; his brown eyes were dilated.
Beth had slumped into a chair beside McCabe. Perturbed, she
watched John-John intently. 'You should take him back to his
caravan, Gerry.'

McCabe got to his feet, but Menson did a smart left turn with
military precision, and marched out of the room. Beth and
McCabe went to the window to stand looking out. They watched
Menson stride down the drive towards the gate.

On his way back to the Fox and Hounds from Abbeyfield Manor,
McCabe noted a car parked in a lay-by up ahead. He needed to
brake sharply as Solomon Quinn stepped out of the car and held

up his hand. Walking up to him, he commented, with a grin, 'Hi, Gerry. You have certainly got your feet under the table at the manor.'

'Only while I ate lunch. I was invited, and it would have rude to refuse.'

'Yeah, yeah,' Quinn said in exaggerated disbelief. He studied his wristwatch. 'An awfully long lunch.'

The colonel had joined them at lunch, but had afterwards left to take a nap. They had then gone for a walk to the edge of the woods where it had been peaceful and quiet. They had spoken little and there had not been a sound in the stillness. Unused to such absolute silence, McCabe had strained at listening, just to be certain. There were only two faint heartbeats to be heard: Beth's and his.

'What did you find out from John the Baptist?' Quinn asked, pulling McCabe's mind away from that enjoyably innocent time in the woods.

'He didn't say much before walking back into the wilderness,' McCabe replied.

'Nothing on Suzi Duoard?' Quinn asked, continuing when McCabe shook his head. 'Who do you have in the frame, Gerry?'

McCabe shrugged. 'Ryan Pavely?'

'Are you telling me, or asking me?'

'It's just a suggestion,' McCabe explained.

'Sylvester Hartley is the reason I stopped you,' Quinn said. 'Mike Sterne is going to bust the Starland Club tonight. I've given Mike everything on Hartley. Mike's the works in an interview-room, Gerry. If Heaney is Hartley, then it won't take Mike long to prove it. Then when Mike has charged him on the drugs issue, we can get Hartley over to Kilverham.'

'And follow through with Suzi Duoard,' McCabe suggested.

'Hopefully,' Quinn assented. 'But we haven't got anything substantial, Gerry. Do your best to get Menson back from outer space.'

'I don't think that will happen.'

With a friendly slap to McCabe's shoulder, Quinn said, 'See ya,' and walked off.

McCabe sat meditating in his car after Quinn had gone.

Returning to the pub and Sharee Bucholz would be a severe test of his strength of will. Last night he had stepped into some strange world where all the things that governed how he had lived since Ali Quenton had been suspended.

When he eventually returned to the pub it was close to opening time. He delayed entering the building by strolling through the children's garden with its swings, seesaw and slide. Filled with fun and laughter in the summer, it was empty of everything but memories now. A solitary cloud momentarily blacked out the sun, and then, as if unnerved by its own daring, went scudding off across the sky moved by a wind that McCabe couldn't feel. Then bright evening sunlight came chasing over the fields and hedgerows as McCabe turned to walk slowly to the door of the pub.

Sharee was standing behind the bar. Her look as she caught his eye was cool and amused. McCabe felt his resolve weakening. There were a few people present, but the atmosphere was still respectfully subdued. McCabe was continually learning how deeply and widely a death affected an insular community. Abb Perkins sat at a table with a couple of thuggish young men, his arm in a sling and the injuries McCabe had inflicted on his face still very noticeable.

Sensing the conflict in him when he reached the bar, Sharee smiled. 'Don't be afraid, I won't bite.' Careful to make sure it was for his ears only, she added cheekily. 'Unless I get the opportunity.'

'I thought we had an agreement,' he reminded her, as she poured him a drink and pushed it across the polished counter to him.

'We have, Gerry. I was just trying to lighten the mood,' she said, her face serious. 'Rita's funeral is tomorrow. Things should ease then. The run up to Christmas will help.'

'It won't help Rita's husband and her parents, Sharee.'

Face flushing slightly, she said, 'I know that. I didn't mean to sound uncaring or callous.'

'You couldn't,' he assured her. 'You have to endure the void yourself at Christmas.'

'You are a kind and thoughtful man,' she told him. 'Each year

I convince myself that I've learned to accept my loss; each year I learn that I haven't.'

She moved away then to serve a customer. Looking around him at the small gathering, McCabe realized that he was as much a stranger here as he had been the first evening he had arrived. He considered, but only for a moment, that loneliness had been at least partly responsible for him straying with Sharee. But he realized that he was searching for excuses. He couldn't recall a time when he hadn't been completely self-sufficient. Carol was different. She didn't fill a gap in him, but was kind of an extension. They were two people who had once truly become one, and would soon become one again.

Roland Merrill came into the bar. McCabe was disappointed that Beth wasn't with him, and more disappointed in himself for wanting her to be.

Merrill went to the bar and unrolled a fluorescent orange poster and showed it to Sharee. They had a short conversation that ended when Sharee gave a nod of agreement and took the poster. Merrill left the bar without looking either to his left or right. Sharee carried the rolled poster to McCabe.

Shaking her head in disbelief, she unrolled it on the counter in front of McCabe saying, 'Roland Merrill asked me if I'd put up this poster for the carol service. What do you see wrong with it, Gerry?'

Expecting a misprint of some kind, McCabe scanned the poster and found nothing. The name of John Menson was included as a vocalist. 'It looks fine to me, Sharee.'

'It's this bit here,' she said, tracing with her finger a line as she read aloud. 'The Kilverham Senior School Choir by kind permission of Mr Roland Merrill, Headmaster.'

'I must be slow in the head, Sharee, as I still can't see what you mean.'

'Take another look, Gerry,' Sharee insisted. 'Merrill designed these posters and had them printed. Which are the largest letters on the whole poster?

McCabe got it then. The wording 'Mr Roland Merrill, Headmaster' was in lettering at least double the size of the type all else on the poster had been printed in.

Seeing enlightenment on McCabe's face, Sharee rewarded him with a pat on the shoulder. Pushing the poster to one side in disgust, she said, 'That is typical of that self-seeking man.'

Sharee was saying something else, and another person was joining in the conversation, but for McCabe it was all going on at a distance. Inside of his head he could hear John-John's words of earlier that day. "Soon we shall gather to exalt the birth of Christ in joyous song, yet already we see the sinner voluntarily indulging in pride." The gathering in joyous song had to be the carol service, so it was logical to conclude that Roland Merrill was the prideful sinner.

The following morning, Solomon Quinn had breakfast with McCabe at the pub, courtesy of Sharee. Having company eased things for McCabe, as conversation with Sharee had become stilted. Their intimacy had turned them into semi-strangers. As they ate, Quinn reported on the Starland Club drugs bust. Soon after arresting Piers Heaney, the neighbouring police force had proved beyond doubt that Sylvester Hartley was his true identity.

'My guv'nor's dusted off the fraud case against Hartley,' Quinn said. 'And we'll be ready to go once Mike Sterne's dealt with the drug offences. According to Mike, who did some surreptitious probing on my behalf, Hartley could have been responsible for Rita Pavely's pregnancy, but, of course, there is no criminal offence involved there. However, he is ruled out as a suspect in both Suzi Duoard's pregnancy and her murder. Hartley was definitely away from the area when both events occurred.'

'More coffee, gentlemen?' Sharee asked, refilling their cups without waiting for an answer.

'A lovely lady,' Quinn remarked when she left them. 'You have it made here, Gerry. Good food and a good woman. It's not surprising that you are in no hurry to go back to London.'

Aware that Quinn had spoken only half in jest, McCabe didn't rise to the bait. He had been attempting to avoid thinking about his situation with Sharee, so he certainly wasn't about to discuss it. To allow time for Quinn's remark to fade, he glanced out of the window. The early morning shadows had shifted and the weak sun of autumn was higher. Then he said, 'I may have a tentative lead on the Duoard murder, Sol.'

'How tentative?' Quinn's eyes were alive with interest over the rim of a raised coffee cup.

'Just about as tentative as it can get. I was asking Menson about Suzi Duoard when he was rambling, and he mentioned a carol service that's going to be held at that place out in the country. He said that a "sinner" had already allowed his pride to spoil the event.'

'Who is the sinner?' Quinn enquired.

'The poster advertising the carol service has Roland Merrill's name on it in giant letters.'

Making a derisive sound with his lips, Quinn said, 'This isn't tentative, Gerry, it's pie in the sky.'

'Merrill designed the posters.' McCabe staunchly defended his theory.

'Everyone knows that Roland Merrill is up himself, as our Aussie friends term it, but that hardly makes him a murderer.'

'The mistake everyone makes, including you, is not listening when John-John talks,' McCabe advised.

'To do that would mean ending up as mad as he is.'

'That's not so,' McCabe disagreed. 'I have learned that there is always a serious message underlying even his wildest rambling.'

No longer scoffing, Quinn was serious as he said, 'In the short time that I have known you, Gerry, I have come to respect your remarkable detective abilities. So let us say, just for the sake of argument, that I go along with your theory that Menson has fingered Merrill. How do we proceed from there?'

'Merrill's DNA. I could pick up something belonging to him at the manor, and no one would know.'

'Come off it, Gerry,' a despairing Quinn pleaded. 'You know that we couldn't do a DNA test on a sample obtained illegally. We first need to find some hard evidence against Merrill, and that isn't going to be easy after all this time.'

'I've been giving that a lot of thought, Sol.'

'And?'

'I'm pretty sure that Katrina Farquahar knows something,' McCabe replied. 'I'm going to drive up to talk with her again.'

'It could prove useful,' Quinn conceded. 'When do you intend going?'

'Straight after Rita's funeral. Will you be attending?'

Shaking his head, Quinn answered, 'No. I'm but a lowly detective inspector. The Pavelys carry a lot of weight around here. Superintendent Peter Rendall, resplendent in his uniform, will be representing the police.'

The funeral of the young Rita Pavely was a traumatic experience. His sense of guilt made it additionally harrowing for McCabe. Tom and Beryl Jenkins patently avoided as much as a glance in his direction. This both relieved McCabe and paradoxically made him feel even more responsible for the death. When, in late afternoon, he left Abbeyfield, the immense sorrow of the occasion journeyed with him to Staines. He had telephoned in advance so Katrina would be expecting him. That was the easy bit. He would be treading on dangerous ground when attempting to voice his suspicions about her sister's husband.

Parking the car at the kerbside outside her house, it required an immense effort for him to get out. He had overdosed on the grief of others that afternoon, and shrank from stirring up further emotion. Had he not phoned Katrina earlier he would have restarted the engine and driven away.

Though it was small, Katrina had a lovely home, decorated in tones of mauve with small accents of old rose and touches of muted green. There was an image on a television screen but no sound. She picked up a remote and switched off the set completely.

'This must be important to have you come all this way, Gerry.' she remarked worriedly.

'I'm afraid that I have some unpleasant news, Katrina,' he began. 'It was Suzi Duoard's body: she was murdered.'

'I suppose that I should be terribly upset,' she said, adding candidly, 'but it's all so far back in the past that Suzi means little more than a name to me. Is that a horrid thing to say, Gerry?'

'No, of course not. As the past fades it takes our old feelings with it.'

'But you didn't come here to tell me that.'

'I didn't,' McCabe said. 'Do you remember Rita Jenkins?'

'Yes, she was one of our crowd. I heard that she married Ryan Pavely.'

'That's right. Rita died this week, Katrina.'

Lowering herself on to the edge of an armchair, she murmured, 'That's terrible. She was a little younger than me if I remember rightly. Was it sudden?'

'Rita committed suicide,' McCabe said regretfully.

'Good Lord! How, and why?'

'How, was by jumping off that viaduct some miles from Abbeyfield. Why, is a long story.'

'Something to do with your reason for calling on me, and something connected to Suzi?'

'It is connected. Back at the time when you were in Abbeyfield, Rita fell pregnant. Her parents arranged for Doctor Ronan to terminate the pregnancy, and it was kept secret.'

'I am surprised,' Katrina said, on a long, slow exhalation. 'I recall that it happened to another girl. Gail Potter was up the duff, as we termed it in those days. But Rita Jenkins, phew! Who was the boy?'

'It wasn't a boy, but a man.'

'Who could also have been responsible for Suzi's condition?'

'No, that isn't likely. Everything points to the man who made Suzi pregnant being the man who killed her.'

McCabe's answer made Katrina's face go an almost translucent white. Her lips moved several times but no words came out. Then she asked, 'Do you know who that was?'

'I'm fairly certain that I do.'

Watching Katrina closely, McCabe could tell that she was struggling to conceal an attack of nerves. On impulse she said, 'I usually have a nightcap around this time. Would you care for a whisky, Gerry?'

He accepted with thanks, and Katrina poured them each a full glass. Passing McCabe's drink to him, she spoke lightly. 'You have me intrigued now as to why you are here.'

'To tell you requires the kind of diplomacy that I know I lack.' McCabe excused himself in advance. 'Do you remember Roland Merrill?'

'Of course,' Katrina answered calmly, appearing to have

regained control of her emotions. 'I did get news of a sort from Abbeyfield for a while after I left, so you don't have to tell me that Beth married him.'

'You don't have a very high opinion of him?'

'I disliked the Merrill family in general,' Katrina said vehemently. 'In my hippie days I was ashamed of my own bourgeois family, but the Merrills had the Farquahars beaten where snobbery was concerned. I have never been able to understand why Beth married Roland. I suspect it was a marriage arranged by my father and the Merrills, Abbeyfield's royal families. Is Roland Merrill the reason for you calling on me?'

Katrina had become suspicious and withdrawn once more. McCabe guessed that she had at first previously feared that it was Merrill who was responsible for Rita Jenkins's pregnancy, but now dreaded that McCabe was going to link him with the Suzi Duoard tragedy. Unsure of how best to answer her question, he decided to take a chance. 'Yes, I was hoping that maybe you could give me some background on him.'

'That's a weak excuse for coming all this way.' Katrina sounded almost hostile. 'Surely there are plenty of people in Abbeyfield you could have asked.'

'Not the sort of questions that I have in mind.'

'But why me? I only knew him as a teacher when I was a schoolgirl.'

'What was your impression of him?'

Refilling their glasses, Katrina replied, 'As teacher he was a very strict. In retrospect, I would say that his major fault was that he was obsessed by the status of the school rather than the education and welfare of individual pupils.'

'How did he react to the hippies?'

Katrina suddenly looked very tired and rubbed a hand across her eyes. 'That seems an odd question for you to ask.'

'I often have to ask odd questions in my line of work, Katrina,' McCabe said. 'Was he friendly with any of the hippies?'

'I take it that you have met Roland Merrill?'

'On a few occasions, yes,' McCabe replied.

'Then you should have the answer to the question you came here to ask me,' Katrina said with a short, harsh laugh.

She was remarkably astute, McCabe silently acknowledged. Astute and defensive. Having deduced that he was trying to establish a link between Roland Merrill and Suzi Duoard, Katrina had clammed up. She was a strong-minded person and her line of defence stood firmly against his investigation.

'I apologize if I have been intrusive,' McCabe said. 'It's getting late. Maybe we could talk again tomorrow at some time, Katrina?'

'I have no wish to be rude, Gerry, but I feel that wouldn't serve any purpose.'

'But we are parting as friends; I trust that we will meet again at some time soon.'

'I hope that we do, Gerry,' Katrina said. 'You're not going back to Abbeyfield now?'

'No, I'll find myself a room for the night here in Staines.'

'I feel guilty because you came all this way for no reason.'

'There's nothing for you to be guilty about, Katrina. It was good of you to see me.' Wishing her 'Good night,' McCabe added, 'I hope that one day when I call I will be able to take you back to Abbeyfield with me.'

'There would need to be a lot of changes before that could happen, Gerry.'

'What sort of changes?' he enquired hopefully.

'Too many to list,' was Katrina's enigmatic reply.

The sound of his mobile became a part of the dream that McCabe was dreaming. As he floated up to the surface of consciousness, so did the dream instantly fade. The glow of a streetlight filtering weakly through the blind on the room's single window gave no hint as to the time of night. The digital figures on his travel alarm clock were just a green blur. Blinking his eyes only succeeded in changing the pattern of glowing green. Things were becoming clearer in his head, though. He had asked a car-park attendant where he could get a room for the night, and he had directed him to an old lady's house beside the river.

With his mind now functioning properly, his eyes quickly caught up. It was twenty minutes past three. He reached fumblingly for the phone. It could only be Sol Quinn, and it had to be serious for the detective to ring him at this hour.

But it was a distressed and apologetic Katrina.

'It's me, Gerry. Forgive me for calling you at this time, but my Jiminy Cricket has been giving me gyp. I'm useless as a liar, and I wasn't honest with you when you were here this evening. When we were talking I wasn't sure where my loyalties lay. Even though Roland Merrill is my sister's husband, if he has done the terrible things you obviously suspect him of doing, then I owe it to Elizabeth more than anyone else to speak out.'

'That's true, Katrina. What is it you have to say?'

There was a long pause at Katrina's end, and the sound of a glass clinking. McCabe guessed that his caller required Dutch courage. Then she was speaking again. 'Merrill had a crush on Suzi. More of an obsession rather than a crush, I suppose. He was careful not to have anyone find out, but for quite a few of us young people it was a standing joke.'

'What was Suzi Duoard's reaction?'

'I think that she was flattered, having a wealthy man after her,' Katrina replied slowly and thoughtfully.

'So, Katrina, Merrill had the urge and the means, but what about opportunity? He couldn't spend nights in a hippie camp without the whole of Abbeyfield hearing about it.'

'Suzi was away from the camp for two nights a week, three weeks in succession, at the same time Roland was attending a teacher training college on some kind of course for potential head teachers.'

'Are you sure this wasn't just girlie gossip, Katrina?'

'I'm certain it wasn't. Sophie, one of the girls, was a close friend of Roma Langley, whose elder sister, Elsa, was a teacher at the same school as Roland Merrill.'

McCabe was convinced. It all fitted together. Elsa Langley was now the head teacher at Kilverham School. The woman Beth and he had spoken to just a few days ago.

'Do you recall where the college was that Merrill was attending, Katrina?'

'I'm sorry, no. I don't think that Sophie ever found that out. If she did, then she didn't tell me.'

Satisfied that he could trace the college, McCabe thanked Katrina for telephoning him.

'How badly do you think that all of this will eventually affect Beth, Gerry?'

'If we are right about her husband, then it is plainly in Beth's best interest to expose him,' McCabe advised. 'I think that the time when I take you back home to Abbeyfield is drawing closer, Katrina.'

'Why are you so persistent where that issue is concerned, Gerry?'

'Because I think the colonel, Beth, and you are very nice people. And I do like a happy ending.'

'You never struck me as being a romantic,' Katrina joked.

'You're kidding. I went to see When Harry Met Sally five times.'

'I don't think that film comes under a romance heading,' Katrina giggled.

'Doesn't it?' McCabe asked, in mock innocence. 'It's been great talking to you, Katrina, but I think we should both try to get some sleep before the night is over.'

'I agree. Good night, Gerry.'

'Good night, Katrina.'

A few miles short of Abbeyfield the following morning, McCabe took a right turn for Kilverham. He had telephoned Quinn before leaving Staines to give him an outline of Katrina's information, and explain that he wanted to find out what college Merrill had attended on some kind of refresher course. The detective had given him the name of Tom Sheppard, his contact in the education department at County Hall.

Tom Sheppard was short in stature, unhealthily obese, and balding. He advanced warily towards McCabe.

'Good morning. My name is McCabe.'

'You asked for me by name, but I don't know you, Mr McCabe,' Sheppard said curiously.

'Forgive me, I should have explained,' McCabe apologized. 'Detective Inspector Quinn suggested that I see you.'

Lifting a flap in the counter, Sheppard said reluctantly, 'You had better come through.'

McCabe followed him into a small office. A girl secretary with a 1920s look about her smiled a 'good morning' at him. Sheppard pointlessly shifted some papers on his desk. 'Well, Mr McCabe, how may I help you?'

'My enquiry concerns one of your head teachers,' McCabe explained.

'I am afraid I'm not at liberty to divulge personal details such as that, Mr McCabe.'

'There is nothing sinister in this, Mr Sheppard. I am a private detective working for an insurance company. The information is required for a particularly expensive life insurance policy.'

'I see. And what was it specifically that you need to know?'

Taking a notebook from his jacket pocket, McCabe made a pretence of scanning it intensely. 'It appears that in 1969 the person applying for the policy had to attend hospital some distance from here as an out-patient over several weeks, but did not disclose.'

A frowning, Sheppard mused, 'That's odd. You have a name for this person?'

McCabe checked his notebook. 'Ah, here we are. It's Merrill, Roland Merrill.'

'I'm prepared to go so far as to check for you, without giving any details.'

'I would be very grateful, Mr Sheppard.'

Turning to his secretary, Sheppard instructed, 'Could you look something up for me please, Helen? It's the 1960s, so you'll find it in Archives over at D Wing.'

'What name is it, Mr Sheppard?' Helen asked, picking up a pad and standing waiting with pen poised.

'Roland Merrill.'

Helen left, and Sheppard made small talk. 'Have you known DI Quinn long, Mr McCabe?'

'We have been friends for quite a while,' McCabe replied, on a roll where lying was concerned. 'Is he a friend of yours?'

'In a kind of way,' Sheppard shrugged. 'I got to know him through the local schools. The police give the pupils very interesting talks from time to time. They are very good in that respect.'

They continued in this light conversational way until Helen returned to pass a file to Sheppard. Opening it, he fingered his way studiously through the papers it contained. Then a smile twitched at the corners of his mouth, extending into a grin as he turned to McCabe.

'I think I have an answer for you, Mr McCabe,' Sheppard

chuckled. 'For two days a week, for three weeks running in 1969, Mr Merrill was on a special course at the Arrowmead Teacher Training College.'

Feigning amusement, McCabe exclaimed, 'That's a relief. My client will be pleased. You have made my life less complicated, Mr Sheppard, thank you. And thank you, miss.'

'Glad to have been of service,' Sheppard said, and Helen joined him in a smile for McCabe.

At the door, McCabe stopped as if struck by a sudden after-thought. 'Just to make certain that I have it right. This training college is not here in Kilverham?'

'You can pocket your fee with a clear conscience, Mr McCabe,' Sheppard assured him, his grin even wider than before. 'Arrowmead is located at Huddlestone, a pretty little half-village, half-town, one hundred and twenty miles from here as the crow flies.'

'An absolute waste of petrol, Gerry,' Quinn remarked, as he returned from the bar and placed their drinks on the table. 'Merrill was at this place in Huddlestone in 1969, for Pete's sake. There isn't much chance that you'll bump into someone who remembers Merrill was there, and that he had a girl with him.'

'I've got to try, Sol. I'm determined to put Merrill in the frame for the Duoard murder.'

Quinn lowered his eyes and his voice. 'You can make a start right now. He's just come in.'

McCabe couldn't resist a quick look. With her husband a couple of steps behind her, Beth was heading for their table. She greeted them with, 'Starsky and Hutch. We won't intrude on you for more than a few minutes. Just long enough to catch up with the news. Roland will get the drinks in.'

'You're welcome to join us,' 'Quinn said, standing up. 'Let's make it my shout.'

'That's kind of you,' Merrill forced himself to say, but failed to make it sound convivial.

'Most kind. I'd like a Tia Maria, if I may,' Beth said. Merrill requested a lager.

As Quinn headed for the bar, Beth, in one of her impulsive

moves, walked to the jukebox. Taking a long time to make her selection she dropped a coin in, and was back sitting down beside her husband when the tune started. It was an old number, the Sherelles singing *Will You Still Love Me Tomorrow*? Beth glanced secretly and meaningfully at McCabe. He avoided eye contact.

'Have you been busy, Mr McCabe?' Beth enquired mildly.

'The colonel has been worrying because you have not visited him at the manor,' Merrill complained.

'I've been out of the area, Merrill,' McCabe said, then addressed Beth. 'Please tell the colonel that I should be able to get to see him later tomorrow, and I will have something to tell him then.'

'Excuse me,' Merrill said, standing up from the table. 'I have a telephone call to make.'

Beth went deadly serious when she and McCabe were alone. 'What will you be able to tell my father, Gerry, that Katrina will be coming home?'

'I don't want to raise your hopes, Beth, but that is a real possibility. There is something else.'

She glanced around her. Quinn was still at the bar, waiting, and Merrill was nowhere to be seen. 'Then tell me, please.'

'Well …' he began, fearing that he would soon come to regret the course he was about to take. Katrina had accused him of being a romantic, and she had to be right. He hadn't been hired to reunite the whole Farquahar family. 'This is mere supposition at the moment, Beth, but do you think it possible that the colonel would take your mother back?'

Speechless for a moment, Beth then asked a little breathlessly, 'Why do you ask, Gerry?'

'Because Hartley deserted her soon after they left Abbeyfield, and now he is in custody and both your mother and the colonel will see justice done.'

'So it was Sylvester Hartley in Fenton,' Beth gasped.

'At the moment he is held on drug charges, but Sol Quinn and his guv'nor are preparing to have him on the fraud charges that have been on the books for years.'

Beth then spoke speculatively. 'Much of my father's bitterness towards my mother is a façade. Having her back would be really good for him. If you can do that, Gerry, get both Katrina and my mother back to the manor, I will be the happiest woman alive.'

Looking at her smiling face, McCabe felt a dark and heavy sense of responsibility descend on him. Since arriving in Abbeyfield he had inadvertently caused suffering for a number of people, and right now he seemed to be setting Beth up as his next victim. McCabe was about to say something important to Beth, though he knew not what, when Merrill and Quinn returned to the table.

eleven

illing his car with petrol in preparation for his trip to Huddlestone, McCabe's body tensed as he saw Silas Pavely pull into the filling station. The sight of the father-in-law of the recently dead girl filled him with dread. He would have to endure an uncomfortable conversation, an unofficial inquest into the tragedy. It made McCabe uneasy when Pavely didn't pull up at the petrol pumps but parked to one side in a spare area. He watched him sit for a moment, head back, eyes closed. McCabe guessed that this was no accidental meeting.

Pavely got out of the car and walked towards the shop. But it was a ruse. Pretending to notice McCabe suddenly, the farmer did a half turn to head in his direction. McCabe's intuition hadn't let him down. This meeting was definitely planned. McCabe experienced a sudden and inexplicable feeling of disquiet.

'Good morning, Mr McCabe,' Pavely said in greeting, holding up his right hand like a man taking an oath. His eyes were a lot older and more tired than when McCabe had last seen him.

'Good morning. How is your son?' McCabe responded. His enquiry sounded like the platitude McCabe was ashamed to accept that it was.

'Bearing up,' Pavely replied. 'The doctor's given him some tablets, two of which get him off to sleep in no time. The problem is that the same two tablets mean that he's drowsy for about three hours after waking up. In the morning he just blunders around the farm. It's pitiful to see a man in such a sorry state.'

'It must be distressing for Mrs Pavely and you,' McCabe sympathized.

'There is something that I believe you might be able to help me with.'

'If I can, then I will,' McCabe promised.

'It's about this Sylvester Hartley fellow.'

McCabe was bewildered. He had told only Katrina and Beth of Hartley's arrest. Katrina had no contact with Abbeyfield, and he trusted Beth not to have told anyone. He guessed the information that Hartley had been arrested must have the police at Kilverham as its source. Certain that it hadn't come from Solomon Quinn, McCabe identified Peter Rendall as the culprit. Narrowing his eyes he gained thinking time by watching the spinning digital figures on the pump so as to stop them when they reached £25.00. Then he asked, 'What about him?'

'Well, you know that he has been arrested at Fenton. You have been in liaison with the police at Kilverham since you came here, McCabe.'

The absence of the title "Mr" warned McCabe that Pavely's civility had come to an end. He admitted, 'I am aware that a man named Piers Heaney has been arrested.'

'One and the same,' Pavely said emphatically. He slanted a glance at McCabe. 'I'm not a man to beat about the bush, so I'll come straight out with it. I know about Hartley and Rita, Ryan's wife, all those long years ago. That man is in a position to stir up a scandal, McCabe. I will not permit any further distress to be caused my son.'

'What do you want from me?' McCabe enquired.

Pavely caught McCabe's gaze and held it. They stared hard at each other. Some kind of psychological exchange. Taking a deep, angry breath that swelled his narrow chest, Pavely rasped, 'My understanding of the situation is that the police at Fenton are charging Heaney, or Hartley if you like, on the drugs thing. Kilverham police lack the evidence to pin the old fraud charges on Hartley, and I understand that they are going to inform the Crown Prosecution Service of this.'

A car had pulled in at the pump behind McCabe's car, and he reached into his jacket for his wallet. He said to Pavely, 'Then I'd say that you don't have a problem.'

'But I do.'

'What is it?'

The driver of the other car tooted his horn impatiently, and McCabe moved off towards the shop to pay for his petrol.

'My problem is you,' Pavely called, his voice frosty. 'I'm told that for some reason you are intent on having Hartley prosecuted, and your insistence might well force the police to drag up a past that is best forgotten.'

'Though I can understand your concern, Mr Pavely, I do have a duty to my client,' McCabe turned to say.

'Your client is Colonel Farquahar, to whom I spoke on the telephone this morning. The colonel engaged you to find his missing daughter, and he is satisfied that you have done that. Consequently, you have no further business here.'

Not responding, McCabe walked into the kiosk and paid for his petrol. Coming back out he was ready to shift his car and discuss things further with Pavely. But all he saw of him was the brake lights of his vehicle glowing redly as he waited in the exit to join the main road traffic. Then the brake lights went out and the engine roared. Pavely and his car had gone.

Neither a town nor a village, had Huddlestone made up its mind which of the two it wanted to be, it wouldn't have been an impressive example of either. The teacher training college comprised two modern adjoining buildings of smooth white stone. In the pale light of an autumn afternoon it was a Legoland construction. Set in spacious and well-kept grounds, the place held no interest for McCabe. He had established that Roland Merrill had attended here in 1969. What he needed to know was where Merrill had stayed with Suzi Duoard.

That quest brought him to Huddlestone's only boarding-house, a redbrick building of modest size. Standing on a veranda that had ornate metal columns, he rang the doorbell and offered up a little prayer that whoever answered the door would be old enough to have been running the place in 1969.

A raw-boned, grim-visaged woman whose excessive use of powder made her face as white as a clown's, opened the door. In her late 60s, she was the right age but appeared to be the wrong type. Her appearance was intimidating. McCabe's mentally rehearsed bogus enquiry about lodgings for a daughter who would soon be attending the local college, disintegrated inside of his head. He decided that a direct approach held the less risk.

'Good morning,' he began politely. 'I wonder if you can help me.'

'I take it that you are not wanting a room.'

The trace of a smile had a dramatic softening effect on her face, encouraging McCabe. 'No, I'm making some enquiries.'

'You are a policeman?'

'A private detective. My name is McCabe, Gerry McCabe.'

'I'm pleased to meet you, Mr McCabe,' she said, her cordiality surprising McCabe more than her smile had. 'I'm Maude Harrison. How can I help you?'

'Have you been in business here long, Mrs Harrison?'

'September 1956. Is that long enough for you?' she enquired, and her earlier smile returned, wider than before and all but eliminating her formidable countenance.

Returning the smile, McCabe said, 'I'm trying to trace someone who most probably stayed here in 1969.'

'My word!' Maude Harrison exclaimed. 'I have already forgotten who stayed here last night. Nevertheless, you had better come in.'

McCabe followed the landlady to a beautifully furnished, lushly carpeted, room. Everything was neat and tidy. There were a dozen limp roses in a vase on a highly polished table. A scattering of black-edged petals lay on the table around the vase. Maude Harrison fussily scooped them into one hand and tipped them into a bin before gesturing for McCabe to sit in an armchair, then taking a seat herself.

'Now,' she said, dabbing with a finger at a real or imaginary speck of dust on the table beside her. 'What is it you want to know, Mr McCabe?'

'In 1969 a man stayed here for two days a week, three weeks running, while attending the training college.'

'Most of my boarders are students at the college,' she pointed out.

'I suspected that, of course,' McCabe said. 'But the person I am interested in was a mature student; a man who had been a teacher for a number of years and was doing some kind of refresher course for promotion.'

'That does narrow it down a little, Mr McCabe, but 1969 was some time ago.'

'If my information is correct, Mrs Harrison, he would have been accompanied by a girl. A girl much younger than him.'

'That doesn't help much,' Maude Harrison mused. 'I run a tight ship here, Mr McCabe, and though the girl may have been with this man, they would most certainly have had separate rooms.'

'Your high standards were obvious from the moment I stepped inside the front door.'

'Thank you. It is very kind of you to say so.'

'The girl,' McCabe said. 'She would have been a hippie.'

Maude Harrison was emphatic. 'Then I can assure you that I wouldn't have accepted her into my house. Those people were involved in drugs and all manner in those days.'

'She could well have toned down her appearance when she came to Huddlestone.'

'That's true. What a pity you don't have any names.'

'But I do,' McCabe exclaimed delightedly. 'Does that help, Mrs Harrison?'

'Yes, but it does present me, or rather my daughter, with a formidable task.'

'I don't understand,' McCabe confessed.

'Well, you see,' Maude Harrison explained. 'I am an inveterate hoarder, Mr McCabe, and I have kept every one of the registers through the years.'

McCabe gasped. 'That is great news.'

Giving him a wan smile, the landlady warned, 'It is for you, but not for Violet, my daughter. Violet is brilliant with figures while I have to confess to being barely numerate. Consequently, she has the registers I told you about stored at her place.'

'Does she live far away?' McCabe enquired, spirits sagging.

'Oh no. She and Richard, her husband, have a bungalow on the far side of Huddlestone.'

'Do you think she'd mind if I called on her, Mrs Harrison?'

'Not at all, but it would need to be this evening. Violet works full-time in the office of Sam Wilton's haulage company, Huddlestone's only industry. Are you staying in Huddlestone overnight?'

'No, I have to get back.'

McCabe contemplated ringing Beth to put his meeting with Colonel Farquahar off until tomorrow. But he dismissed the idea immediately. The colonel was paying the piper, so the colonel could call the tune.

'Oh dear,' Maude Harrison frowned. 'I could telephone Violet at work and see what she thinks.'

'Would you mind?' McCabe asked. First impressions certainly can be deceptive.

'No trouble at all,' Maude Harrison assured him, coming partly up out of her chair to reach for a telephone.

McCabe heard the ringing tone at the other end, and the click as a receiver was lifted, but not the voice that answered.

'Hello, Vi, it's me,' Maude Harrison spoke self-consciously into the mouthpiece. 'I have a problem that you should be able to help me with. What? No, you cheeky monkey, I didn't forget to pay the electricity bill.' She gave McCabe a sideways smile. 'Listen, Vi. I have a gentleman here who is interested in two guests we may have had many years ago: 1969, in fact. Yes, I realize that.' Putting her hand over the mouthpiece she spoke to McCabe. 'What are the names of the people you are looking for?'

'Roland Merrill and Suzi Duoard.'

Asking him how to spell Duoard, Maude Harrison then relayed the names to her daughter. After some more talk on the telephone, she hung up and turned to McCabe. 'She's going to start going through the registers as soon as she can, but warns that it will take some time. Violet said to take your address and we'll send the details on to you immediately she finds them. That is, of course, providing the people you are interested in did stay here.'

'I can't thank you enough,' McCabe said appreciatively. Taking out his notebook he wrote down the Fox and Hounds address at Abbeyfield and passed it to Maude Harrison.

Taking the address and glancing at it, the landlady nodded. 'I am sure that Violet won't waste any time,' then shrank back as McCabe held out a £50 note.

'I hope that will cover it,' McCabe said.

'I can't take your money, Mr McCabe,' Maude Harrison protested.

'Please accept this. I'll feel better about having imposed on you.'

'No. Thank you, but no.'

'Then please buy your daughter's children something,' McCabe said, placing the £50 on a table and walking to the door of the room.

'There were complications, Gerry,' Sol Quinn said pensively, 'and as you will know, complications don't come anywhere as complicated as they do in the police.'

On the return journey McCabe had diverted to the police station at Kilverham. Hearing what Quinn had to say, a fragmented fear that had been lurking unfocused in his mind came rapidly to the fore. Peter Rendall had informed him that though the police at Fenton were proceeding against Piers Heaney on the drug charges, it was likely that his true identity of Sylvester Hartley would not be revealed.

'We can't let that happen, Sol,' McCabe complained. 'Silas Pavely had a go at me this morning, and he knew about this.'

'This isn't the Metropolis, Gerry. Pavely and others like him pull the strings around here,' Quinn said. Lying back in a chair with his hands cradled behind his head, he continued, 'Don't be fooled by Pavely's concern over Rita and Ryan. It goes much deeper than that. When Hartley was a solicitor here he did a lot of people some big favours, including Silas Pavely. Hartley knows where all the dead horses are buried in these parts.'

'It seems that those indebted to him will rescue him, Sol.'

'Exactly. Where the drug offences are concerned, Hartley, or Heaney, will probably get away with a fine. But if he goes down for fraud, then he'll make sure that he ruins the lives of quite a few other people.'

'But neither they nor Hartley should be above the law,' McCabe protested.

With a snort of derision, Quinn said, 'You'll know all about two-tier policing.'

McCabe said, 'I know about it, and I don't like it. Anyway, I'm not a policeman now.'

'No, but I'm a detective inspector in a small community, and I'm likely to go back to being a constable real fast if I kick against the traces,' Quinn observed glumly.

McCabe declared, 'I'm not going to let this happen.'

'That's what is worrying Rendall, Gerry,' Quinn said. 'He's under orders to leave the Hartley thing alone, and he knows that as his subordinate I'll fall into line. But you are the wild card in this, with the knowledge to cause quite a ruckus. But that wouldn't be a sensible thing to do.'

'Whatever, I want to tie up all the loose ends before I leave Abbeyfield, Sol.'

'Your brief is Katrina Farquhar,' Quinn complained. 'I don't see how Hartley became a loose end for you. Is it connected to your involvement with Beth Merrill?'

'I am not involved with Beth Merrill.'

'Yeah, yeah.' There was total disbelief in Quinn's tone.

'I don't intend to be stopped on this,' McCabe declared. 'I have nothing to lose, Sol.'

'I wouldn't be too sure of that,' Quinn advised. 'But remember that professional respect and friendship are not necessarily joined to the same body. Don't expect me to stand by your side.'

'I won't.'

McCabe's critical tone brought a deep sigh of regret from Quinn before he said, 'Let's leave that aside. What did you come up with at Huddlestone?'

'Probably nothing,' McCabe answered. 'There's a chance, of sorts, that Merrill and the Duoard girl stayed at a B & B there, but I'll have to wait to find out.'

'I did say that you didn't have much hope,' Quinn said wearily. 'We've lost Hartley and, bar a miracle, Merrill is likely to get away.'

'I can't afford to lose either of them.'

'Take great care, Gerry,' Quinn advised with a sincerity that took the edge off McCabe's dislike of the tough detective's acceptance of partial law enforcement. 'Finding out how the other half lives is always traumatic. A word of warning that I beg you to heed: watch out for Ambrose Merrill, Roland's old man. He's the local godfather, as it were, and won't allow you to queer his pitch.'

This was a stark reminder for McCabe that he was in alien territory. He was an outsider among people living in one another's laps in the depth of the country. He could never fit in here. All the hysteria of hate and love – that was something he could never adapt to.

He asked grimly, 'How do you see my immediate future, Gerry?'

'What future?' Quinn laconically replied with a question of his own.

'No, seriously,' McCabe said. 'I don't expect to end up dead in a ditch.'

'The way I see it, Gerry, Pete Rendall will be asked to have a quiet word with you.'

'And then?'

'You'll probably end up dead in a ditch.'

'Have you ever had the eerie feeling that something has happened before?' Beth asked mysteriously, with one of her special smiles.

She had opened the door of Abbeyfield Manor to him, just as she had when he had first arrived. He replied, 'That seems an awful long time ago, Beth.'

'Almost as if it was in another lifetime,' she mused.

McCabe was well aware that Beth had a brilliant mind. In Abbeyfield and district circles she was an intellectual amazon among mental pygmies. Possibly Solomon Quinn was an exception, but his intelligence potential was limited by his being a member of a disciplined force.

'Can we agree that it was in this lifetime?' McCabe said, sometimes finding her fondness for the abstract confusing.

'If we must.'

'Good,' he said with a grin. 'Then can I come in to see the colonel?'

Stepping back she did an exaggerated sweep of her arm to invite him in. But when he was in the hall and she turned to him after closing the door, there was a troubled expression on her face.

'Is something wrong?' he enquired worriedly.

She said dubiously, 'Nothing I can put my finger on, but when you see my father be prepared for anything.'

'Such as?'

'I don't know,' she replied with a shrug. 'It's just that things have been happening. Silas Pavely has telephoned a few times, and Ambrose Merrill, my *dear* father-in-law, came to see my father earlier today.'

'But you don't know what all this was about?' McCabe queried.

'No, but old man Merrill hasn't lowered himself to come to the manor for more than twenty years, so whatever he wanted from my father is important. It's left him more muddled than usual and terribly worried. They have put some kind of pressure on him, Gerry.'

'Let's go to see him. Maybe together we can discover what's happening,' McCabe suggested. 'If I tell him that I've visited Katrina again and that she was asking about him, it might help.'

'We can hope that it will, but I am not looking forward to this.'

They entered the colonel's study to find him sitting behind his desk leafing through some papers. He recognized his daughter right away, but had a few minutes' difficulty in identifying McCabe before being able to greet him with, 'McCabe, my dear fellow.'

McCabe said, 'I thought you would like to be brought up to date, Colonel Farquahar.'

Eyes blank, the colonel peered at McCabe then swung his wizened head to look questioningly at Beth. A tic pulled rhythmically at the right side of his face.

'You remember that Mr McCabe has been looking for Katrina,' Beth reminded her father.

Deciding to use a shock tactic, McCabe announced, 'Sylvester Hartley has been arrested.'

The change wrought in the colonel was astounding. The twitches were gone, the eyes were clear; the expression on his wrinkled face was now as lively as a gypsy dance. 'I care nought about that damned rascal. But I do appreciate you telling me. You have done excellent work for Beth and myself. We are very appreciative. I will be grateful if you would call tomorrow morning and present me with your account. Don't stint yourself, my dear fellow. I will write you a cheque at once in the morning, and then you can be off back home to London straight away.'

Totally unexpected, Beth and McCabe glanced questioningly at each other. For a former diplomat, the colonel had displayed a distinct lack of tact in his haste to get McCabe out of the area.

He said, 'There are still one or two things that I need to clear up, Colonel.'

'Nonsense. As I said, McCabe, you have done an excellent job of work. After so many long and stressful years, I now know that my second daughter is safe and well. Take your well-deserved money and go home.'

Prepared to argue further, McCabe saw that the old man's attention had ebbed swiftly away. Head bent, his face seemed to flatten out into a mask and he was once again engrossed in his scrapbook. Beth put her hand lightly on Mcabe's arm to guide him out of the room.

As they left, McCabe heard the old man say, 'You know, he looks very much like a film star from the old days, Anthony Steel.'

Miming the name 'Sylvester Hartley' at McCabe, Beth made a sign that said her father had been talking to no one in particular.

When they were in the passageway and she had closed the study door, McCabe referred to the colonel's eagerness to pay him off, asking, 'What do you make of that?'

'As I said, someone is brining pressure to bear. He would never do anything underhand, Gerry,' Beth said in a fearful, quiet voice. 'Yet I would say that he is frightened, very frightened.'

'Frightened of what, Beth?'

'Not *what*, but *for*,' was her enigmatic answer.

'You've lost me, Beth,' McCabe confessed.

'He's frightened for you, Gerry. It's almost as if he wants to get you away from here before you come to harm.'

He brushed away her suggestion. 'That's an extreme theory, Beth. This is little old Abbeyfield, not New York.'

'You're probably right,' she partially accepted with a nod. 'I don't seem able to think straight any more. You have changed things here, Gerry.'

'I'm sorry if I've made you unhappy,' McCabe apologized.

'I didn't say that,' she replied quickly. 'Forgive me, I'm becoming maudlin. Come to the drawing-room for a drink.'

A surprised McCabe asked. 'Isn't your husband at home this evening?'

'No.' Stopping, Beth turned to him. 'I think that he could be having an affair.'

'If that is the case, then I'm deeply sorry, Beth.'

'Don't be. My biggest shock came from realizing that I just don't care.'

'Whatever makes you think that he is playing away?' The idea of the dour Roland Merrill having an affair struck McCabe as inconceivable.

'He has been very on edge of late. Then earlier this evening he had a phone call. It got him into quite a state, and he hurried off out without saying a word to me. He left his mobile behind and I checked who had made the call.'

'A woman?' McCabe raised both eyebrows.

'In a manner of speaking,' Beth said, pulling a face. 'Helen Petters is an anachronism. She looks as if she's stepped out of the pages of an F. Scott Fitzgerald book.'

Mind racing, McCabe saw an image of Tom Sheppard's secretary. A 1920s flapper about to dance the Black Bottom. But it seemed too much of a coincidence, so he asked Beth an innocuous question. 'Does this Helen live locally?'

'Kilverham,' Beth said flatly. 'She works in County Hall.' Then the Beth that McCabe liked returned. 'Let's go and have that drink.'

It was plain that Roland Merrill would by now know that McCabe had been making enquiries about him. The game had become a dangerous one that had to be played out to the end, and the rules had just changed dramatically.

Beth fixed him with a steady look as she poured two drinks. Momentarily, she was no longer poised and talkative. There was a tremor in her hand as she reached for one of the glasses and passed it to McCabe. Lifting her own glass she drank deeply, coughed on the straight alcohol, and drank again.

Having regained her emotional balance, she enquired with a tinge of flippancy, 'So, it will be a case of you loving me and leaving me in the morning?'

'That is unlikely,' McCabe said, hoping that she had simply used an old adage, and the word 'loving' was innocent. 'My work here isn't finished.'

'My father seems to think differently.'

'He'll learn differently in the morning when I don't arrive to collect my cheque.'

'I don't want you to go, but I fear that you may regret staying,' she said unhappily.

'I'd better be going before your husband gets back,' he heard himself say, and it sounded really crass.

'Don't let him worry you,' she murmured, her voice as soft as a kitten's fur. 'We may live, exist rather, under the same roof, but that's it. I have my own bedroom, and when he does come home I won't see him until breakfast-time.'

Trying to convince himself that there wasn't a covert message in what Beth had just given him, McCabe failed. Draining his glass he went to place it on the table. Nervousness made him bang it down hard.

Embarrassed, he said, 'I'm sorry, Beth. I have to be on my way.'

'Stay for just one more drink,' she half pleaded.

'Some other time, Beth,' he promised, walking slowly out of the room.

Turning to see her framed in the doorway, her disappointment was so obvious that McCabe had to wait for a wave of guilt to pass before he could make his way across the hall to the door.

'Some other time,' she listlessly agreed. 'There may well not be another time, Gerry.'

Aware that she was right, McCabe was tempted to turn back to her, even if it was only to say something reassuring. Gaining a victory over his basic instincts, and whatever else it was that Beth aroused in him, McCabe reached and opened the door.

'Good night, Beth,' he said without turning.

She didn't answer. It seemed a million miles to the dark night outside and, as he went, it felt to McCabe as if his legs were shackled.

McCabe was perplexed as he drove away from the manor. To give himself time to think he deliberately chose a long route back to the Fox and Hounds. Roland Merrill had been alerted. There was no way that Merrill could cover his tracks across the ground of the 1960s. What did worry McCabe were Ambrose Merrill's efforts to keep Sylvester Hartley out of the picture. But to uncover local corruption more than three decades old would cause barely a whimper. So why was the older Merrill going to such lengths, obviously putting pressure on both Silas Pavely and Colonel Farquahar? One explanation, perhaps the only one, was that the father was aware of the sins of the son, and was desperate to save him from a charge of murder.

Pulling into the pub car-park, McCabe didn't get out of his car. Instead he reached for his mobile and tapped in Quinn's number. Even though his thinking about the Merrill father and son had started to come together, the need to form a connection between them, Suzi Duoard, and Hartley eluded him. There was no delay in the detective answering.

Quinn was too busy to speak at length. He invited McCabe to his home, and gave him directions.

McCabe discovered that Quinn's home was a top-floor flat in a modern building that was tall by Kilverham standards. Though not expensively furnished, it was given more than a touch of class by the creative way in which the furnishings had been arranged. The décor was tasteful although subdued, and there were no pictures or paintings on the walls. There wasn't one elongated police group photograph in sight, a fact that pleased but didn't surprise McCabe. Quinn was something of a loner.

Solomon Quinn's wife was not what McCabe had expected, although he admitted to himself that he'd had no idea what to expect. Stella Quinn was a sophisticated woman whose person-ality struck a balance with her rough diamond, yet poised and cultured husband, to make them a perfect couple. With short-cut black hair, slender shoulders, slender arms, and long slender legs, she had worn a frown on McCabe's arrival. But her face had swiftly lightened into an easy smile and the trouble lines were gone. Her eyes had met his evenly when Quinn introduced them, and the grip of her slim, cool hand was firm.

She poured drinks for all three of them, and they sat chatting. To begin with there was a certain amount of guarded talk at cross-purposes, with Quinn obviously apprehensive about the angle from which McCabe would bring in the subject of Sylvester Hartley. But having been made to feel at home, McCabe found it easy to broach the subject. 'You told me a little while ago, Sol, that Hartley couldn't be responsible for the Duoard girl's death because he wasn't around here at the time.'

'That's right,' Quinn nodded as he sipped his drink. 'Why do you ask? Have you got him in the frame now instead of Merrill?'

'No, Roland Merrill's the one, but do you remember where Hartley was around the time of the girl's death?'

Brow creasing, Quinn answered, 'With forensic evidence and the fact that the Farquahar girl's purse was buried with her and the money inside was exactly in the amount that Beth Merrill said, we are pretty certain that Suzi Duoard was killed on or close to the day Katrina left Abbeyfield. At that time Hartley had been in London at the Old Bailey for several weeks representing Kilverham businessman Harold Benfield on a tax evasion charge. Alibis don't come any better than that, Gerry. Why this interest in Hartley's whereabouts?'

'I believe that he has something on Roland Merrill.'

'Concerning the Duoard girl?' Despite himself, Quinn had become keenly interested.

'Yes. Ambrose Merrill has given me an indirect get-out-of-town message through Colonel Farquahar.'

'Which you are going to ignore,' Stella Quinn guessed.

'Of course he is,' a smiling Quinn agreed with his wife. 'All of this will end with my friend Gerry as a hero, and me as a traffic warden.'

twelve

Letting the humorous remark pass, McCabe pondered aloud, 'I can see how old man Merrill might have known that his son had committed a murder, but it is unlikely that either of them would have confided in Hartley. To do so would at the very least lay them open to blackmail.'

'From what I've read about Hartley in his file I know he's a scrote,' Quinn said. 'The Merrills would know him much better than that. So you are right, Gerry. I agree that it is difficult to come up with a reason why Hartley would have old Merrill so worried.'

'Would you mind if I said something, Gerry?' Stella Quinn asked.

'Please feel free. I welcome any help I can get,' McCabe admitted.

Stella studied both her husband and McCabe for a moment, then asked a question. 'If you had a pregnant unmarried daughter in the sixties, or a son who had got a girl pregnant, and couldn't bear the disgrace, what would be your first response?'

'Arrange an abortion,' Solomon Quinn volunteered.

'Exactly,' his wife concurred. 'So how do you go about it?'

'Have a discreet word with a midwife or a doctor,' Quinn suggested.

Accepting this with a pleased smile, Stella said, 'But not personally if you are one of the Abbeyfield aristocracy as Ambrose Merrill is. He has an OBE now, and he probably had it then. The possibility that he might approach the wrong medical person wouldn't allow him to take a chance.'

'So he'd have someone try to fix up the abortion for him.'

Quinn's hand sought and found his wife's hand as he looked at her admiringly.

'Sylvester Hartley,' McCabe breathed out the name in a long sigh of satisfaction.

'It's just a theory,' Stella modestly reminded them.

'A brilliant one,' McCabe congratulated her. 'But the search for a termination was unsuccessful, so the girl was murdered.'

'Probably by a panicking Roland Merrill,' Quinn remarked.

'And his father found out,' McCabe said, developing the theme.

Quinn nodded. 'Most probably guessed.'

'But Hartley would have definitely put two and two together,' Stella concluded.

'Exactly,' her husband affirmed. 'It is in the best interests of several people around here to keep Sylvester Hartley happy, but Ambrose Merrill has the most to lose if Hartley faces charges under his real name.'

'I can almost feel sorry for the old man,' Stella sighed.

'Only if you forget what happened to the girl,' Quinn observed.

His wife, regretting her expression of sympathy, murmured. 'True.'

'Obviously Roland Merrill's father is the one to put pressure on,' McCabe said. 'That is just what I intend to do.'

Quinn made his position clear. 'On your own as the man-in-the-street, Gerry. Don't expect any official support from me. I've already told you that Sylvester Hartley is a no-go area as far as I am concerned.'

'Don't panic, Captain Mainwaring,' McCabe urged him with a grin.

Though Stella Quinn smiled at this, she defended her husband. 'You do understand the position Sol is in, Gerry.'

'I do,' McCabe said. 'But I could use your advice on how to get near to Ambrose Merrill, Sol.'

'That's easy, Gerry, Sharee Bucholz. It's the Licensed Victuallers' annual do here in Kilverham tomorrow, so get her to take you with her.'

Having concentrated on putting distance between Sharee and

himself, McCabe's first thought was to reject Quinn's suggestion. But time was running short for him here in Abbeyfield and he couldn't afford to miss any opportunity. He enquired, 'Was Merrill a publican?'

'No, he was the Kilverham Council's chief executive,' Quinn explained. 'The fact that he's been a magistrate ever since he retired guarantees that he'll be there tomorrow night. The publicans will be keen to keep old Ambrose on side, and he won't turn down a free meal and free booze.'

'Then I had better be there,' McCabe said. 'Which means I have a busy day tomorrow, so I had better make a move now. Thank you both for your hospitality.'

Quinn shook his hand. 'It's been a pleasure. But remember, Gerry, You are on your own with the Sylvester Hartley thing.'

'I've a feeling that you won't let me forget it, Sol,' McCabe said.

'You can count on it, Gerry.'

Opening a low wooden gate to enter the front garden, McCabe followed a footpath that changed into a series of steps leading up a grassy rise. A row of well-tended evergreens formed a screen that concealed both Dr Ralph Ronan and his bungalow home until the last moment. Wearing a blue smock overall, the old man stood at an easel in the subtle sunlight of an early winter morning. He held a palette in one hand and a long brush in the other.

Standing fairly close but unnoticed, McCabe took a deep breath. Everything had gone wonderfully well so far that morning and he wanted his good fortune to continue. He had received an encouraging letter from Carol, asking him to spend Christmas with her and Cindy. It was a long time since they had been together at Christmas, and Carol had stated rather than hinted that this family Yuletide would be a new beginning for them.

The fact that before he had received the letter, Sharee had readily agreed for him to escort her to the Licensed Victuallers event that evening had diluted McCabe's delight. He had since been working hard to convince himself that his date with the vivacious Sharee was in the line of duty.

More good news had arrived in the same mail delivery. An A4 envelope had contained three photocopied pages from the boarding-house ledgers of Maude Harrison. On each of the three pages were entries for Roland Merrill and Suzi Duoard, with accompanying signatures. This evidence smoothed the jagged-edged pieces of his investigation so that they began to fit together.

'Good morning, Doctor Ronan.'

Startled, the old man half turned towards McCabe. Speechless for a few moments, he then spoke jerkily. 'Ah … yes … good morning. Please give me a moment … yes, I have it. Mr McCabe, isn't it.'

'That's right,' McCabe said.

As they shook hands, McCabe glanced at the canvas on the easel, and instantly wished that he hadn't. Staring at him was Rita Pavely. Her eyes were mesmerizing. Dark-lashed and terribly innocent, they were also terribly wise with a perverted wisdom that altered the innocence to mocking knowledge. It had been a fleeting illusion. In a split second, the image returned to being an almost finished portrait with unseeing eyes. But the initial effect still unsettled him.

'I'm a total amateur, as you can see.' The doctor gestured at the portrait and unnecessarily excused himself. His talent was patently evident. He pointed at a glossy magazine held open by a paper clip that was fastened to the easel. 'Rita appeared in the area's National Farmers' Union magazine, and I thought it was a particularly good likeness of the dear girl.'

'It is,' McCabe agreed. 'And you have captured more of her than appears in the photograph, Doctor Ronan.'

Going to great lengths to conceal the pleasure caused him by the compliment, Doctor Ronan said. 'How kind of you to say so, sir. My advanced age is probably responsible for a fear I have of late that my dreams and daydreams have become mixed with reality. My hope was to complete the painting by Christmas as a gift for Ryan. But now I am not so sure.'

'I know very little about art,' McCabe admitted. 'But it appears to me to be just about finished.'

'Oh, there's no problem with that. It will be ready and

framed well in time,' the old doctor exclaimed. 'My problem has grown as the painting has taken on life, so to speak. My original intention was for this to be a therapeutic gift for a widower. Since then I have come to fear that it may be the opposite – a constant and harrowing reminder of his terrible loss. What is your opinion, Mr McCabe? As a gift would the portrait heal or harm?'

Though at first not wishing to venture a judgement, McCabe was moved by the distress the dilemma was causing the old man. He spoke consolingly. 'You have put something special into that portrait, something of your spiritual self. I have no doubt that it will be accepted as a much-welcomed gift.'

'You have restored my confidence. Thank you.' Leaning back to study his work of art, Ronan went on, 'Now, as much as I would welcome a social call from you, I know that this isn't one. What can I do for you?'

'I'm afraid it's loosely connected with the subject of your painting, Doctor.'

'Oh dear,' Ronan sighed. 'That's a period of my life that returns regularly to haunt me.'

'I don't enjoy bringing it up again,' McCabe assured him.

'Not at all. We can neither ignore nor change the past,' Ronan said, pausing in thought for a moment. 'Nothing is all bad, Mr McCabe. That was an age of hope, a time of great opportunity. Young, non-militant people made contact with the spiritual and blended it with universal love. Sadly, it didn't last. The new mysticism was annihilated in an explosion of narcotics, free love and self-interest. A golden opportunity was squandered, condemning us to life in today's insane world.'

An impressed McCabe said, 'Much has been said about the 1960s, Doctor, but I have never heard it summed up so brilliantly and succinctly.'

'The babbling of an old fool, more likely,' Ronan said in self-deprecation. 'Now, you are investigating yesterday today, so how can I help you before I attempt to leave my shame back in the past?'

'I remember you saying that at the time you were approached by others as well as your friends the Jenkinses.'

'To the best of my remembrance, the parents of just one girl did ask for my help. I turned them away, of course.'

'Of course,' McCabe acknowledged. 'I have recently spoken with the girl concerned.'

It was the doctor's turn to compliment McCabe. 'You are very good sleuth. Did you perchance learn from her if someone had been willing to terminate the pregnancy?'

'She gave birth to a son, Doctor Ronan. He is now an airline pilot, married with children.'

'Hearing that both pleases and terrifies me, Mr McCabe,' the old doctor said in a half-whisper. 'None of us fully realizes what a frightening responsibility we have for one another. If I, through greed or moral laxity, had carried out that abortion, I would have deprived a woman of a son, another woman of a husband, and their children of lives. That is an awesome thought even without considering their children's children.'

Disturbed by Ronan's philosophy, McCabe tried to make light of it. 'It certainly is a reminder of the responsibility we have to each other.'

'Quite so, Mr McCabe,' Ronan argued. Made melancholy by his own reflections, he looked at the canvas on the easel for a long minute. 'What of Rita? What if her parents, my dear friends, had put a new life above their vanity and pride? How different would everything now be? Would I be enjoying the company of a living Rita instead of creating an icon, a lifeless image?'

Realizing that he had been, at least in part, responsible for pitching the old doctor into a black mood, McCabe made an unspecified apology. 'I am sorry, Doctor Ronan.'

Concentrating on washing his brushes, Ronan shook his head. 'There is no reason for you to be sorry, Mr McCabe.' Staying silent for some time, he then said. 'There is one favour I would request of you, but in doing so I fully accept that I have no right to ask.'

'What is it, Doctor?'

'The evening of the carol service out at the abbey is not far away,' Ronan said. 'Will you be attending the event?'

It wasn't McCabe's scene, but Beth would be there and he reasoned that it would make a fitting finale to his stay in Abbeyfield. So he replied, 'Yes.'

'Oh.' The doctor sounded disappointed. 'You see, I thought that I would present the portrait to Ryan on that evening, before the service. It seemed quite fitting to me. However, I am ashamed to admit that I would like someone to accompany me. I suppose it is psychological support I seek. Having someone with me would lessen the hurt should my gift be rejected. I have no one to ask but you. Yet I was taking a liberty in doing so.'

'Not at all,' McCabe protested mildly. 'I will go with you, Doctor Ronan.'

'If you are sure.' The old man's relief seemed mingled with a fear that McCabe might suddenly change his mind. 'I could pick you up at the Fox and Hounds on my way to the Pavelys, and drop you off on the way back in plenty of time for you to collect your own car, and any companion you may be taking with you, and drive to the abbey.'

'You'll find me waiting for you when you arrive,' McCabe promised.

Though he had come here with the sole purpose of making enquiries about Sylvester Hartley, McCabe didn't feel that he could raise the subject now as Ronan went back to his artistry. McCabe reasoned that he could make his enquiry while accompanying the doctor when he delivered the painting.

'Now, Mr McCabe, I have put myself in your debt,' Ronan said, as he brushed a subtle shade of red to Rita's bottom lip, shaping a slightly more generous mouth than she had in life. 'You called on me for information, so I will do all I can to help. Short of breaking the confidentiality of former patients, that is.'

The opening this presented was too good for McCabe to ignore. He asked, 'Was Sylvester Hartley a former patient of yours?'

'Thankfully, no.' Ronan was watching McCabe narrowly. 'Dear me, Mr McCabe, lies are said to have a limited lifespan, but that rumour, which I regret you have been caught up in, has indeed become a survivor.'

'What rumour is that, Doctor Ronan?'

'That it was Hartley who got Rita Jenkins into trouble. The man was a cad, Mr McCabe. Oh yes, he made a play for Rita, who was a very attractive girl. But she spurned him.'

'Then who ...?' McCabe began, as his theories crumbled.

'John Menson.'

Stunned, his Sylvester Hartley theory blown, McCabe gasped, 'But he denied it and I believed him.'

'He believed it when he denied it to you,' the doctor explained. 'Most of the time he doesn't remember, but very occasionally he does. I am just as responsible for his mental condition as I feel that I am for Rita's suicide.'

'I don't follow,' McCabe said, certain that the old man was being too harsh on himself.

'In those far off days, Menson was a man who loved to live life, and lived life to love,' Ronan spoke softly in reminiscence. 'He was a very religious man even then. Menson was truly a person whom it was easy to admire, and I enjoyed many a philosophical and psychological discussion with him. Even so he was a hippie, which made him totally unacceptable as a son-in-law for Thomas and Beryl when their daughter fell pregnant. Menson was determined to do the right thing by her. Abortion was abhorrence to him, and he didn't learn of Rita's termination until after the event. He regarded it as murder, Mr McCabe, just as I did then and I do now. But Thomas and Beryl were distraught, and I felt that I had to ease their distress. How easy it is to do the wrong thing for the right reason. It was all too much for John Menson. He went on a drug-fuelled journey from which he never returned.'

The John Menson of the 1960s was someone McCabe would like to have known. He said quietly, 'That is a very sad story, Doctor Ronan.'

'It's one that continually plays on my mind, Mr McCabe. My wrong act as a physician is equally, if not more to blame for John Menson's mental breakdown as the drugs.' Recovering a little from his misery, Ronan said, by way of an apology, 'But I am wrong to involve you in my self-pity. Is the rumour that Hartley was responsible for Rita Jenkins's condition your reason for asking about him?'

'Not exactly,' McCabe confessed. 'I was going to enquire if Hartley had ever made an approach to you on the subject of abortion?'

'How on earth do you find out about obscure matters such as this? Hartley was a womanizer, and he did have reason to telephone me on the subject of abortion.'

'He didn't reveal on whose behalf he was enquiring?'

'No, I assumed it was his own,' Ronan replied. 'I gave him short shrift, of course. No doubt he had caused some poor girl grief.'

McCabe had got what he had called on the elderly doctor for. Hartley would have had to return to the Merrill father and son with the bad news. But it saddened him. Everything he experienced in Abbeyfield was tinged with sorrow. Was it so because he was wandering through the eerie dark tunnel between the past and the present?

He walked slowly away. Pausing at the gate to look back, he saw Doctor Ronan working on the portrait again, holding a long brush in the stance of an *en garde* fencer. He doubted that the old man had noticed him leave.

'If I do something for you, Gerry, will you promise to return the favour?'

An unsmiling Sharee asked the question as they stood together in the entrance to the function room of Kilverham's only hotel. It was a spacious room, plain and unadorned, but able to reflect and hold the congenial atmosphere. Other guests were covertly eyeing them. McCabe assumed that they knew Sharee well, and were curious about him. The serious way Sharee had asked the question made him fear that she was thinking of coercing him into some sort of commitment. He would permit nothing to menace his reconciliation with Carol.

'I don't want to make any rash promises, Sharee,' he replied cautiously.

'You idiot,' she chided him laughingly. 'All that I'm saying is that I have some influence here. I can arrange for us to be seated at Ambrose Merrill's table.'

This was more, much more, than McCabe had hoped for. At a meeting he'd had with Peter Rendall that afternoon, the police superintendent had come close to being hostile. Rendall's suggestion that McCabe should 'leave well alone', collect his money from the colonel and return to London had been ener-gized by fear of the possibility of a backlash. At no time while he was at the police station had McCabe seen Solomon Quinn. When he had enquired about Quinn's whereabouts, Rendall had replied that the detective inspector was busy. Having intended to show Rendall the evidence he had of a serious relationship between Roland Merrill and Suzi Duoard, his cold reception at the police station made McCabe postpone the idea.

Denied the co-operation of the police he had decided to employ unorthodox methods to ensure Sylvester Hartley's pros-ecution and ensnare Merrill for murder.

'What is the favour you want in return?' he asked, now a little more at ease.

'Just that you at least combine business with pleasure,' Sharee answered. 'I want us to enjoy this evening. Which mode are you in, 1969 or 2005?'

'I suppose that I'm stuck somewhere in between,' he confessed.

'Where do you place Beth Merrill?'

'Simply as the daughter of my client.'

'You are pants as a liar, Gerard McCabe,' Sharee criticized him smilingly.

She took his arm as they entered the room. The buzz of conversation gained volume. Sharee was greeted from all sides as they passed through a throng of people waiting to be seated for dinner.

'Please point Ambrose Merrill out to me should he appear,' McCabe requested.

'You are going to be sorely disappointed, that's for sure,' Sharee informed him.

'Why?'

'You are expecting some kind of ogre; the Creature from the Black Lagoon,' Sharee explained with a wry smile. 'I've always found Mr Merrill to be polite, although in a remote kind of way. He is absolutely devoted to his wife. She's very ill now, and he spends every available minute with her.'

This unexpected character reference didn't shake McCabe's resolve. He said, 'Thanks for the information, Sharee.'

'I hope that it has helped.'

'It has pushed me closer to 2005.'

'Good, so now get closer to me.'

McCabe was guiding Sharee through the crowd when he saw Peter Rendall coming towards them, in evening dress and with his steel-framed glasses completing an image of sophistication. Catching sight of McCabe stopped Rendall in his tracks.

'Mr McCabe,' Rendall smiled warmly. 'I didn't expect to see you here. Have you bought yourself a pub?'

Amused by the unexpected joke from the normally dour Rendall, McCabe introduced Sharee. 'I didn't need to. This is Sharee Bucholz, landlady of the Fox and Hounds, Superintendent.'

Rendall introduced them to his wife, a tall, greying woman, and then Sharee excused herself. Telling McCabe she would only be a few minutes, she left them. At the same time, Mrs Rendall turned away to speak to an elderly couple who had come up to her.

'Let me offer a few words of friendly advice, Mr McCabe,' Rendall said conversationally, his aloofness of that afternoon now absent. 'Be extremely careful to whom you mention the name Sylvester Hartley this evening. Better still, don't speak the name at all.'

'If I do, I will be discreet,' McCabe replied.

'Please take care.' Rendall added a final caution as his wife and Sharee returned simultaneously.

'You are going to be pleased with me,' Sharee murmured, smiling at McCabe as they left the Rendalls. 'Although I couldn't work the ultimate miracle of having you sit at the right hand of the local god.'

'But?' McCabe questioned, desperate for her to have secured seats for them at Ambrose Merrill's table. He wanted to press home the advantage that Sylvester Hartley had unknowingly given him.

'Wait for it,' she said teasingly. 'You will be sitting next to Merrill, on his left.'

This news elated McCabe. 'I don't know how you did it, Sharee, but I can't tell you how grateful I am.'

'We're all going to the zoo tomorrow,' Sharee meaningfully

sang the first line of a Julie Felix song before looking questioningly at him.

'I don't know that one, but it sounds like an oldie,' McCabe told her, aware that he was being tested. 'After all, this is 2005.'

Laughing, she said. 'That's what I wanted to hear. Come on, I've asked Cecil Yelton, who keeps the George Inn here in Kilvereham, to introduce you to Merrill.'

Grey hair naturally wavy, Ambrose Merrill had a tendency towards obesity that his skeleton hadn't been designed to support. His flesh seemed to sag from his bones. He dressed well, but the quality of his suit was negated by his poor physique. Ageing in a couple is rarely synchronized. The husband usually fares better that the wife, and this was very true with the Merrills. White-haired, Mrs Merrill, despite showing the indelible marks of a terminal illness, was a pleasant woman. She had a motherly look that painfully reminded McCabe that what he was planning would ruin yet more local lives.

When Yelton, a Danny DeVito look-alike, introduced Sharee and McCabe, Merrill accepted the introduction in the distanced manner of someone bored with continually having to suffer social formalities. His reedy voice was intellectual but burred slightly by a West Country accent.

McCabe suspected that Merrill had forgotten both Sharee and him the moment he had turned away. Neither did the local celebrity speak or pay any attention to McCabe throughout dinner. But when the meal had ended and the diners had endured a succession of lacklustre speeches, Merrill did a quarter turn in his chair to look sideways at McCabe through baggy, sunken-in eyes. Smoking a cigar, he had a comfortable halo of smoke above his head. He took off his glasses with a practised, gentlemanly gesture.

'Please do forgive me if I appear to have been rude,' Ambrose Merrill apologized. 'Mrs Merrill finds these occasions to be quite demanding at present. Nevertheless, she still likes to socialize as often as possible. Consequently, I like to pay attention to her.'

Merrill's consideration for his wife supported what Sharee had said earlier, but refused to fit together with the image McCabe had formed of the man. He managed to say, 'I fully understand, Mr Merrill.'

'Most gracious,' Merrill said. 'Would you be kind enough to extend my apology to your lady.'

Hearing this, Sharee leaned forward to smile politely at Merrill and he smiled back. A surprisingly warm smile from so obviously cold a man.

'Quite a splendid meal I thought,' he said.

'Most enjoyable,' McCabe concurred.

'You are this detective chappie who discovered the body of a girl buried on Colonel Farquahar's estate,' Merrill stated rather than enquired. 'It was a terrible shock for everyone. A young life wasted.'

'Two lives, Mr Merrill,' McCabe said. 'The dead girl was pregnant.'

Realizing his error caused Merrill to gasp, 'Of course. Do you know, probably because I haven't really recovered from first hearing the awful news, I overlooked that. I fully accept that you were acting in your professional capacity when you made this gruesome discovery, but I feel it would be better had it never come to light.'

'I don't follow you, Mr Merrill.'

McCabe had to wait for a response from Merrill, due to the tables being cleared. A quartet played soft, sweet music from a niche that could double as a stage, and most of the diners were moving out on to the dance floor.

'Well,' Merrill spoke hesitantly, 'it happened so long ago, and we were literally swamped by an army of anarchists at the time.'

'Let sleeping dogs lie, in other words?'

'Perhaps not the phraseology I would have chosen, Mr McCabe, but that is the gist of it. The girl was one of our itinerant population of those days, as was the person responsible for her death, I don't doubt.'

'Most probably,' McCabe agreed. 'But we are compiling a short list of local males who knew the girl.'

'We?' a poker-faced Merrill questioned.

'I have been working with the local police.'

'It pleases me that they have helped you,' Merrill said. 'I must say, from experience that I have nothing but immense admiration and respect for the local force.'

Noticing that Merrill's wife was trying to attract his attention, McCabe realized that time was running short. Needing to introduce Sylvester Hartley into the conversation, he said, 'They have been most helpful, and I'm sure that when—'

Merrill interrupted him. 'I do beg your pardon, Mr McCabe. Please do forgive me.'

Turning away, the old man was pouring a glass of water for his wife. Disappointed, McCabe joined Sharee as she stood up. She smiled at him. 'Maybe now we can start enjoying ourselves, Gerry.'

'Up to a point.'

'You coward,' she chided him with a laugh. 'I suppose that if I buy you a drink later you'll suspect I'm planning a date rape.'

'That possibility is certain to occur to me,' he said with feigned gravity, making her laugh gaily as she led him on to the dance floor as the small band struck up a waltz.

'I'm no great dancer, but I can manage a slow number like this,' she warned him.

The lights dimmed for the beginning of the dance. Despite her modesty, Sharee was a good dancer but, like McCabe, their agreed truce in their relationship made her hold her body stiff and distanced. As they moved rhythmically to the brilliance of Irving Berlin, their tension slowly unwound. Sharee danced with her head held high. Her looks and full figure, shown to advantage by a white sheath dress, attracted the attention of the couples gliding across the dance floor. McCabe felt vibrant and alive holding her.

'Well?' she enquired. 'What was your impression of Ambrose Merrill?'

'The jury is still out,' he replied truthfully.

'I'm not prying, Gerry, but you didn't seem to have the chance to talk with him at any length.'

'No, but we might be able to have a drink with him later.'

Though that had been McCabe's original intention, its appeal was fading fast. Every time he thought of pinning Ambrose Merrill down and frightening him by mentioning Sylvester Hartley, he had an image of Mrs Merrill's illness-wearied face.

When the music stopped and the lights came up, he was very

aware of Sharee's watchful brown eyes on him. They held their dance embrace for a few seconds too long before breaking away from each other jerkily.

The failure of McCabe's Ambrose Merrill plan faded into insignificance in the realization of the many temptations the rest of the evening would hold.

'This is dangerous ground,' Sharee warned herself aloud, as McCabe drove through the moonlit night.

'Just a quiet country road,' he observed, deliberately misunderstanding her.

She was as aware as he was that it was easier to talk while he was driving. The lack of eye contact made it less intimate. She shrugged, a gesture wasted in the darkness. 'I suppose that joking is one way to get through it.'

There had been no opportunity for McCabe to speak with Ambrose Merrill again. It had been Sharee, the odd brightness in her eyes and plainly as aware as he was of the temptation they were both about to face, that had filled his mind. Now that they were alone together in the night, he guessed that she shared his feeling that they were heading towards the inevitable.

The bubbly Sharee had been great to be with at the social gathering. It perplexed McCabe that the two of them found it so easy, so natural, to be in each other's company. Concerned by his quietness now, she asked, 'What's troubling you, Gerry? I understand your situation, and I'm not expecting any commitment from you.'

The December moon reached down into the car to touch her face. It was beautiful, almost mystically so, in its desire. Head back, eyes closed, she could have been thinking of another time, another place, but McCabe knew that she wasn't. A row of cottages that they drove past was mostly dark, a reminder of how late it was. A sign reading "Lay-by ½ mile ahead" reflected in the car's headlights. Hating himself and dreading the consequences, McCabe felt his resolve ebbing fast. Though it was too soon for him to reduce the car's speed, Sharee seemed to pick up telepathically on his intention.

'No, Gerry,' she said. Reaching out she placed her hand on his, and he liked the touch of her fingers, and knew what she was thinking. 'That isn't a no in capital letters. It just isn't a good idea. The back seat of a car would make it cheap, tawdry.'

'So?' McCabe asked, his scalp tingling electrically.

'Jenny will be staying over for the night.' Sharee stretched her arm so as to read her wristwatch in the dim light from the dashboard. 'She'll have cleared up and be settled in her room by now. That's all I'm saying, Gerry. The decision is yours.'

She had made it sound fair and simple. But McCabe knew that the situation was both complicated and hazardous. There was no conversation for the remainder of the journey, and he practised mind control by employing thoughts and images of his wife and daughter. By the time they reached the pub he had regained some of his reasoning powers. But it was a fragile arrangement. A man's conscience was the first casualty in the battle of the sexes.

thirteen

The interior of the pub was in darkness as the wheels of McCabe's car left the metalled road for the crunching gravel of the car-park. Sharee gave a little frightened gasp as they saw a motor-cycle under the exterior light over the pub's door. There was a figure sitting sideways on the machine, waiting. The motorcyclist stood up as McCabe drove closer to the door. Facing them, blinking in the car's headlights, was the massively built Abb Perkins.

'Does this mean trouble?' Sharee asked worriedly.

'Not for you, Sharee,' McCabe replied. 'Come on, I'll see you inside and then I'll find out what it is Perkins wants.'

'Will you be all right, Gerry?'

'Don't worry about me,' McCabe said, as he guided her past Perkins to the door.

With Sharee safely inside and the door shut behind her, McCabe walked up to the big man. They stared at each other, not speaking. Ready for anything, McCabe issued a challenge. 'Make your move, Perkins.'

'No, no, you've got it wrong,' Perkins said quietly, shaking his head. His arm was no longer in a sling. 'I'm here about John-John.'

'What about him?'

'He went missing early this morning, and I'm really worried.'

'Was he in a worse state than usual?' McCabe asked, surprised that a brutish man such as Perkins could be worried about another human being, particularly an outsider like John Menson.

'No, that's the strange thing, McCabe. He was upset about something, but he was more normal than I have ever known him to be.'

'But he didn't say where he was going?'

'He didn't. I know that you care about him, and thought that where you have connections with the police, you might be able to find him.'

'There isn't much I can do tonight, Perkins,' McCabe said. 'But leave it to me. I'll get on to it first thing in the morning.'

'Thank you,' Perkins said, turning to his motor cycle, then coming back to face McCabe. He spoke hesitantly, almost boyishly. 'I know this is asking a lot, McCabe, but could I shake your hand?'

'Why would you want to do that?'

'Because you have given me every reason to respect you,' Perkins answered sheepishly.

Something instinctive in McCabe made him hold out his hand without hesitation. The big man smiled and took McCabe's hand in a warm handshake. Then he put on his crash helmet, gave McCabe a friendly pat on the shoulder, and started up the motor-cycle.

Standing in the doorway of the pub, McCabe watched the bike go out of the car-park on to the road. Desperately in need of thinking time, he stayed watching until the machine went over a distant hill and its lights were swallowed up by the night. Then he went reluctantly inside, closing the door behind him. His earlier upbeat mood had been changed completely by his encounter with Abb Perkins.

Finding Sharee in the kitchen, McCabe stood in the doorway, somehow unable to enter the room. She looked searchingly at his face, her eyes slightly unfocused. Then her glance fell away.

'Would you like some coffee?' she asked.

He hesitated, wondering exactly where lay the borderline that he shouldn't cross. Walking slowly into the kitchen he said, 'Yes please.'

She made them instant coffee and placed two mugs on the table.

'You have no need to say anything, Gerry,' she said, then stared off into space as if unaware that he was there.

His hands round the hot mug remained cold. 'I'm sorry, Sharee.'

Though she managed a slow, weak smile, dejection crossed her pale face like a quick shadow.

McCabe left the pub on a morning that was cold and made ugly by a dirty grey sky. Anxiety over John-John Menson and a need to avoid facing Sharee prompted him to leave early. The opportunity to resurrect his marriage was intact, but his behaviour in encouraging Sharee and then rejecting her had been more than unfair.

He had driven less than a mile through the dawn when his mobile phone bleeped. A disgruntled Solomon Quinn was the caller. He had heard from Inspector Mike Sterne that Menson was at the Fenton police station causing trouble. McCabe explained that he knew Menson had gone missing, and was driving to the scrap-yard to see if he had returned home.

'Forget that and make haste to Fenton, Gerry.' Quinn said. 'They've got your pet nutter in a cell. Have you told him anything about Heaney?'

'Not a thing.'

'That's odd. He knows that Piers Heaney is really Sylvester Hartley, and he's shouting it to the rooftops. That's likely to have everything about Hartley explode in our faces.'

'Not in my face, Sol,' McCabe pointed out.

'This isn't a time to gloat, Gerry. Get Menson back to his hovel of a caravan before he can do any further damage.'

'I'm on my way, and I'll do my best, Sol.'

'Thanks,' Quinn said, then suddenly sounded contrite. 'I really had no right to ask you to help, Gerry, after refusing to give you back-up with the Hartley thing.'

'Don't let it bother you. I place a high value on friendship,' McCabe said sarcastically.

Anticipating humility and gratitude as a response from Quinn, McCabe told himself that he should have known better. The policeman switched off his phone without uttering another word.

Doing a three-point-turn on a long stretch of deserted road, McCabe jabbed his foot hard on the accelerator as he drove off in the direction of Fenton.

*

Fenton police station was a large, ugly building with grey stone walls. The year 1882 was carved in the keystone over the arched door. Due to the building's crumbling state of disrepair, this was more an apology than a boast. The age-discoloured dial of the wall clock behind the desk-sergeant's desk told McCabe that it was 9.30. Some fault with the central heating made it as cold inside as it was outside, possibly colder. The sergeant behind the desk didn't look happy about still having his outdoor clothing on. He studied McCabe suspiciously when he asked to see DI Sterne.

'May I ask in what connection, sir?' the sergeant enquired.

'My name is McCabe,' he explained. 'DI Solomon Quinn at Kilverham was in contact with DI Sterne earlier this morning, so he will be expecting me.'

Picking up an in-house telephone, the sergeant asked for DI Sterne, nodded his head to whomever he was speaking, then shook it for McCabe's benefit as he replaced the receiver. 'Detective Inspector Sterne is not in his office.'

'Any idea where he might be, Sergeant?'

'Could be anywhere …' The sergeant shrugged, then looked across at the street door as it opened. 'Here he is now. Someone to see you, Mike.'

Dark-skinned, smartly attired in a suit of dark-grey material, Mike Sterne had a heavy-set body, and the look of a mobster from America's prohibition days. He glanced at McCabe, his eyes impatient and impersonal, before approaching him.

'Mr McCabe, I take it?' he said, grasping McCabe's hand.

'Pleased to meet you,' McCabe responded. 'I'm not sure what I'm doing here.'

'Hopefully to relieve us of the clown that Sol Quinn calls John the Baptist,' Sterne said. 'He doesn't exactly preach peace and goodwill, Mr McCabe.'

Waiving aside the formalities, McCabe said, 'Make it Gerry. I've never found John-John to be an in-your-face kind of guy.'

'Then he must have switched over to his *alter ego* when he arrived here,' Sterne said with a grimace. 'Come on up to my office and I'll bring you up to speed.'

As McCabe followed him up a flight of wide stairs, Sterne

turned his head to use excuse the dilapidated building. 'We should be moving out of here early next year. They are building the new station about a mile out. What's with this modern idea of building supermarkets and police stations outside of towns?'

'Probably to make the former more accessible and the latter less accessible to the public,' McCabe suggested.

'A cynical theory, but no doubt accurate, ' Sterne commented, as he ushered McCabe into a small unoccupied office and pulled out a chair for him. The room was cold and the distempered grey walls were depressingly monotonous.

Sterne took the seat behind a bulky wooden desk from the era of gaslight and Neville Chamberlain stand-up shirt collars, and riffled uninterestedly through some unopened mail. He crossed his legs, then straightened them again. Two pre-World War II radiators in the room made a series of explosive sounds.

'We didn't have enough on Piers Heaney to charge him as a supplier, but we've got him on intent to supply.'

'Which hardly qualifies him as Public Enemy Number One,' McCabe remarked sarcastically.

Sterne argued defensively, 'That's true, but it's just as the Kilverham lot wanted it to be. He would have stood trial as Piers Heaney and been sentenced as Piers Heaney.'

'But not now?' McCabe raised one eyebrow.

Sterne shook his head slowly and regretfully. 'That would have been the end of the story had that latter-day Elijah not come bursting in here ranting on about Heaney's real identity being Sylvester Hartley.'

'No one ever takes any notice of a word that John-John Menson says,' McCabe advised.

'Maybe that's true on Sol Quinn's patch, Gerry, but it's the talk of the station here. This guy may be a nutter, but he makes sense. The *Fenton Herald* will be running the story by teatime. Imagine how it will make us look. And that's not all. Your crazy friend claims that Hartley was involved in the Duoard murder.'

'He couldn't have been. Sol Quinn says Hartley was in London at the time.'

Sterne apologized. 'He said that Hartley was *involved* in the murder. I took that to mean that Hartley knows who the killer was.'

'That's possible,' McCabe nodded. Menson had certainly put the proverbial cat among the pigeons by coming here to Fenton. Hartley had agreed only to keep silent as long as his true identity remained concealed.

'What happens now?' Sterne asked worriedly.

With a shrug, McCabe said, 'The Kilverham lot won't be able to keep the lid on the Hartley thing now.'

'That's obvious,' Sterne groaned. 'But you were in the job, and you know how these things work. The buck in a cover-up stops with the guy at the bottom of the heap. In this case it's me that's the patsy. Police work makes good televiewing, but the real thing is all a fat fake.'

McCabe could sympathize with Sterne in his bitterness. As the arresting officer in the Piers Heaney case, he would be held responsible for concealing his prisoner's true identity. The anonymous people who arrange these things would make Sterne pay for the failure.

'They might give you the opportunity to retire early due to ill health,' McCabe suggested.

'They might not,' Sterne commented realistically.

McCabe enquired, 'What do you want me to do with Menson?'

'There's only one thing you can do.' Sterne's eyes tightened for a moment.

'You mean some way of shifting the blame to someone in Kilverham?'

'Exactly,' Sterne exclaimed, instantly brightening.

Disappointing him, McCabe said, 'I know of no way of helping. You're on your own in this, Mike.'

'Then get him out of here quick,' Sterne urged. 'I'll get one of the uniform lads to fetch your car round to the back door, and you can smuggle him out that way. I won't have him using the front desk as an altar.'

'John-John isn't that bad,' McCabe defended his strange new friend. 'His is a pretty sad story.'

'And he's made sure that mine is going to be the same,' Sterne complained.

*

There was no space for small talk between the two of them. A melancholy Menson had remained silent from the time when McCabe had collected him from a cell until they had travelled five miles out of Fenton in the direction of Abbeyfield. Not having had breakfast, McCabe was hungry. But the thought of pulling into a roadside café with a robed John-John as a companion was prohibitive. Passing through a village, he pulled up at a small shop and bought sandwiches for them both. Guessing that Menson would be a vegetarian; McCabe got him cheese and tomato.

It was then, with fingers gripping the bread so hard that tomato squashed out juicily to drop on his robe, soiling it, he spoke mumblingly, with his mouth full. 'I fear that I may have hindered your work in some way, Mr McCabe.'

'No, John-John, you possibly did me a favour,' McCabe said, grateful that his companion was coherent.

'Suzi was a close friend of mine, you see,' Menson continued, as he ate. 'She was a very special person, Mr McCabe. When we first met, a very long time ago now, it was in mysterious circumstances. I still remember that time well. It was a moonless night. Drawn by the light of my camp-fire, she had come drifting out of the blackness like a ghost.

'In all the years I knew her, Suzi never spoke of where she had come from that night. Her past forever remained a mystery, but she surely must have lived a grand way of life, for she was filled with knowledge that can't be got from books.'

'You sound as if you loved her,' an intrigued McCabe remarked.

'I did,' John-John replied quietly, 'but not in the usual sense of that word. It would be a sin to love an angel in that way, and Suzi Duoard truly was an angel. That is why the man who ended her life must be brought to justice.'

'Roland Merrill.'

No longer staring at the sky, Menson jerked his head round to look at McCabe. He said, 'You know. I sensed that you did. What does this do to Beth Farquahar and yourself?'

Astounded by how acute was Menson's perception despite the long hours he spent in a rambling disoriented state, McCabe parried the question. 'There is no Beth and myself, John-John. I shall be shortly returning to London, where my life is.'

'But where will your heart be?' Menson shrugged, but that simple gesture implied much.

This was a question that McCabe didn't want to hear, let alone answer. Still feeling uncomfortable about his situation with Sharee, Beth was coming into his mind more and more as his departure from Abbeyfield drew nearer. He objected mildly to what Menson had said. 'We are supposed to be discussing Roland Merrill, not me. Sylvester Hartley can point to him as Suzi's murderer, isn't that so?'

'Assuredly.'

'But what if he doesn't?'

Menson's dark-blue eyes turned black as he looked at McCabe. Yet despite this odd feature he answered sensibly. 'Then I hold evidence that will beyond a doubt prove that Merrill killed poor Suzi.'

'How long have you held this evidence?'

'Since before Suzi disappeared.'

'Then why ...' McCabe began, 'haven't you passed this evidence to the police before this?'

'There was nothing to show that Suzi was dead, Mr McCabe. It was possible that she had walked out of my life in the same mysterious way she had entered it. At the time I was seriously and sadly involved with another girl, but I have been planning to avenge Suzi's death from the moment you discovered her body.'

'I am not being disrespectful, John-John,' McCabe ventured, 'but where does "Vengeance is mine saith the Lord" come into this?'

'This will be the Lord's vengeance, Mr McCabe, as I believe that He is working through me.'

Stumped by this, McCabe changed tack. 'What is this evidence, John-John?'

'The letters that Merrill wrote to Suzi. She gave them all to me for safekeeping. The last ones refer to her pregnancy and his proposed solution to the problem.'

'Which was?'

'An abortion,' Menson replied dully.

'That's really something,' McCabe exclaimed, barely able to breathe.

'I realize that, Mr McCabe, but how can I persuade someone to listen to me?'

'I can make the police listen,' McCabe assured him.

Considering this for a few moments, Menson then spoke dubiously. 'That would entail me passing the letters over to you.'

'It will only be necessary to use them if Sylvester Hartley doesn't shop Merrill, which I feel sure that he will. I'd take great care of them, John-John.'

'Oh, I trust you completely, Mr McCabe,' Menson assured him. 'But what if the police refuse to give them back to you?'

'That won't happen, I promise you that, John-John. One of the senior officers at Kilverham is a good friend of mine. He will ensure that the letters are returned to me.'

'Then when we get back to Abbeyfield I will hand them over to you,' Menson said.

Elated by this, McCabe started the engine and moved his car away. Eager to get Menson to his caravan before he could return to his usual muddled mental state, McCabe's high spirits took a dive from the high board as a sudden thought hit him. Bringing the killer of Suzi Duoard to justice had been such an overwhelming prospect that he had temporarily overlooked what it would do to Beth. It was plain that any true feelings she may have held for Roland Merrill had long since fled, but it would be a terrible blow for her to learn that she had shared her life with a murderer.

The problem of Beth increased, causing McCabe real trouble on the journey along country roads. He would have to call to see her that evening, but what could he tell her? Where could he find the words to convey to her the enormity of the trauma she would suffer shortly?

Slowing the car to make a sharp turn to the left, causing the tyres to squeal, McCabe drove up on to the grass verge. On each side of them green-velvet hills rolled and tumbled away. Switching off the engine, McCabe looked down. Below them buildings of a village were pink and ugly and unfledged, like young birds in a crowded nest. The sight made him long for the familiar London environment. It made him hate the ghastly ugliness and cruelty of country life, and pine for his wife and daughter. Menson's voice cut in on his morbid thoughts.

'The only way is to tell her the truth in the least hurtful way, Mr McCabe.'

With his amazing perception akin to mind reading, Menson was aware that he was troubled by Beth. McCabe said glumly. 'There isn't a least hurtful way to tell her, John-John.'

'The most injurious, the most callous thing you could do is not prepare her for the inevitable.'

Menson was right: McCabe had no choice. He had to go to Abbeyfield Manor that night and tell Beth that her husband would soon be revealed as a murderer. Turning the ignition key, he reversed the car out on to the road. Pulling away so violently that the rear wheels of the vehicle spun and kicked up loose gravel, he headed for Abbeyfield.

The determination showing in the set of his features masked the quaking dread that he felt deep inside.

Casually dressed in a short, blue-denim skirt and a white blouse tied round her bare waist, just under the outstanding curve of her breasts, Beth's whole attitude was slightly nervous. Arranging flowers in a tall vase to create effortlessly a fabulous explosion of brilliant colours, concentration accentuated her high patrician cheekbones. The lounge was as shiny and bright as a temple of faith, with icons that were ornaments and heirlooms and pictures lovingly displayed. It was alien to McCabe. But being with Beth bridged the chasm between this world and the one he inhabited.

'Do you mind if I don't disturb my father, Gerry?' she asked. 'He's had a trying day.'

'That's OK, Beth. It's you that I've come to see.'

She studied him as if trying to predict his reaction to what she was about to say. 'In that case, can I postpone playing the perfect hostess and suggest that we go to the pub for a drink. We can talk there.'

Her suggestion appealed to McCabe. It would be easier to say what he had to tell her when among other people. But there were risks involved. Sharee was likely to get the impression that he was on an ego trip flaunting a relationship with Beth in front of her. Roland Merrill was likely to present the greatest problem if he found Beth and him together.

'What about your husband, Beth?'

'The carol service is tomorrow night, and he's out making the final arrangements,' she answered. McCabe noticed that her eyes were bright and smoky at the same time, hiding the thoughts behind them. 'He won't know and probably wouldn't care if he did.'

'Do you still suspect that he's playing away?'

'I'm not sure, and since earlier this evening I am past caring.'

'It's none of my business, but what was different about earlier today?' McCabe ventured, recognizing this as a crucial moment. When they had reached his caravan, John-John had passed him Merrill's love letters to Suzi Duoard, and they were damning.

'It is your business,' she responded with a wry smile. 'It has been since my father engaged your services. For your sins, Gerry, you became part of this dysfunctional family the day you arrived at the manor. Roland had changed for the better recently. Then he returned home from work this evening in a terrible state. I don't think that he spoke two words, either to me or my father, between coming home and going out again.'

'Probably he's under pressure at work,' McCabe falsely suggested.

He guessed that the truth was that Merrill had become easier to live with on being assured that Sylvester Hartley presented no danger to him. Then today he must have been warned that the situation had been radically changed by John-John Menson's intervention.

'Whatever,' Beth shrugged. 'I need a break from this place tonight. If I take my Land-Rover and you go in your car, you won't have to come all the way back out here, Gerry.'

Realizing that by this time Roland Merrill's mind was unlikely to be stable, McCabe couldn't allow Beth to return to the manor alone late at night. Particularly as it was possible Merrill would learn they had been out together.

Not wanting to alarm her, he told her, 'I wouldn't dream of not seeing a lady home.'

'You, Gerry McCabe, are an absolute gentleman.'

'You may have to change your mind before the evening is out,' he warned.

'I do hope so,' she quipped, with more than a touch of her old flippancy. 'If you trust my driving, we'll take mine. Just give me a minute to fetch my coat.'

'What would you say if I told you it's not what you think?' McCabe asked an unhappy Sharee, after he had seated Beth at a table and come up to the bar.

'That's the first thing anyone caught doing naughties comes up with,' she replied.

'Believe me, Sharee,' he said earnestly, 'I'd rather be anywhere doing anything tonight, than have to be here with Beth because of what I have to tell her.'

'You don't have to explain yourself to me, Gerry.'

'I want to, Sharee.'

He could tell that she accepted that he was being honest, and the look they exchanged as he left the bar gratified him.

'Sharee looks sad tonight,' Beth remarked, who had slipped into a morbid mood soon after they had driven away from the manor. 'I suppose that it's to do with her memories of a Christmas past. What a world this is, Gerry! There's Sharee living with a ghost that she desperately wishes was the husband she once had, and me living with a husband I don't want and desperately wish was a ghost.'

'That's a depressing, if not macabre, way of looking at things.'

'I shouldn't have asked you to take me out tonight, Gerry,' she said apologetically. 'I'm abysmal company. Worry over Katrina got us all involved in trying to recapture that past, and we dragged you into it the moment you arrived in Abbeyfield. The nostalgia game is a dangerous one, Gerry. The present always colours the past, and you're likely to finish up ruining the future.'

'That's most profound, Beth,' he complimented her.

'There's nothing clever about me. If I was brighter I'd have stopped all this nonsense before it started.' Pausing to sip her drink, she changed the subject. 'What was it you wanted to speak to me about?'

McCabe paused, for too long. Beth had given him the perfect opening by speaking of Sharee's tragedy and her own marital unhappiness. But he had let the moment slip past. Cursing himself for his abject cowardice, he said, 'I just wanted to say that I think the time will soon be right to persuade Katrina to come home. I make no promises, of course. Maybe then you and I can find a way to have the colonel consider letting your mother return to the manor.'

'That would be wonderful,' Beth exclaimed, her face lightening. 'Do you think that will be soon?'

'Depends whether all goes well tomorrow,' McCabe replied, momentarily caught off guard.

'What's happening tomorrow, Gerry?'

'Just some odds and ends I have to tidy up,' he fibbed, aware that she hadn't been fooled by his answer. He went on, 'Possibly the day after I will be going up to London. With luck, I will be able to call on your mother and Katrina with some firm proposals.'

'I do hope so, Gerry,' she said. 'It is good of you to go to all this trouble. It's above and beyond the call of duty, as it were.'

'A little bonus for the colonel, Beth.'

'He's likely not to thank you for it,' she cautioned.

'At least I'll have tried.'

The bar had become more crowded. Several locals came over to their table to speak to Beth, and there was always someone within earshot to prevent McCabe from broaching the main subject. He was honest enough with himself to admit that he probably wouldn't have had the nerve to do so if the two of them had been isolated from the other drinkers.

Beth had loosened up a little more with each drink, and they passed the rest of the evening with small talk. When they left to walk to the car, she became quiet and reserved once more, although her depression of earlier did not return.

She spoke little on the return journey, but on entering the manor gates she slowed the Land-Rover and looked at McCabe to ask, 'What is it that you really want to say to me, Gerry?'

'I'm not sure that this is the right time, or even if it is my place to do so.'

Pulling up outside the door of the manor, Beth applied the handbrake and switched off the engine. Doing a quarter turn towards him in her seat, she said in a shaky voice, 'It's about Roland, isn't it.'

He nodded, aware that she was able to see the movement in the dimness. Even with her having half-guessed what he had to tell her, he couldn't bring himself to continue. No woman should have to hear such terrible information about her husband. She prompted him.

'This has something to do with the murder of Suzi Duoard, hasn't it?'

'How on earth could you know that?' McCabe was worried that he had brought up something in Beth that she hadn't suspected was there.

'Intuition, Gerry. I have always relied on it. Please go on.'

Trying to do so, trying hard, McCabe had to admit to himself that he was defeated. 'I'm so sorry, Beth. I just can't bring myself to tell you.'

Staying silent for a long time, not looking at him, she then asked a question, her voice so low that he only just caught her words. 'Was it Roland who killed her?'

Tension built inside of the car as she waited for his answer. After a struggle, he managed a one-word reply. 'Yes.'

At least five minutes must have passed, agonizingly slowly, before either of them uttered another word. It was Beth who spoke first, her voice sounding strange after the prolonged silence.

'I think that I've known since soon after Suzi's body was found,' she said. 'Different little memories starting linking up in my mind to present me with a picture that I just couldn't accept.'

'Can you accept it now?' McCabe enquired sympathetically.

'All I needed was for someone to give me a shove in the right direction.'

'I'm sorry that someone had to be me, Beth.'

'I'm glad it was,' she said. 'I don't know how I feel. It's not that I have any feelings left for Roland, but it's all a terrible shock.'

In the half-light, McCabe could see tears glistening on her cheeks. Automatically reaching out with his right arm, it seemed right when she leaned towards him to bury her face in his shoulder. He heard her sob lightly, then she raised her head to look at him. Something special flashed between them. It was something that neither of them could comprehend. Their lips touched and then parted again. The two of them gazed at each other, each seeking the permission of the other to continue.

As if moved by an invisible force, they came together again. McCabe gave way to a long-held desire, but only momentarily. Terrified of his own lack of willpower, he struggled for common sense to overcome his passion. He was gently moving Beth away in order to break the kiss, when a car swung into the drive. Headlights like sweeping searchlights lit up the interior of the Land-Rover as the car passed by. A startled Beth broke away from McCabe to twist in her seat and look out of the rear window.

'Oh no!' she cried on recognizing the car. 'It's Roland. He's certain to have seen us.'

fourteen

Kilverham's dreary Christmas decorations depressed McCabe as he drove to the police station the next morning. He was tired. Concerned for Beth's safety, he had patrolled outside the manor on foot after she had followed her husband indoors. McCabe hadn't left until the manor lights had been extinguished. Back at the pub a reaction to his first pulse-racing physical contact with Beth had hit him. With sleep elusive, he had telephoned Carol. Icy at first by having been woken up in the early hours, his wife had thawed swiftly. They had talked, becoming closer than they had been in years. It had ended with an agreement that he would return home on 23 December so they could spend Christmas together.

When he had switched off his mobile, Beth had not been so distinct in his mind. But she was there now in the growing morning of a cold December day as he reached the police station. In Quinn's office he immediately sensed something was wrong. Quinn was behind his desk, on an edge of which Peter Rendall was perched like a bespectacled predatory bird. Staring at the ceiling he made a blunt announcement. 'Sylvester Hartley has died in police custody at Fenton. It was death by natural causes.'

'That sounds convenient,' McCabe commented.

Rendall stared stonily at McCabe. His voice droned, as though he were bored, 'You are speaking from your experience in the Met, Mr McCabe. We do things very differently here.'

Giving Rendall a tight little smile, McCabe said, 'Human nature is the same everywhere, Superintendent. What about the *Fenton Herald* story?'

'They pulled it.' Quinn's sombre brown eyes were out of tune with his superior's attitude.

McCabe was appalled. The publicity generated by John-John Menson had been effectively quashed. Justice for Suzi Duoard had died with Hartley. The local slate of shame was to be wiped clean after more than three decades. 'So Hartley's identity wasn't exposed.'

'Whose identity?' Rendall queried, faking bewilderment.

McCabe unzipped his briefcase. 'These records show that Merrill and Suzi Duoard stayed together at a Huddlestone boarding-house on three occasions in 1969.'

'Hmm …' Trying to appear casual, Rendall took the photocopies. Barely glancing at them, he said. 'They occupied separate rooms, which proves nothing.'

'Unsupported, maybe not,' McCabe agreed calmly, producing the last two written letters by Merrill to Suzi Duoard. He passed one to Rendall and the other to Quinn.

An oppressive hush settled on the office. The squeaking of Quinn's chair was a mini-riot. Face expressionless, the policemen read before silently exchanging letters. When they had finished, Rendall sighed a world-weary sigh.

'Obviously Roland Merrill was in the process of arranging an abortion, a criminal offence at the time. We know there was no abortion, so no offence was committed.'

'Merrill wouldn't have been involved unless he was responsible,' McCabe argued.

'Spare me!' Rendall groaned. 'This girl was a hippie, Mr McCabe. They were at it like Bonobo chimpanzees. I don't doubt that Mr Merrill was simply trying to help a girl in distress.'

Experience in the police told McCabe he was up against an officially constructed brick wall. It would be pointless to produce the other letters that proved Merrill and Suzi Duoard were lovers. Rendall walked out of the office, closing the door behind him symbolically loudly.

Quinn took a scrap of paper from a drawer before getting up from his chair. He spoke diffidently. 'I feel bad about Suzi Duoard, Gerry. But I have to do as I'm told by them upstairs.'

'Hearing that makes me thankful that I'm a free agent, Sol.'

Quinn handed McCabe the scrap of paper. 'Ali Westwood rang here asking how to get in touch with you. I wouldn't give her any information. So she left her number for you to call.'

'Thanks.' McCabe took the piece of paper.

Quinn said humbly, 'I'd like to think that we are still friends, Gerry.'

'So would I,' McCabe said enigmatically as he went out of the office.

The rendezvous Ali Westwood arranged on the telephone was The Crown Inn, a dingy establishment. It was lunchtime and space was at a premium. Workers from a nearby building site crowded the bar. Pushing through the throng, McCabe saw her standing alone in a corner.

'White wine, please,' she mouthed silently, in reply to his raised-eyebrows question.

As McCabe ordered for both of them, a small table became vacant. McCabe hurried Ali Westwood and himself to two vacant chairs. She had an elegance that had been absent at their first meeting. But a hard mouth and resentful, indrawn eyes spoiled the image. Eyes that watched him, unblinking.

'I told you that I get to hear things. You know Sylvester Hartley is dead?' She paused for McCabe's affirmative nod. 'Sylvester and I went back a long way, Mr McCabe.'

McCabe said. 'My interest in him ended when he died, Ms Westwood.'

'Everybody calls me Ali.' She gave him a smile that died just as it reached her lips. 'I am sorry I was rude to you before. I was protective of Sylvester, but I can speak freely now.'

'Speak freely about what, Ali?'

Ali Westwood's breath caught in her throat sharply. 'About Suzi, the hippie girl. We met by chance at a beauty contest and became close friends.'

McCabe remarked. 'It must have been a shock for you when we found her body.'

Before answering she opened a cigarette case with long, crimson-tipped fingers; McCabe, refusing with a shake of his head, held out a lighted match. When she put her soft-skinned hand on his as she drew on her cigarette, he was surprised to find that she had warmth. He had anticipated the hand being cold, reptilian. She drew on the cigarette, her look cool and composed.

'Not really.' Head back, she blew a long column of smoke up toward the ceiling. 'I *knew* she was dead. Sylvester was forced to help after she was killed, but he would never be a party to murder.'

'You know about Roland Merrill, Ali?' an intrigued McCabe enquired.

'They told me you were good, and I guessed that you would suss Merrill.' She gave a taut little laugh. 'But you can't prove it. I can, because Sylvester recorded everything meticulously.'

Ali Westwood rose up a little from her chair and pulled down the jacket of her light-blue suit. McCabe noticed her breasts for the first time. If he'd thought of her body before then it had been to consider it as lean and hard-muscled, like a fully trained pugilist. In an instant she had become a woman. Intuitively aware of the effect this had on him, she gave a pleased smile.

'He had something on file against Merrill?' Though McCabe suspected her motive, she was simply an opportunist with style rather than a wicked woman. But she could hold all the trump cards to win the frustrating game he was playing with the police.

Not giving a direct reply, she said, 'You'll need the help of your friend Solomon Quinn. There's a local guy called Red Bundy doing a long stretch at Barrack Square in Gloucester. Get Quinn to pay him a prison visit and ask what job it was Sylvester had lined up for him in 1972. He'll remember, and he will talk. Bundy's due out on parole, Gerry, and he'll need help. Have Quinn tell him that I will see him all right when he gets out.'

'But who is going to believe what a con says?' McCabe spotted another flaw in her plan.

'Leave that to me. Just get Quinn to call on me on his way back from the prison. If you're wondering why I want to help, I'm doing it for Suzi.'

As it was too risky to contact Quinn at the police station, McCabe visited his home at lunchtime. Listening dubiously to McCabe, Quinn had said, 'I can fix a visit to Bundy, but Westwood's a whore, and Red Bundy's a low-life.'

'Nevertheless, I've a gut feeling about this, Sol.'

Shaking his head slowly in disbelief at his own stupidity, Quinn had surrendered. 'I must be mad, but I'll do it. But not if Bundy doesn't want to play, or Westwood's evidence is crap.'

'That's understood, Sol.'

'Don't call us, we'll call you,' Quinn had advised. 'Pete Rendall has you off-limits.'

Stella solved this problem. 'We'll see you at the carol service. Sol has agreed to go.'

'My first mistake, Gerry,' Quinn had moaned. 'Agreeing to your request is my second.'

'I'm sorry about this, Doctor,' McCabe apologized, as Ronan turned into Perkins's scrap-yard.

'Don't worry, Mr McCabe. I'm pleased that you care about this poor fellow.'

Coming out of his caravan, Menson called out a question. 'Were we not afflicted by the woes of this world, would we foolishly believe that we are living in paradise?'

'Oh dear,' Doctor Ronan sighed.

'What is the link between what we love and what we hate?' Menson asked, as he came up to bend towards their car and look in at them. 'Have we a desperate need to love what we hate and hate what we love?'

Leaning forward slightly to peer into the rear of the car. Menson's eyes widened alarmingly. McCabe turned his head. The cloth cover had slipped down from the portrait of Rita standing upright on the back seat. The shadows inside the car had brought the portrait eerily alive. Rita Pavely's eyes were staring into the eyes of a quivering John-John Menson.

Lips moving soundlessly, John-John backed slowly away. There was a shock wave of silence in the car that beat against McCabe like a storm-force wind. John-John crumpled down on to the stony ground and lay there. McCabe rushed to lift him to his feet. Menson spoke in a strangled voice, 'Deep inside me it has been easy to live back in those days. But now that has been taken from me.'

Ronan enquired in a semi-professional tone, 'Why do you say that, John-John?'

'Because, Doctor Ronan, the spirit of the girl that I loved; the mother of my never-to-be-born child, has just emerged from the past into the present.'

McCabe asked, 'Can we help you to your caravan?'

'Thank you. No, Mr McCabe. No offence, but I'd like to be alone for a while.'

Watching Menson walk slowly back to his caravan, and climb the steps unsteadily, McCabe asked, 'What do you make of that, Doctor Ronan?'

'It's difficult to say,' Ronan replied. 'John-John has sustained a severe shock that will probably have one of two possible reactions.'

'Kill or cure,' McCabe gloomily predicted.

'A somewhat extreme prognosis, Mr McCabe,' the old doctor reasoned. 'Though an improvement is possible, I think that the chance of a complete recovery is unrealistic. Now, shall we deliver this painting of mine and pray that it will not be the cause of any further trauma?'

An emotional Ryan Pavely had been ecstatic over the gift of the portrait. On the return journey, a delighted Ronan chattered incessantly about Ryan's response. When they reached the Fox and Hounds, McCabe saw Beth's Land-Rover in the car-park. She came walking through the gathering dusk. The strained expression on her face worried him.

'Is something the matter Beth?'

With a failed reassuring smile, she answered, 'Nothing serious. It's just that my father insisted on attending the carol service. He's in my car now. He had to choose a bitterly cold evening like this.' She made a dramatic what-can-I-do gesture to the understanding shadows around them. 'Do you mind going in your car, Gerry?'

'Of course not,' he assured her, and she reached for his upper arm and squeezed it, either as a thank you or a need for security. McCabe could feel relief and tension alternating in her grip. She ran her fingers lightly over McCabe's cheek, tracing his jawline. Then her shoulders made a gesture of resignation and she turned and walked away. McCabe felt a great sadness.

*

The cars huddled together in the wide clearing outside the old church were out of time and harmony with the beautiful landscape that was soft, rounded, and shadowy with the quality of old velvet. The scene was an anachronism that added to the melancholia that had plagued McCabe since leaving Beth.

There was as yet no singing in the crowded church. Roland Merrill was talking with the old choirmaster McCabe had seen on his previous visit to the church. Ambrose Merrill and his wife sat in a sideways pew to one side of the altar. The old lady looked more desperately ill than when McCabe had last seen her. The blue lustre of Menson's robe made him stand out at the centre of the choir in the gallery. Stella Quinn turned in her seat in the third pew to raise a hand in greeting. Her husband stood to hurry up the aisle to McCabe.

McCabe saw Beth and her father in the front pew. To his left, Mary Pavely smiled at him. He was stunned to see Maria Farquahar at her side.

Sol Quinn spoke quietly. 'Do you want to hear this now, Gerry?'

'Is it good news or bad, Sol?'

'That depends on how you see it.' The most significant part of Quinn's answer was in his eyes. 'We'd better go outside.'

Out in the night, he spoke fast. 'You've altered a lot of Abbeyfield folks' lives. What I've learned today forces me to remind you of that, Gerry. In 1972 there were plans to build a gazebo in the grounds of Abbeyfield Manor, taking in the rockery. Ambrose Merrill panicked and had Sylvester Hartley, who still had local contacts, find someone prepared to dig up Suzi Duoard's body for reburial elsewhere. Hartley chose Bundy, but the gazebo idea was dropped and the exhumation was unnecessary. But Red Bundy had been told almost everything. Now he's ready to talk.'

From inside the church the singing of *O Little Town of Bethlehem* began falteringly, then filled the outside night as the carollers gained confidence. Beautifully sung and emotionally charged, the carol echoed far away in the hills, its mysticism more pronounced on the counterpoint.

'It was a long time ago, and Bundy is a convicted criminal,' McCabe remarked.

'That's where Ali Westwood comes in, Gerry. She has Sylvester Hartley's files, including a chart of the manor grounds drawn in pencil, with X marking where the girl was buried.'

This was sound evidence. The note could be dated forensically, but a problem occurred to McCabe. 'There is no way to prove who drew the map.'

'Hold on, Gerry. The house on the map is marked "The Manor" in pencil, and another place is marked "Gardener's Shed". Hartley attached a note identifying the writer.'

'Who was it, Sol?'

'Old man Merrill.'

Now McCabe fully understood Quinn's earlier warning. His quest to avenge Suzi Duoard had suddenly taken on a daunting dimension. To press ahead would result in the sins of the son being visited upon the father. Ambrose Merrill would be arrested. What would that do to the terminally ill Mrs Merrill?

'This puts a different complexion on things, doesn't it?' the detective declared.

It did. For McCabe to pursue the Suzi Duoard murder would mean sacrificing the innocent in his crusade against the guilty.

Quinn suggested, 'Give it some thought for an hour or two, Gerry. I can force my guv'nor to go ahead, but only if you still want to.'

Uncertain as to what he wanted, McCabe followed Quinn inside. He found Maria Farquahar waiting for him. Quinn walked on to rejoin his wife. In front of the altar the choirmaster was conducting a group of schoolgirls in the low-voiced singing of a carol. Roland Merrill stood at the side of his parents, wearing his schoolmaster rank like a cape of royalty.

'I owe you an explanation, Mr McCabe,' Maria Farquahar said excitedly. McCabe saw her as a countrywoman who had for too long missed the smell of new-cut grass and the coolness of an evening breeze sweeping down from green hills. 'Mary Pavely rang to suggest that I came down to spend Christmas with her family. As you know, this is a very sad time for them.'

'It is most kind of you, Mrs Farquahar,' McCabe said. 'What of the colonel and Beth?'

'I still have to face that problem, Mr McCabe. They've yet to learn that I'm here.'

'I wish you luck,' McCabe said lamely. 'Enjoy the rest of the evening.'

Her smile thanked him. 'There is something very special about it. How often it happens that after the most morbid moments of despair we suddenly discover how brilliant life can be.'

'I'm pleased for you,' he said as they parted.

McCabe could see nothing brilliant about life. Having the destiny of several people in his power weighed unbearably on him. Stella and Quinn squeezed up on the pew to make room for him on the end. Beth turned. Seeing McCabe, she smiled. The colonel didn't turn. His white-haired head was visibly shaking, not violently but constantly.

The carol ended and the Methodist minister that McCabe had met in Kilverham stood at the altar. Spreading his hands wide in a gesture of awed appreciation of the carol singing, he smiled beamingly. 'I have been asked to say a few words. But as a comparative newcomer, I am not qualified to address you good folk. So I would ask you to welcome the man without whom this wonderful evening would not have been possible.' Standing with his hand on his father's shoulder, poised to step forward, Roland Merrill smiled down at his parents. The minister continued, 'Allow me to present, Mr John Menson.'

A murmur of astonishment rippled through the congregation. People looked questioningly at each other. John-John Menson stepped up. 'Thank you, Mr Pulman.' Then he faced the congregation. 'Good evening, my dear friends. First I thank you for leaving the comfort of your homes to support the carol service on this unpleasantly cold night.'

The congregation was shocked into staring silence. No one had known what to expect from a figure both feared and ridiculed. No one had expected so coherent a greeting. 'We are here to give thanks in song for the birth of our Lord, but first I ask you to spare a few minutes to join me in prayer. We shall pray that this Christmas will be a happy and a holy one for us all. Your prayers are especially asked for one of our community taken from us so tragically in recent weeks. May our Saviour Jesus Christ care for her. We must also offer our prayers for Suzi Duoard. To have known Suzi was to be touched by a unique, golden experience.' Clasping his hands together in front of his chest, John-John bowed his head. 'Let us pray.'

McCabe lowered his head with the rest of the congregation, but was prevented from praying by the thoughts racing through his head. The portrait of Rita Pavely must have brought about Menson's apparently complete recovery, a recovery McCabe regarded as permanent.

Still racked by indecision, McCabe saw John-John heading for the gallery. Hurrying, he caught up with Menson at the foot of a stone staircase. McCabe called him, 'John-John.'

Turning, John-John exclaimed, 'Mr McCabe.'

'Could I have a quick word?'

'Of course. But I am pushed for time.'

'It's about Roland Merrill,' McCabe began, wondering how he could condense all he needed to say into a few minutes. 'We have evidence now to charge him with Suzi's murder.'

'Praise the Lord,' John-John said with a heartfelt sigh.

'But there's a problem, John-John. Arresting Merrill will mean charging his father, too, either with conspiracy to murder or being an accessory after the fact.'

'Surely his only offence is that of a parent protecting his child,' Menson disputed.

'The law doesn't recognize that sort of thing, John-John,' McCabe explained.

Menson said sadly, 'My thoughts go mainly to dear Mrs Merrill.'

'She is why I'm thinking of taking no action. What is your opinion, John-John?'

The choirmaster came to the top of the stairs to call down to him impatiently. Putting a reassuring hand on McCabe's arm, John-John whispered, 'Leave it with me, Mr McCabe.'

'John-John's giving the problem some thought,' McCabe reported to Quinn on returning to his seat.

As Menson returned to his place in the choir to begin a superb rendition of *O Come All Ye Faithful*, McCabe replied, 'John-John's thinking is fine, but his conscience is sure to be more sensitive than mine, so I'm not expecting him to come up with an answer.'

The rest of the evening passed without McCabe really noticing. It ended with the congregation standing to sing *Silent Night* along with the choir. When it was over, McCabe moved quickly to where Colonel Farquahar and Beth were preparing to leave. Some people McCabe didn't know were talking to the colonel. Beth welcomed McCabe with a smile.

McCabe came quickly to the point. 'Your mother is here.'

'Where?' an ashen-faced Beth querulously asked.

'With Mary Pavely at the back of the church.'

Agitated, Beth had turned to speak to her father, stopping when Quinn suddenly arrived.

'We have a problem, Gerry,' Quinn announced. 'Both Menson and Roland Merrill have completely disappeared. Merrill's car has gone. Could Menson have tipped Merrill off and he's done a runner?'

That was the worst-case scenario in Quinn's reckoning, but not McCabe's. McCabe's titanic fear right then was that he had misjudged the extent of Menson's recovery. John-John might well consider himself to be an avenging angel of sorts, and had decided to deal personally with Merrill.

'He won't help Merrill, Sol,' McCabe said. 'But now we have to go ahead regardless.'

'What's happening, Gerry?' Beth enquired anxiously.

Aware of the difficulties her question presented, Quinn answered swiftly. 'Mrs Merrill, I regret to have to tell you this. It was my intention to arrest your husband tonight on suspicion of the murder of Suzi Duoard. But Mr Merrill seems to have been made aware of his situation, and he has gone. John-John has gone missing, too.'

Beth suddenly looked ill. 'John-John called at the manor earlier today. Shortly afterwards, Bert Jakeman told me that a 12-bore shotgun and a box of cartridges were missing.'

This confirmed McCabe's worst fear. But before he could alert Quinn, the colonel parted from his friends and asked, 'What is all this about? Something to do with Katrina?'

Beth and Quinn left it to McCabe to answer. He said, 'It's

getting late, Colonel, and it's turned very cold outside. Let Beth take you home. I will come out to the manor in the morning to explain everything.'

Nodding assent, Colonel Farquahar allowed his daughter to wrap him up warmly. With a grateful glance at McCabe, Beth had an arm round the shoulders of her father, shepherding him away when McCabe saw a pensive Maria Farquahar heading their way. He signalled Beth to wait.

He said reluctantly, 'There is just one thing, Colonel. Mrs Farquahar is here this evening, and would like to speak to you and Beth.'

A series of expressions flitted across the old man's lined face. Then a connection was made inside of his head. He questioned McCabe angrily. 'Give me a reason why you propose that I should speak to that woman?'

'It could be the first step to having Katrina return to the manor, Colonel.'

Influenced by this, the colonel looked directly at McCabe. Wrinkles of defeat framing his eyes, he applied a fuzzy-headed logic. 'I have found you to be a most dependable fellow, McCabe, and I recognize that I am old-fashioned and therefore in no condition to dogmatize. Perhaps my moral code is outdated. I will speak with Mrs Farquahar.'

Having just reached the little group, Maria Farquahar's sigh of relief at hearing this was audible enough to embarrass her.

As Quinn and McCabe walked discreetly away, McCabe confided in his policeman friend. 'I hope that I'm wrong, Sol, but Menson could have taken the shotgun to kill Merrill.'

'Let's hope that you are wrong. I can't make this official yet, Gerry, so I'll run Stella home and then you and I have a long night ahead of us.'

It was a little after midnight when they started their search to find Menson's caravan unoccupied. From there they drove to Abbeyfield Manor hoping for a sight of Merrill's car. Beth had left her Land-Rover parked in the drive, and the doors of the empty double garage were open.

'He didn't come home,' Quinn remarked.

'I didn't expect him to,' McCabe admitted.

'Are we likely to be collecting bits of Merrill in a bin-bag?' Quinn asked, as he drove out through the manor gates.

'John-John looked to be absolutely normal at the church.'

'Absolutely normal people don't steal shotguns and ammo, Gerry,' Quinn reasoned. 'All we can do now is scout round the area. He's not at home so he has to be out here in the night.'

They toured the district for hours without success. At six o'clock in the morning, Quinn conceded defeat. 'I've got to bring Pete Rendall in on it now. It's a bit early, but I'll ring him.'

Stopping the car, Quinn tapped in his superior's home number. McCabe could hear both sides of the conversation. There was a childish ring of dissatisfaction in Rendall's tone.

Quinn opened with. *'It's me, guv. We can't keep the lid on the Merrill thing any longer.*

'What's happened?'

'I have a witness who will testify that Merrill killed the girl, together with material evidence supporting all the witness says. At least one other person was involved after the fact.'

'We won't be able to put Hartley in the dock, Sol,' Rendall observed sarcastically.

'I'm not talking about Sylvester Hartley, guv. It's Roland's father, Ambrose.'

Confounded into silence, Rendall used a false cough to conceal his delay in responding. At last he spoke shakily. *'We had this contained, Inspector. Have you any idea of the consequences? This will destroy a community. Don't approach Merrill until you see me.'*

'I can't, guv, he's vanished. We've been searching all night for him.'

'We?'

'Gerry McCabe's with me, due to what might be described as a complication.'

Exhaling long and despairingly, Rendall asked, *'What sort of complication?'*

'John the Baptist has also gone AWOL, armed with a shotgun and a desire to do Roland Merrill harm.'

'What a mess!' Rendall exclaimed, before lapsing into another long period of silence. *'This could end up as a complete disaster for both you and me, Sol. Where are you now?'*

'Out at Clouds Mill.'

'Well come straight back to the station. I should get there about the same time as you.'

'Right, guv.'

Starting the car, Quinn sat contemplating something without moving the vehicle. Then he said to himself rather than McCabe, 'Why didn't I think of that before?'

Driving fast, he headed towards Kilverham before turning left into a lane that ended a hundred yards up ahead. McCabe estimated they were less than half a mile from the town. Quinn took another left to drive along a rutted dirt track. The headlights of the car parted the darkness to sweep over the remains of a small stone cottage. It stood in a small notch among some hills, set back in the trees. The windows were no longer glazed. They were the unseeing eyes of the past. A thick-trunked elm, snapped off by some now forgotten hurricane, had fallen on the red-tiled roof, half wrecking it. The chimney had collapsed into a heap of rubble on the ground. Weeds and grass grew through, disguising it.

Stopping the car, Quinn explained, 'A recluse named Billy Shanter used to live here. It was before my time, but I am told that John the Baptist used to visit him regularly.'

'There's someone there.' McCabe saw movement in the open doorway.

Holding one hand up to shield his eyes from the glare of the headlights, a thin man dressed in a fawn-coloured suit with flared trousers, a cream shirt and dark tie, stepped out, shivering in the icy-cold air.

'Who ...?' a mystified Quinn gasped, before he and McCabe saw the shotgun the man held in his other hand. Quinn identified him. 'It's Menson, Gerry.'

Unrecognizable without his robe, and with his hair pulled back tightly and secured in a ponytail. Menson instructed, 'Switch off the car's lights and walk towards me.'

Quinn turned off the car's lights and, when they got out of the car, Quinn shouted, 'Put the gun down, John-John.'

'No.' A faint figure now in the starlit early morning, Menson spoke in a strong voice.

'Then just tell us where Roland Merrill is,' Quinn said.

'Merrill is safe and well,' Menson replied.

'Where is he?'

'I can't tell you that right now, Mr Quinn. As soon as it was light I was coming to the police station. If you could drive me there, I can establish some conditions and settle this swiftly.'

'You will have to surrender the shotgun first, John-John,' Quinn stated.

'I can't do that, Mr Quinn. I will need this weapon in order to negotiate at the station.'

'We don't negotiate with guns, but I'll ring my boss to see what he says,' Quinn said.

Quinn walked away out of earshot to make his call. When he returned, he moved McCabe back towards the car so that Menson couldn't hear what he was about to say. 'Rendall threatened to have an armed squad waiting for us at the station. I managed to dissuade him.' He called to Menson. 'We'll take you to the police station, John-John, and you can keep the shotgun for now.'

When they were driving away with Menson in the back seat holding the shotgun across his knees, McCabe turned to speak to him. 'It's nice to see that you're feeling better, John-John.'

'Out of my old habit, so to speak, Mr McCabe,' Menson remarked wryly, causing McCabe to smile and Quinn to release an involuntary chuckle. 'I suppose you could say that I've taken a giant step from the past into my own future.'

'Which of those two places would you prefer, John-John?' McCabe enquired.

'Sadly, Mr McCabe, I have discovered both eras to be extremely disappointing. My beloved sixties were not a time of revolution, not the introduction of Eastern philosophies to the Western spiritual psyche, but an illusion. We nurtured the sexual libido, knelt at images of the guru, mistook the weird hallucinations produced by drugs for glimpses of the divine.'

'And how do you see today?' McCabe asked, as Quinn reached the police station.

'This has to be the most exploitative age in history, Mr McCabe. You live by a system of values that are totally devoid of spirituality.'

As Quinn drove his car into the yard of the police station, a weak daylight was dulled by the greyness of winter. Apart from two police cars, the yard was deserted as they got out of the car. Menson was holding the shotgun across his chest. A shouted command reverberated on the morning air.

'Drop the weapon.'

'I trusted Rendall,' Quinn muttered angrily. 'Put the gun down on the floor, John-John.'

Knowing that armed police ringed the yard, McCabe was horrified to see that Menson had no intention of obeying.

'Drop the gun, *now*.'

Quinn moved, fast. Pressing himself close against Menson, he said. 'Get to the other side of him, Gerry.'

'Step to one side, Inspector Quinn,' the officer in charge of the armed squad shouted.

Staying where he was, waiting until McCabe had moved in close on the other side of Menson, Quinn issued an order. 'On my count of three, make a run for the door, but stay close together so that John-John doesn't make a target. One – two – three.'

Dashing across the yard, they crashed in through the doors of the front office, to come face-to-face with Rendall, who yelled, 'What do you think you are doing, Inspector Quinn?'

'Let's get him up to your office, guv,' Quinn pleaded, taking the gun from Menson.

When they were upstairs, Rendall shut his office door by back-heeling it. Picking up the shotgun from where Quinn had placed it, he broke it to find a cartridge in both barrels. Propping the gun against the wall, he asked a now seated Menson, 'Why were you carrying that gun?'

'I used it to force Roland Merrill to come with me from the church last night.'

'Then you shot him.'

With a real grip on reality now, Menson wouldn't let it be snatched away from him. 'No. I took him to his father, so that they could talk things over.'

'Where is Roland Merrill now?'

Facing Rendall across his office desk, Menson hesitated. 'I can't tell you that until you agree to my conditions.'

'I think you should hear what John-John has to say, guv,' Quinn interceded.

'It is quite simple,' Menson said evenly. 'I need only make one telephone call from here to have Roland Merrill come to the station and make a full confession to the murder of Suzi Duoard. But I can only do that if I have your assurance that no further enquiries will be made, that no one but Roland Merrill will either be interviewed or charged.'

McCabe felt a rush of admiration for Menson, who had cleverly determined that, though it was inevitable the ailing Mrs Merrill would lose a son, she would be spared from losing a husband as well. He watched Rendall, whose dislike of doing a deal with Menson showed on his face. But the superintendent was weighing the situation carefully. Though with no choice other than to charge the Merrill son, he would be sparing the father and possibly other important local personages. It had worked out better than he could have hoped. He smiled a smile that had no warmth.

He gestured to the telephone on his desk. 'I agree, Menson. Make your call.'

Speaking guardedly into the mouthpiece in a low tone, Menson then replaced the receiver and turned to face them. 'Roland Merrill will be brought here shortly.'

An anxious Rendall walked to stand looking out of the window down into the yard. The others joined him in his vigil. Fifteen minutes passed and then a car drove slowly into the yard. 'That's Ambrose Merrill's car,' Rendall told them. The car stopped. They saw the two men in the front seats embrace briefly, and then Roland Merrill stepped out of the passenger's side to stand watching the driver turn and drive out of the yard. It was a poignant little drama.

'Come on, Sol,' Rendall said. 'Let's do our duty.'

But before the policemen had a chance to move, Menson grabbed the shotgun and ran out of the room. Rendall hit a panic button on the wall with the heel of his hand. Shouting to Quinn and McCabe above the bedlam of the alarm sounding throughout the station, he told them, 'He's going to get Merrill.'

All three of them started down the stairs after Menson. On the ground floor a constable leapt out from behind the desk to attempt a rugby tackle. But Menson evaded him easily and went out of the door into the yard. McCabe and the others got to the exit to see John-John sprinting across the yard. With the shotgun held high he was running at an angle away from where a bemused Roland Merrill stood, and it was Quinn who first realized what was happening.

'He's not after Merrill,' Quinn told McCabe and Rendall, before jumping out into the yard, waving both arms and shouting, 'Don't shoot! Don't shoot!'

As it dawned on McCabe that the armed police squad was still in position, a single shot rang out. A bullet hit Menson in the back, shattering his spine. Bent over backwards nearly double, he grotesquely continued to run until his knees buckled and he flopped to the ground just as McCabe and Quinn reached him.

'He's dead,' McCabe announced numbly.

'That is what he planned, Gerry,' an awed Quinn said.

McCabe gave a nod of agreement. 'Being disenchanted with his past and with the present, so he had no enthusiasm for the future.'

Detailing two uniformed officers to take Roland Merrill into custody, Rendall strode up to stand beside McCabe and Quinn. Looking down at the broken body of John-John, his face looking slightly sweaty, Rendall murmured, 'How am I going to explain this?'

McCabe and Quinn turned to look at him in disgust.

There was a silence so profound that it seemed to have an echo to it. Though Colonel Farquahar, his wife and his two daughters were there, the huge room in Abbeyfield Manor seemed vacant to McCabe. There had been something oddly dreamlike, perhaps nightmarish about that day. Sharee Bucholz hadn't been able to keep her promise not to weep when they had earlier said their farewells. That had been difficult, but very soon he would face a far more intimidating farewell.

'My hope is, McCabe,' the colonel said, 'that you will be able to put the unfortunate incidents here from your mind, and forever have pleasant memories of Abbeyfield in your heart. You have brought us together as a family again, and we shall all be eternally grateful.'

Taking his hand, Maria Farquahar smiled warmly. 'Goodbye and God bless. You have a long journey ahead of you, Mr McCabe, so we mustn't delay you.'

'Thank you for everything you have done, Gerry,' Katrina said, kissing him on the cheek.

Then he was walking with Beth to the front door, keenly conscious that he was to face the toughest part of his leave-taking.

'*Déjà vu*,' she said, when they were at the door. 'We are finishing where we started, Gerry. You said then that happy endings are rare.'

'You have your sister and your mother back with you, Beth.'

'For that I am thankful, but it has taught me that the past can't be reassembled in the present. At this very moment I'm happy to be standing here with you and nowhere else.'

'This moment will slip into the past when I walk away.'

Close to tears, Beth tried to say something, but her voice splintered into the shards of mounting hysteria. Wanting to comfort her, McCabe knew that to take her into his arms would trigger an emotional nuclear explosion, the fall-out from which would surely last an eternity. He put out a hand to brush back tenderly the silken hair that had fallen loosely across her face. The backs of his fingers traced the pronounced cheekbones. Running the tip of one finger over her wide mouth, he committed it to memory.

Breaking away, not saying a word, McCabe strode to his car. Without even a backward glance he got in and drove away. Having travelled only a few yards, his resolve collapsed. Stopping the car, he got out to stand looking back. The door was closed and the manor as dark and unapproachable as it had been on the evening when he had first arrived.

Getting back into the car, McCabe drove off into a future that would be forever coloured by the memory of his sojourn in Abbeyfield.